Deadly Betrayal

ANGUS BRODIE AND MIKAELA FORSYTHE MURDER
MYSTERY
BOOK EIGHT

CARLA SIMPSON

OLIVERHEBERBOOKS

Cover art by Dar Albert at Wicked Smart Designs

Published by Oliver-Heber Books

0 9 8 7 6 5 4 3 2 1

Prologue

APRIL 1891

THE CALL CAME LATE in the evening as Angus Brodie was preparing to leave the office on the Strand.

The shrill ring of the telephone stopped him at the door. It had been a long day, in a dozen or more of them lately in his work for the Agency. Now a new inquiry case over counterfeit currency that had been found circulating among merchants in London.

He had sent round a message to Sir Avery at the Special Services Agency several hours earlier with an update delivered by Mr. Conner, a retired officer of the MET whom he'd worked with in the past, regarding the counterfeit currency case.

He had a particular distrust for telephones, knowing how the system worked. A call initiated by one person was put through to an operator at one location, then transferred to another operator in another part of the city, and eventually to the person the call was intended for.

In the interest of the Agency and the work they did, it was best to send round messages by trusted persons, rather than rely on a system where several others might be able to listen to the conversation.

The irritating clanging sounded again, and he thought it might be his wife, Mikaela. He had sent her home to Mayfair earlier, after she made her notes in the case on the blackboard. That was hours ago.

She understood the nature of the work from past inquiry cases, and it was not like her to ring up the office and remind him that he was late for supper or some social engagement, particularly social engagements which he had a particular dislike for.

Still, the persistent sound seemed almost urgent in itself. He returned to the desk and lifted the earpiece. The call was scratchy, a crackling sound as it was put through by the operator, then he heard a frantic voice.

"*I saw him again as I was getting ready to leave!*"

Brodie recognized the voice, the tension, and more.

"Did ye see his face?" he asked.

"*No, but it was the same man! He was there like before, at the carriage park across from the service entrance as I was about to leave. When I looked again, he was gone!*"

The fear reached through the telephone connection from the hotel.

"Stay where ye are!" he told her. "I will meet ye there!"

It was the third time in as many weeks, always the same and included that first note he had received from her—someone was there watching, waiting, then disappearing.

He had urged her not to return, that it might still be dangerous, but she hoped the past was in the past.

"*What if he knows where I live?*"

"All the more reason for ye to stay at the hotel where there are others about until I get there!"

"*I can't take the chance!*"

"Stay where ye are!" he told her again, and then as the connection crackled, "Ellie?"

Brodie cursed. The call had gone dead at the other end.

He grabbed the revolver and the hand-held lamp from the desk drawer, then his coat.

It was late, even for the nearby theater district, most of the coach and cab drivers already gone with a last fare of the night.

He eventually found a driver on his way to the yard where the drivers put up their rigs for the night. He thrust a five-pound note into the man's hand. Instead of the hotel he told him to take him to Charing Cross.

How long had it been since that call, he thought, as the driver let him off at the square where those five streets met, including Charing Cross?

An hour or more, he realized, as he set off toward Craven Street and the row of tenements where Ellie lived.

Would she have already arrived? Very likely, he thought. There were always cabs at the hotel, no matter the time of day or night, for guests arriving or departing.

He quickened his pace, past Northumberland House, darkened for the night, then past the Lane. Craven Street was just beyond.

He slowed, cautious as he rounded the corner, staring through the misty glow of a street lamp at those tenements that lined the opposite side of the street. They were often crowded with more than one family to a room, rubbish over-flowing on the street, a cat skittering from an entrance into the shadows.

It was Friday, the work week end. Workers who returned to

those flats would have collected their pay, then spent an hour or two at the local pub or tavern.

It was a place of families, with a child's trolley made of wood and skate wheels propped against a wrought iron rail outside one of the buildings, where a boy's or girl's play took them to the streets.

The entrance to number twenty-eight Craven Street was lit from the ground floor to the third, the shadows of those inside suddenly appearing at a window amid shouts of alarm that reached the street.

Instead of entering by way of the street entrance, Brodie ran down the steps behind a wrought iron rail, to the basement door. The lock gave easily and he quickly entered the building. The beam from the hand-held fell across stairs that led to the upper floors.

He paused in the shadows on the ground floor, heard voices just beyond, footsteps urgent on the floor above, then the slam of a door.

He crossed the hall to the stairs, the smell of coal oil and fish for someone's supper thick in the air, along with a haunting memory that suddenly returned, of another place and another woman.

Ellie's flat was on the second floor. The door, always bolted, now stood ajar. Had she only just returned in spite of what he'd told her, and forgot to set the lock?

He kept his voice low when he called out. When there was no answer, he eased the door open and stepped inside.

It was dark inside the one-room flat, except for the thin shaft of light that spilled through the open doorway from that single fixture in the hallway. He cursed softly. She would not have left the door unlocked, not even for a moment.

The flat had electric, the button beside the door. He didn't turn it on. There was no need as he slowly swept the beam from the hand-held across the usually well-kept room. It was now in disarray, the table turned on its side, utensils scattered across the floor. And then he saw her.

She lay on the floor, her eyes sightless as she stared back at him, her head twisted at a sharp angle. Not satisfied with that, the murderer had also cut her, the bodice of her gown stained dark with blood.

He knew before he touched her that she was dead.

"Why wouldn't ye listen!" he whispered.

He touched her cheek, her skin cool to the touch, that old memory sharp as if it was yesterday.

He pulled his thoughts back to the here and now.

She had fought her attacker. Not that it had done her any good. Whoever had been there had easily overpowered her.

It would have been quick, he thought. Those years with the MET and before, pushing their way back through memory.

This had been done by someone who chose to overpower and silence her quickly, and had then slipped away—someone who was experienced in such things.

If only he had gotten there sooner!

"Ellie, girl. I'm so very sorry," he whispered even though she was past hearing anything.

The sound of a constable's whistle, distant at first, then much closer, cut the silence.

He scanned the looming darkness of the flat, eyes narrowed in the meager light.

Where was the boy, Rory? Had the killer taken him? His head came around at the creak of a floorboard.

There was only the one room in the flat with the sleeping area curtained off in the corner.

That faint sound came again.

He rose and aimed the hand-held in the direction of the alcove with that curtain drawn across. He pulled the curtain back. The alcove was empty.

He heard it again, along with another muffled sound from the wall beside the alcove.

Brodie ran his hand along the scarred wood of the wall, caked with an accumulation of grime and soot from a coal fire she, and countless others before, had cooked with.

It wasn't unusual for people who lived in these places to hollow out a space behind a wood panel or behind a counter to hide something of value—coins, a trinket, or a bauble that might be of value—against thieves who were known to frequent these places when those who lived there were away.

Or possibly something more precious than a trinket or a handful of coins?

He rapped gently on the wood panel, the wall behind hollow.

"Ye can come out, lad," he said gently.

The panel creaked, then opened a narrow space. A pale face appeared in the opening, a boy with a mop of dark hair and large, dark eyes.

"Yer safe now," Brodie told the child.

There was a hesitant nod as the lad, small and thin for his age, stepped out of the narrow space between the wood panel and the stone wall behind it.

When he would have glanced past, Brodie stopped him.

"Dinnae look, lad." Rory, a strong, fine name. He would need that strength now, and for all the days to come.

"Is she...?" The rest of the question caught in the boy's throat.

Brodie pulled him against himself and held him tight, Rory's face pressed into his shoulder.

He knew only too well what it was to have that image forever burned into one's memory. That old memory of finding his mother's body in a place very much like this swept back at him, painful and raw as if it was here and now. He forced it back. Back over twenty years earlier, where he kept it carefully hidden.

How did the murderer find Ellie after all these years? Did he know about the boy?

Until Brodie found who had done this, he had to assume that Rory wasn't safe.

He heard the constable's whistle, closer now.

"We must go," Brodie gently told him.

Rory pushed against him, surprisingly strong.

"No! I won't leave her!"

Brodie heard the tears along with the anger in the lad's voice, something he knew only too well.

"There's nothin' to be done for her now."

"I want to find him!" Rory cried. "I want to make him pay for what he did."

The same words he had screamed into the shadows as a boy a long time ago.

Was it possible Rory had seen the man? In that case, he might very well be in danger.

"I will find him," Brodie promised, as he stroked Rory's back. "Ye have my word. But we must go now."

The fight eased out of that thin body and ended on a sob.

"I don't want to leave her!" Rory said as he fought the tears.

Brodie would see that her body was provided for. It was the least he could do. He couldn't bear for this to be the boy's last memory. But for now, they needed to go.

"Yer not leavin' her, I am."

One

"MORNIN', Miss Mikaela," Mr. Cavendish greeted me as I arrived at the office on the Strand.

I smiled. It had been '*Miss Mikaela*' since our first meeting and still was, in spite of the change in my relationship with Brodie. And I was quite all right with it.

Before stepping down from the cab, I handed him the wrapped package that contained cakes as well as biscuits with sausage from breakfast that Mrs. Ryan, my housekeeper, had sent.

Food was always a good strategy to prevent my clothes from being muddied when Rupert the hound grinned a greeting at me from the sidewalk.

Others, Brodie in particular, would of course have argued that what I considered a grin was in fact a snarl. Nevertheless, Mr. Cavendish, keeper of the alcove and the latest word on the street, knew better, and so did I.

The hound and I had a special bond, although those same '*others*' who claimed to be such experts would have called it my imagination.

We had our own language which he usually obeyed. *Usually,* because there had been times when he was not of a mind to obey, most particularly in taking down an attacker on the street, for which I was most grateful.

There had been an extra basket of cakes for him after that episode, most particularly my housekeeper's sponge cakes which he was particularly fond of.

And, despite Brodie's argument against it, he had proven himself to be most capable in tracking down people—namely those of a criminal sort—in our inquiry cases.

He had also warded off other potentially dangerous situations when I was out and about London on my own—Rupert's presence a precaution Brodie insisted upon, despite his criticism of the hound's investigative talents.

"He's a bloody animal with a brain no larger than a walnut," Brodie had argued in one of our conversations.

"He has excellent instincts," I had replied in the hound's defense.

I had then pointed out that according to Mr. Brimley, who had studied medicine before opening his pharmaceutical shop, some of the *human* species—notably men—seemed to possess a brain no larger than a walnut.

To say that had not gone over well is an understatement. In his usual way after one of our conversations with differing opinions, Brodie had thrown up his hands, declared that there was no arguing with me, and had immediately changed the subject. I did so enjoy our conversations.

As for the previous day and several more before, Brodie had been deeply involved in our most recent inquiry case, regarding counterfeit currency that had been found circulating at several business establishments in London.

I had left him with his report to Sir Avery the previous

afternoon, while I had followed up on an appointment with my great-aunt's personal banker, Aldous Trumble, at the Bank of England.

My great-aunt was also a stockholder of the bank, so our inquiries had a dual purpose, and I attended on her behalf.

"Not that I'm concerned about the matter," she had told me. "If the entire English currency was worthless, I always have the family jewels."

The *family jewels* were a collection of gems, gold baubles, and other valuable pieces from over the centuries, and also included several pieces of armor and weapons that her lawyer insisted belonged in a museum rather than the game room at Sussex Square.

Her family included William the Conqueror, along with a list of other noteworthy and notorious persons, one well-known highwayman, and a pirate who had done some rather nasty business in the Caribbean.

I didn't ask how the family jewels had been acquired. Possibly best to leave that part of our family history just that— to history.

She did have a particular affection for Scotland, that wild, untamed place, just as I did, and was in favor of self-rule. I had visions of family treasure hidden in some cave near Old Lodge in Scotland.

"The English tried to conquer Scotland," she had once told me over one, or possibly several, drams of whisky produced at Old Lodge, her estate in the north.

"But they will never conquer that spirit. Take Mr. Brodie for example, or Mr. Munro."

Mr. Munro was manager of her estates, and had a somewhat shadowy past that included Brodie.

The short version of their boyhood together on the streets

of Edinburgh had included working odd jobs to get by until they found their way to London.

The somewhat longer version, that I eventually learned from Brodie, had included a bit of petty thievery—mostly food, occasionally a coin or two someone had dropped on the street, and running numbers for gambling.

And then there was murder, most particularly in the case of Brodie's mother, that had left him to the care of his grandmother for a short time.

As for Munro's history before he joined Brodie in that life of crime, that was, as they, say a somewhat blank slate.

His background, dealing with all sorts, made him the perfect manager of my great-aunt's estates. There was never a farthing or a keg of whisky unaccounted for, or the party responsible was made to account for it. I didn't ask how that was done, only that the party involved was not seen again, according to my great-aunt.

"He takes care of the matter," she had once explained. "I don't ask the details."

And in consideration of my great-aunt's somewhat eccentric life, from rumors of a wild girlhood, three marriage proposals—none accepted—and the 'love of her life,' who had disappeared under somewhat mysterious circumstances and about whom little was known, I didn't pry.

It was my aunt's connections and long history with the Bank of England that facilitated my meeting with the stockholders of the bank regarding the counterfeit currency that had surfaced about London.

The currency had first been discovered some weeks earlier, through banking made by a reputable merchant, and then several other subsequent incidents.

It appeared that it was not a crime of some low-level

amateurs as first thought. The counterfeit notes were of extremely fine quality that had been difficult to recognize unless one was familiar with such things, and always the same in twenty- and fifty-pound notes.

That had prompted the bank's president to contact the Agency. In the weeks since, counterfeit hundred-pound notes had begun to appear. The total, as far as could be determined, could have a devastating effect on the economy and in trade abroad. It was a most serious affair.

I had not seen Brodie since the previous afternoon and wanted to update him on my meeting with the stockholders.

He previously resided at the office on the Strand, where I stayed over from time to time in our past inquiries. Of late, he had been spending more and more time at my town house in Mayfair even though I knew that he was not comfortable with the arrangement.

"I will not have people thinkin' that I am livin' off ye," he had commented over a supper of my housekeeper's Irish stew —a favorite that had persuaded him to stay at the time.

I pointed out that I could just as easily move to the Strand, which had not gone over well either.

"And have people thinkin' that I canna take care of ye?"

Take care of me? It was something that I found amusing. The question of where to live had not resolved itself.

For now, I had the town house in Mayfair and he had the office on the Strand.

"Is he about?" I now asked Mr. Cavendish.

He shook his head. "Not since late the evening before, miss. He left real sudden. Didn't say where he was going. He hasn't been back."

That seemed somewhat curious, although it wasn't unusual for Brodie to be out and about on some matter or another, particularly with a new case, and most particularly for Sir Avery at the Agency.

It was possible that he had returned later and decided to stay over at the office, unnoticed by Mr. Cavendish, who was in the habit of frequenting the local taverns until quite late of an evening.

I gave the hound a scratch behind the ears and headed for the stairs that led to the office on the second-floor landing. I unlocked the door and stepped into the office.

It looked much as it had when I left the previous afternoon. A pot sat on the coal stove, the contents quite cold. A file folder had been returned to the cabinet, obviously somewhat hastily, part of the folder protruding from the edge of the drawer.

A note pad lay on the desk where it appeared that Brodie had been making notes. And the adjacent bedroom was empty at a glance, the bed neatly made. Whatever the reason, it did appear that Brodie had not returned the previous night.

I looked at the blackboard where it had become a habit for me to make my notes when we were working on a case.

To his credit, Brodie found it to be useful and had taken to adding his own notes. If there had been a development in the counterfeit case, there was nothing new written on the board to indicate that.

Whatever reason, he had obviously left the office quite suddenly, as Mr. Cavendish described. However, at a glance, there was nothing to indicate what that was.

I removed my gloves and laid them on the desk. I had received a message this morning from Mr. Trumble, president of the bank, that a man with an account for his business had made a deposit that had contained a good amount of counterfeit notes.

He claimed to know nothing about the fifty- and hundred-pound notes. Still, Mr. Trumble thought it might be important to speak with him.

I had sent round a note to the customer who owned the well-known leather goods shop just near St. James's, and hoped to meet with him later in the day.

With the intention of adding the man's name to the board, I opened the right-hand desk drawer that contained Brodie's pouch of tobacco, an assortment of bits and pieces of paper with notes scribbled on them that he was in the habit of writing down, and a box of chalk.

Still, two items were very obviously missing—his revolver, and the hand-held lamp he carried when out and about at night.

It was a habit to carry both since his time with the MET, encountering all sorts of criminal types on the street as a police inspector, and then in his own inquiry business.

He had also provided me with a small revolver that I carried in my travel bag, along with a particularly impressive knife Mr. Munro had given me when I set off on my first travel adventure some years before.

"I almost pity the man who makes the mistake of approaching ye," Mr. Munro told me at the time. Then added, "Almost."

Since Brodie was not at the office, there was nothing to do but make my notes, then leave a message for him before I departed for my meeting with the owner of the leather goods shop.

I spent the next hour at the chalkboard, making notes that included my most recent conversation with Mr. Trumble at the bank regarding the other counterfeit notes that had now surfaced across the city. That also included a significant amount of counterfeit notes found at City Bank, Barclay & Company, and Westminster Bank, in addition to the Bank of England.

It was very near midday when the service bell on the landing rang, an invention by Mr. Cavendish, installed to let us know when someone arrived.

I barely had time to set down my pen from the notes I was making on my notepad when Constable Dooley entered the office.

He was not wearing his uniform. Instead he was plainly dressed, in the trousers and jacket that he wore when working on some matter for Brodie. He looked quite flustered.

"Pardon, miss. I called round to Mayfair this mornin' and was told I might find you here. Have you heard from Mr. Brodie? There's somethin' I need to let him know," he added, quite urgently.

Constable Dooley had worked with Brodie when he was with the MET. He'd remained a good friend since, as well as being an *'inside'* source for information, as Brodie called it, in past inquiry cases. And neither of them had any regard for Chief Inspector Abberline of the Metropolitan Police.

The Chief Inspector was a political animal, as Brodie referred to him, far more keen on becoming the next Commissioner of Police than solving crimes, unless it could advance his career. I had encountered just that side of the man in the matter of my sister's disappearance two years before.

And he had a particular dislike of Brodie. Their enmity went back to the last investigation he had participated in just before he left the MET, some issue which Brodie chose not to speak of.

"The past is the past," he had told me, when the matter came up during that first case to find my sister. Abberline had been less than cooperative in the matter, trivializing her disappearance as undoubtedly a *'marital disagreement.'*

It was the first inquiry case where I joined Brodie, refusing to be set aside by a bureaucratic imbecile with the intellect of a centipede—the Chief Inspector, not Brodie. Although I will admit that Brodie had been reluctant to have my participation.

Actually, *reluctant* was a bit of an understatement. He had initially refused to allow me to join the search at all, and then had conceded only when I informed him that I would carry on by myself.

During that investigation, I had eventually convinced him that I had something valuable to contribute, in addition to the fact that I could take care of myself in most any situation. That was still a point of discussion that came up from time to time. I was working on that.

Now, it seemed that something serious had most definitely happened. Had Brodie gone off to pursue some piece of information in the counterfeit case and then found himself in a bad situation?

Granted, that was not like him. Brodie was thorough, careful, and far too experienced in matters of crime to be caught in a dangerous situation.

An accident perhaps?

"Do you know where Mr. Brodie is?" Mr. Dooley repeated. "It's important."

"No," I replied. "What is it? Is there a message I can give him when I see him?"

Mr. Dooley was exceedingly uncomfortable.

"I need to warn him. It's most urgent, miss."

An uneasy feeling tightened my stomach as he twisted his cap in his hands, obviously reluctant to tell me. Yet, I have been known to be most persistent.

"Warn him about what?" I demanded. He was still reluctant.

"Since I may very well be the first one to speak with him, you must tell me what this is about."

I had to admit that he looked quite distressed.

"It's the Chief Inspector...he has a warrant for Mr. Brodie's arrest, and a good many of the men in the department searching for him. He has a man on his way here now."

Arrest?

"For what?" I demanded.

Mr. Dooley shifted uncomfortably, and the uneasiness tightened in my stomach.

"For murder."

Two

"MURDER?!"

"It's in the matter of that old case Mr. Brodie was investigating a long time ago, before he left the MET," Mr. Dooley explained.

"There was a witness, a young woman who saw the murderer. Mr. Abberline was Assistant Chief Inspector then," he continued.

"He was determined to have the matter resolved, as he was hoping to be promoted. But he needed the witness to make the case. Mr. Brodie wouldn't give the woman up."

"That was almost ten years ago," I replied as I tried to make sense of all of this with the few details that Brodie had shared with me.

Mr. Dooley nodded. "Mr. Brodie told him at the time that she had left London and he didn't know where she was. That didn't sit well with the Chief Inspector, as you can well imagine."

"Please continue," I replied.

"The Chief Inspector threatened him with charges then,

for withholding evidence. You can well imagine what Mr. Brodie's response was."

I knew well enough what had followed. He had resigned rather than divulge who the young woman was and risk endangering her, merely to promote Abberline's career.

I forced myself to remain calm.

"It seems that the woman returned to London some time ago," Mr. Dooley continued. "Now, she's turned up dead, and Abberline is set to bring charges against Mr. Brodie for tampering with evidence all those years before, as well as the murder of the woman."

"That's ridiculous!" I protested. "He is not a murderer."

"I know that and you know it as well, but according to the warrant, the murder charge is for evidence discovered at the scene where her body was found."

"What evidence?" I demanded.

"It seems the woman who collects the rents heard a commotion in the woman's flat and then saw Mr. Brodie leave."

Had Abberline gone mad? A warrant for murder?

"That's the reason I'm here, miss. We need to find him before Mr. Abberline, or one of his men," he continued.

The first shock was beginning to wear off as I forced myself to think.

"Abberline is like a crazy man," Mr. Dooley continued. "He'll have him hunted down and a good chance that Mr. Brodie will never see the inside of a cell. If you get my meanin'."

The terrifying part of all this was that I knew exactly what he was saying.

"You should leave, miss. Before Mr. Abberline's man

comes round with the warrant. There is no telling what the man will do."

Even though I refused to be intimidated, I agreed. There was no way of knowing what Abberline might do.

"He mustn't find you here, either," I told him, and thanked him for taking the risk to come to come there.

"Mr. Brodie has done right by me, more than once. I don't go forgettin' things like that. And I don't hold with the charges for a minute." He put his cap back on.

"You take care as well, miss. I might work in the same district as Mr. Abberline, but there's many of us have no regard for the man and his ways."

I laid a hand at his arm. "You'll bring word if..."

I couldn't bring myself to say the rest of it—*if* Brodie was found and arrested before I could find him.

He promised that he would.

When Mr. Dooley had gone, I forced myself to think.

I needed to find Brodie, but first I made a thorough inspection of the office that included the file cabinet, the desk drawers, and the adjacent room, searching for anything that might reveal clues to Abberline or one of his men if they searched the office.

I then looked at the chalkboard. The notes we'd made about the counterfeit case had nothing to do with that past situation. Still...

I had most of the same notes in my notebook. That would have to do until I could find Brodie. I quickly erased everything on the chalkboard, tucked Brodie's notebook into my bag, and then locked the office behind me.

I encountered Mr. Cavendish on the sidewalk.

"If Brodie should return, I need to speak with him immediately. And if anyone else inquires, you haven't seen him today."

"I haven't seen him," he replied.

"It's just that..."

"No need to explain, miss. I'm just a poor street beggar, livin' in that alcove." The grin deepened and he winked. "I don't know anything about Mr. Brodie's work or where he is."

"Mr. Dooley spoke with you?"

He nodded. "I've known Mr. Dooley a long time. For all he's with the MET, he's a good man."

"Be careful," I cautioned.

He nodded. "Best to have the hound with you. Mr. Brodie would insist on that." He turned and whistled for Rupert.

The hound suddenly appeared from the alcove, an old boot hanging out of his mouth. I did hope there hadn't been a foot in it.

"I might just take meself off to another place for a while," Mr. Cavendish added. "But I'll have people I know and trust keep watch for Mr. Brodie and warn him if he should come back here."

"How will I find you if I need to get word to you?" I asked.

"The hound will find me sure enough. Just bring him round if you need my help." He waved down a cab for me.

"I've locked the office door," I told him as I climbed aboard and the hound followed.

Mr. Cavendish nodded. "Right you are, miss. Not that it would make a difference with the likes of Mr. Abberline."

"Do be careful," I told him.

He tipped his cap. "And you as well, miss."

I kept my appointment later in the afternoon with the owner of the leather goods shop, regarding the counterfeit case, and made notes that included the name of the customer who had paid with those counterfeit pound notes to pass on to Sir Avery at the Agency.

A legitimate excuse to go there and hopefully find out when they had last heard from Brodie. Or at least what he was off and about, even as what I'd learned from Mr. Dooley kept turning over and over in my head.

Who was the woman? Whom had she seen murdered almost ten years before? Why had she come back to London? And who would have killed her?

Abberline was obviously determined to connect Brodie to her death. And it was worrisome that I had no idea where he was.

So much for happily married bliss.

Then again, I was not the dutiful wife waiting at home for the husband to return. Most particularly if Brodie was in trouble.

We arrived at the high street near the Tower. I say 'we,' as that included my companion. It was difficult to ignore the hound, either by size or the smell that usually accompanied him. It did seem that fish, with the underlying scent of old boot, was the fragrance of the day.

Perhaps I could persuade one of the groomsmen at Sussex Square to give the hound a bath, since it seemed very likely that we were going to be spending some time together.

As we approached the Tower, a coach drew up at the street-side entrance, and two men stepped down from the coach, one in a constable's uniform and the other...Chief Inspector Abberline!

The man was nothing if not persistent, apparently turning over every stone in search of Brodie. And this in spite of the fact that there was no love lost between Abberline and

Sir Avery Stanton, who was head of the Special Services Agency.

I had detected the dislike on Sir Avery's part in the past. Something mentioned about *'meddling incompetence and over-reaching one's intelligence.'* Which I thought described Abberline quite well. I was inclined to agree.

Under any other circumstances, I would have continued to the Tower entrance and simply ignored Abberline. He *was* rather easy to overlook.

Yet, with the information Mr. Dooley had shared with me, it was safe to assume that Abberline had only one reason for calling on Sir Avery, since he knew that Brodie worked for the Agency from time to time.

"Most interesting," I thought. Rupert appeared to agree.

Then, as if he was determined to do something about it, he started forward. I immediately called him back.

"Not today," I said, as much to myself, heeding Mr. Dooley's earlier warning.

The hound looked up at me as if he might have made a comment to that.

"We'll come back later," I replied, as if he understood, while I watched Abberline and the constable enter the Tower from the alcove at the entrance of a building. I made a mental note to speak with Sir Avery as soon as possible.

When they had disappeared inside the Tower gate, I immediately waved down a driver. There was someone else who was usually very well informed about Brodie's whereabouts.

I climbed aboard the coach. I caught the disapproval of the driver as Rupert jumped in after. The brief discussion that followed, regarding the usual sort of passengers and that he would need to clean the coach afterward, quickly ended with the promise of additional coin.

"And quickly," I added after informing him of my destination.

It was late afternoon. The sun that had warmed the day earlier had dropped below the rooftops when I arrived at my great-aunt's residence at Sussex Square. I paid the driver as Rupert loped up the steps to the front entrance.

He was most anxious in anticipation of whatever food might be cooking in the kitchens. However, the same could not be said for my aunt's staff.

Along with an appetite for whatever might be the fare for supper and a fondness for rummaging through the solar as if there might be a creature to be found there, he was in the habit of making himself quite at home.

As for the solar, one could never tell what might be found there. My aunt had a monkey in residence for a time in preparation for her safari. It had since been returned to the London Zoo after it escaped the solar and went about terrorizing the housemaids.

Mr. Symons, my aunt's head butler, greeted me at the entrance and Rupert charged past him.

"Good day, Mr. Symons."

"Good day, miss," he replied. "Good to see you, as always," he added as he collected himself from the hound's enthusiastic greeting.

"How is my aunt today?" I asked. Mr. Symons was always a good source for that information.

"In excellent health, miss. She is presently rearranging her wardrobe for her upcoming safari."

That was at least the dozenth time that I was aware of. Always an adventure in itself. I could only imagine what she was taking with her—hunting costume, along with the requisite head gear.

"*One never knows when one might encounter a dangerous beast,*" she had explained when I arrived on a previous occasion to find her trying on various pairs of boots while still in her dressing gown. A most curious sight to be certain.

In the end, she chose to include all six pair of handmade boots—just in case. Of what she had not explained, and I didn't ask.

"And Miss Lily?" I inquired of the newest addition to our family.

"She has gone to the theater," Mr. Symons replied. "There was mention of attending the rehearsal for Miss Templeton's new play. She has decided that she may want to be an actress."

She had escaped her lessons again. And now with aspirations to be an actress. I could hardly fault her in that. I had entertained that as well when I was very near her age. As I knew only too well, such ambitions had a way of changing.

Lily had arrived from Edinburgh after contributing to one of our inquiry cases. She had worked in a brothel known as the '*Church*' as a '*ladies' maid.*'

When it burned to the ground, I persuaded her to come to London as my ward, with the plan of providing her an education. I couldn't bear the thought that her future might be limited to work in a brothel, as a maid or *otherwise*.

She was quite spirited and gifted with a photographic memory, as Alex Sinclair, who worked for the Agency as their code breaker and had assisted us previously, had described. That had proven quite extraordinary in resolving our last inquiry case. She was also somewhat headstrong, as Brodie had pointed out. Yet, he approved the arrangement.

"*God knows the girl has no future in a whorehouse.*"

For now, considering my involvement with inquiry cases, and the fact that neither Brodie nor I had figured out where we were going to live, Lily resided at Sussex Square. It was convenient for her lessons, and my aunt was delighted with the arrangement.

Now, after several conversations regarding the boring lessons with a succession of tutors my aunt had provided, Lily had decided on a career in the theater.

To be discussed at another time. There was a far more urgent matter at hand.

"Is Mr. Munro about?" I inquired.

"I believe he's in the office going over the accounts, miss."

I thanked him and turned toward the long hallway that led to the servants' area, the kitchens, and the office.

"Will you be taking the animal with you?" Mr. Symons inquired.

Rupert had disappeared into the solar, no doubt following the scent of the now-departed monkey.

I assured him that I would.

As I passed the formal salon that was adjacent to the solar, Rupert suddenly reappeared with a large piece of some exotic plant hanging from his mouth. I reprimanded him which brought the usual grin. He then ran ahead toward the back entrance of the manor.

I found Munro in the office, muttering to himself as he stared down at a bill.

With dark brown hair and sharp blue eyes, he could be intimidating to anyone with just a glance. However, behind the disapproving frown and that blue gaze was someone who was '*loyal to the bone,*' as Brodie once described. That came from their shared childhood on the streets.

And quite simply, I knew that I could trust him, particularly when it came to Brodie.

He looked up from the pile of invoices and receipts in front of him. The frown eased as he came out of his chair just as the hound shot past the doorway toward the gardens at the back of the manor.

He knew quite well that Brodie insisted I take the hound with me whenever I was out and about the city unescorted, something that I found off-putting though I didn't argue the matter. He had been right on more than one occasion.

That piercing blue gaze narrowed. Munro stepped past me and closed the door, then pulled out a chair for me.

"Somethin' has happened?"

I explained about Mr. Dooley's visit to the office that morning.

"Do you know where Brodie is?" I asked with an attempt to keep my voice steady.

"I would think that under the circumstances, ye would know best where to find him before anyone else," Munro replied.

"No, not since yesterday at the office," I replied.

He frowned. "What is it then?"

He knew better than anyone the animosity between Brodie and Abberline in the past. that had led to Brodie leaving the MET.

"Abberline has a warrant for Brodie's arrest."

It might have been my imagination, nevertheless it seemed that the air inside the office was suddenly quite cold. Or possibly it was the expression on Munro's face.

"For what?" he asked.

"For murder."

He cursed as he came out of his chair.

"The man will not be satisfied until he has Brodie in Newgate!" He looked at me then. "Who is he supposed to have murdered?"

I explained everything that I had learned from Mr. Dooley about the death of the woman from that old case years before.

"There's more," I continued, forcing myself to remain calm. "According to what Mr. Dooley was able to learn, Brodie was seen there that night just before the police arrived.

"Why is Abberline doing this?" I asked. "I need to understand why this is happening."

"What has he told ye about it?"

I repeated what little I knew about that old case—that there was a witness to a murder. Brodie refused to hand over the witness because of threats that were made. Abberline then threatened to have charges brought against him. Rather than reveal the woman's name, Brodie resigned, and left the MET.

From my own experience with Abberline, it wasn't difficult to understand the reason he had made that decision.

Munro nodded. "Afterward, he was able to send the woman away where she wouldna be found, and with a different name."

"But she recently returned," I pointed out.

"Aye. He found her a place to live, someplace where no one would ask questions."

"At Charing Cross," I commented.

He nodded. "He also found her work to support herself." He hesitated, then added, "Brodie was never one to speak of the cases he worked when he was with the MET, and most particularly not this one, after he left the service."

All well and good, still Brodie needed to know about the warrant.

"We have to find him and warn him. Then figure out what is to be done." I refused to believe that he had any part in the woman's death.

Munro's sharp gaze met mine as he stood and retrieved his jacket from the coat rack.

"It's best that I try to find him. If he heard of it on the street, there are places he might go..."

I stood as well. "I'm going with you."

"No," he replied.

What was it about men, Scots in particular, who had a way of using one word with such irritating effect. I wondered if it was something they were born with.

He shook his head when I would have argued the matter with him.

"When the man needs to disappear, he's like a ghost. Ye learn that when ye live on the street. And he would not want ye to go about London searchin' for him. And knowin' him as I do, I would not want to explain the reason I let ye."

Let me?

Munro promised to let me know if he was able to find Brodie. Waiting was not something I was good at.

Three

I RETURNED to the town house in Mayfair, much to Rupert's approval. He immediately headed for the kitchen, where Mrs. Ryan had just taken a fresh-baked cake from the oven, while I went into the parlor where I kept a desk.

"There was a telephone call a short while ago," Mrs. Ryan informed me. "A young man by the name of Alex. He said it was most urgent."

Was it possible that he knew about the reason for Abberline's visit to the Tower? Was it also possible that he had heard from Brodie?

"Did he say anything else?"

"He said that he would try to reach you again later."

Instead of waiting, I put a call into Alex at the Tower. I was most anxious to learn if he knew where Brodie might be, not to mention finding out about that visit by Chief Inspector Abberline.

There was the usual wait as operators made the necessary connections, and I thought of Brodie's warning that it could be possible for others to listen to conversations.

Alex was quite anxious when he picked up my call. He insisted that he needed to see me as soon as possible. Instead of asking about Brodie in case anyone might be listening, I asked if he could join me for supper.

The town house was far more private for the questions I had, whereas a tavern or restaurant might draw attention.

He was to have had supper with Lucy Penworth that evening.

I knew Lucy quite well. She had once worked for the Times of London and now worked for the Agency. She had also assisted Brodie and me in an early inquiry case. I liked her very much, but far more important, I trusted her. I insisted they both join me.

We agreed for them to arrive at the town house at eight o'clock, and I informed Mrs. Ryan that they would be joining me for supper.

"And Mr. Brodie as well?" she asked.

"Not this evening," I told her with a frown and a vague excuse. "He is following up some matter in an inquiry case."

I left it at that. She was quite used to his hours when on a case, and there was no need for details that might upset her. She was quite fond of him.

The truth was, I didn't know anything beyond what Mr. Dooley had told me, and then the brief information Munro had provided about that unsolved murder case years before.

That, and the fact that I hadn't had a word from Brodie since the day before, and then only a vague explanation that he was following up some information in the counterfeit case.

Today, all had changed, and I needed to know everything Abberline had told Sir Avery.

We exchanged the usual pleasantries over supper.

Whatever Alex knew, he chose to keep to himself until after we had eaten and retired to the front parlor, where Mrs. Ryan served dessert with coffee and tea.

Alex and Lucy both commended her on a fine meal. I waited until she had closed the sliding doors behind her, then set aside my plate, my dessert untouched.

"I cannot imagine how you are so calm," Lucy commented once we were alone.

"Have you heard from Brodie?" Alex asked.

"I was hoping that you had heard from him."

"Not since yesterday," he replied. "We received a note regarding the latest developments in the counterfeit case. There was nothing new in that regard, other than someone he was to see who had business dealings in the East End.

"He thought the man might know who had been passing the counterfeit notes, or at least know something that he could follow up on."

I explained that I had intended to stop by the Agency earlier and saw Abberline as he arrived.

Alex exchanged a look with Lucy. Agency business was highly confidential and not to be shared beyond those imposing stone walls. However...

"He was looking for Brodie," Alex explained, then paused, obviously hesitant. "He has a warrant for his arrest."

I nodded. "I received word earlier at the office on the Strand."

"Then you are aware of the charges against him?"

I inquired what Sir Avery's response had been.

"He listened to what Abberline had to say, and then reminded him that he had no authority over the Agency. He also reminded him that he must send word ahead when he intends to call in the future."

I could well imagine how that went over, for a man who considered himself to be the ultimate authority in all matters.

"You must know that I don't believe the charges," Alex added most vehemently.

I did appreciate that.

"What about Sir Avery?" I inquired. "What was his reaction?"

"He sent Abberline on his way. As you know, he is not one to share his thoughts on matters. He spoke at great length after Abberline left, saying that the Agency cannot afford to be associated with such a situation."

I was not surprised.

"I have heard from one of the reporters at the newspaper," Lucy added. "The Times will be carrying an article about the murder in the morning crime section, along with a statement from the witness who claims to have seen Mr. Brodie there."

Alex nodded. "And we've heard that Abberline has brought in another private inquiry firm to look for Mr. Brodie, in addition to the police who are looking for him."

No stone unturned.

It was obvious that Abberline was determined to find him, no matter where that took the search or what it required.

However, this was Brodie. He had lived on the streets, including the East End of London. I had no doubt that he knew people and places where he could simply disappear. But for how long? And then?

Knowing him, he would be determined to find the murderer in spite of the arrest warrant Abberline had taken out for him. But one man against a substantial number of constables and a private inquiry firm? The odds were not in Brodie's favor.

"What else were you able to learn?" I asked Lucy.

"According to the person I spoke with at the paper, the landlady where the woman lived heard a horrible disturbance from the woman's flat. She went to check on her afterward, and that is when she saw Mr. Brodie and the boy."

"A boy?"

Lucy nodded. "According to the landlady, the boy is about ten years old."

The woman had a child, now caught up in this dreadful business?

What had he heard, or perhaps seen? Not unlike what Brodie had experienced years before in the death of his mother? It was no surprise that he had taken the boy with him.

But where would they go? Who would Brodie go to for help?

He had not come to Mayfair or gone to Sussex Square to enlist Munro's help. I was not surprised. Munro had already spoken of it—that the search for Brodie would extend to me. But that didn't mean that I was going to sit by and wait for the outcome.

"What was the woman's name?" I inquired.

"Ellie Sutton, apparently not her real name." Alex frowned, then, "You cannot think to find him yourself. Abberline is most determined. He'll want to speak with you as well considering...your relationship with Mr. Brodie," he added. "He will assume that he has been in contact with you."

I was grateful for his concern, still I refused to be intimidated by the fact that I might receive a visit from the Chief Inspector.

"Then, Mr. Abberline will also be aware that I cannot be

forced to provide information about my husband." Even if I knew where to find him.

"He told Sir Avery that he wouldn't let anyone stand in his way."

I did appreciate Alex's concern. However, I refused to be intimidated by Chief Inspector Abberline, or anyone else.

"I have no intention of '*standing*' anywhere," I replied.

"How can I help?"

I did appreciate his offer of assistance.

"If I were to tell you that, it could be useful to Abberline if he merely thought you were helping me."

"I do see your point," Alex admitted. "You will call on me if I can be of assistance? I owe Mr. Brodie that and...I could always go to work for the two of you, if Sir Avery gives me the sack." That boyish smile briefly reappeared.

I promised that I would contact him if needed and thanked them both. Then I walked with them to the door as their driver arrived.

"Do be careful," Lucy told me.

I assured them both that I would.

I watched as their cab moved off down the street and turned at the corner, the hound beside me at the entrance to the town house.

When I went to close the door, I caught a sudden change in the hound's manner, ears perked, that usually friendly demeanor suddenly alert, the ruff of fur at his neck standing up. His attention was fixed across the street in that line of town houses across the way.

I saw nothing there, the windows darkened in the residences, as it was quite late of the evening. But then I was not accustomed to roaming the streets of London late at night.

There followed a low rumble from Rupert and he was off

as he charged through the opening then across the thoroughfare.

I didn't attempt to call him back as I knew well enough that was pointless when he was on the chase of something. Or perhaps some*one*?

I thought of Alex's warning regarding Abberline and his determination to destroy Brodie as I glanced once more into the shadows across the way where Rupert had disappeared.

I saw nothing. Still...

I closed the door and bolted it. Rupert would return when he chose, as he had in the past and let me know with either a scratch on the door, or a howl if I didn't promptly let him in. Out of respect for my neighbors I was usually most diligent in that.

I returned to the parlor and went to my desk. I needed to make notes about what I had learned about the counterfeit case, and then decide precisely how I was going to help Brodie.

I did wish that I had a chalkboard at the town house. It always helped to see everything more clearly written out where I could consider it from every angle.

Quite often something I had not thought of seemed to pop out at me. In the matter of finding Brodie, it was undoubtedly best that I didn't write down anything that might be seen by others.

I wouldn't put it past Abberline to simply barge into the office on the Strand or the town house, in his search for him. Best to simply add my notes into my notebook.

I opened the desk drawer where I kept an assortment of writing implements along with an extra notebook in search of a pen and frowned at the elegantly carved wooden box that had been a gift from Brodie. I opened it. The fountain pen was the color of dark red wine with my initials in gold lettering, *M.F.B.* —Mikaela Forsythe Brodie.

He had purchased it from Hancock's Jewelers, for a sum I could only imagine. He had given the pen to me on my birthday, just after we had returned from Scotland.

"For ye to make yer notes, and so that ye know that ye are now part of me," he had added.

To say that I was surprised was an understatement. Hancock's was an exclusive jeweler in London, and notably carried only the finest jewelry and accessories.

I was not given to wearing jewelry other than the pendant, a medallion that had great meaning that he had given me, and the simple bronze wedding band. But more than that, Brodie was not a man given to excess sentimentality, and he had grown up painfully poor.

He had chosen something that held deep meaning to me, and had reduced me to tears at the time. And I never cried.

I had put it in the drawer to be used when I was working at my desk, but hadn't the opportunity yet. I removed it from the box. It wasn't the gift itself, but what it represented.

I had never needed or wanted anyone before. My family was my great-aunt and my sister, and more recently Lily.

But now...?

The seriousness of the present situation was not lost on me, and my throat tightened.

Where the devil was Brodie? Who had killed Ellie Sutton? And where had he taken the boy?

I gathered my thoughts, then sat at the desk and began making my notes about what I knew.

It was long after midnight when I finally heard the scratch of paws at the door. I set the pen aside and went to the front entrance. Rupert had returned.

He trotted past me, then sat down, and dropped what appeared to be a large piece of cloth on the floor in front of the hearth.

My first thought was that at least it wasn't some poor dead creature that he'd scavenged. Such as Mrs. FitzHugh's prize Pekingese, which she let out at night to relieve itself. Something that was a source of aggravation among the other residents.

"What have you got there?" I asked the hound. Not that I expected an answer. Still, that grin...

The scrap of cloth was dark blue, almost black, and made of wool, most definitely not the sort of rag that would have simply been found lying about. Particularly in this part of London. And in spite of the fact that it was torn about the edges, it was in excellent condition considering it had been in the teeth of the hound.

I picked it up and inspected it. The scrap of wool looked very familiar, the same sort of fabric in a police constable's uniform.

It was rare for a constable to be out and about in Mayfair, unless there was some incident that required their presence. There were other areas of London that required their presence due to a great deal of crime.

I thought of the hound's reaction just before he charged off across the street after Alex and Lucy left, and there had been Alex's warning that I might receive a visit from Abberline.

It seemed that I had. Or at least one of his constables, keeping watch if Brodie should pay a visit?

I set the lock on the door, and returned to the parlor.

Neither my guests nor I had touched Mrs. Ryan's raspberry cake. I set the dessert plates on the floor.

Rupert was quite pleased. He was very fond of Mrs. Ryan's cakes.

"Good boy," I told him as I tucked the piece of wool into my notebook. "Well done."

The rail car lurched sharply around a curve as it sped through the night.

Away from London.

The boy slept on with his head against Brodie's shoulder, occasionally jerking awake as memories slid into dreams, a thin hand twitching as if he wanted to grab something.

Something, anything, to fight off the nightmare dreams and the people that were in them, Brodie thought. He understood well enough.

Kings Cross station, then north.

He wanted to tell Mikaela where he was going, the one person he trusted above all others. But then there was the warrant Abberline put out. He couldn't, wouldn't involve her in this.

This was something only he could do. He needed to get the boy out of London, to a place no one would think to look for him.

The answer came from his old friend—the chemist, Mr. Brimley.

Late the previous night he had showed up at the back entrance to the chemist's shop, the boy exhausted and shaking beside him.

There were no questions.

With his medicines, microscopes, and medical knowledge from an education at Kings College, Mr. Brimley had assisted in previous inquiry cases.

The bond was more than merely professional with the care

and assistance the chemist provided to the poor in the East End.

"I'll not be forgettin' that you saved my boy from the gaol," the chemist told Brodie at the time.

"When the time comes, I will see that you're repaid for what you did."

The East End of London, running with those who had little care for anyone but themselves. More bad choices, and young Brimley was the only one identified in the robbery of a smoke shop by a group of lads.

Mr. Brimley had come to him, desperate to save his son from gaol, or worse.

Brodie knew someone, a man of some means who had contributed financially to one of the foundling homes.

He had helped the man before, someone whose career would have immediately ended if it was learned that he had assisted more than one young person escape the legal system that was flawed, and a sure sentence to prison.

But this was different. Young Brimley had needed to leave London before he was arrested. Brodie went to the man. Young Brimley was given a choice—remain in London where he would most certainly be arrested, or leave.

It was a situation where there was no real choice. Arrangements were quickly made, and he left London with Brodie for Leeds and a position with a man of some property who raised sheep.

It was far from London and far from the streets. Safe. And in time, the young man admitted that it had saved his life.

He had stayed in Leeds, worked hard, and saved his wages. He eventually acquired a small plot of land of his own and then another, along with a small herd of sheep. He was married, and now had two boys of his own.

No telegram was sent, no telephone call was made, to a small community where those things would have been known by all in a matter of time.

Instead, Brodie boarded the train at King's Cross Station with young Rory. And not a word from the lad the entire trip.

It was the middle of the night when they arrived at the station in Leeds, the only passengers that left the train that time of the night.

He found a room at the local inn, where the woman at the counter appeared in her nightcap and dressing gown. He provided a story about traveling to visit his *'sister.'*

He spent the night watching over Rory. The boy only cried out once in sleep. The rest of it stayed buried in his dreams.

The following morning, the owner of the tavern provided the name of a man who rented out his horse and cart at the local livery.

Young Brimley, a man full-grown now, well-muscled from life on the sheep farm, was already far afield when they arrived. His wife greeted them at the door, two young boys racing about.

"I know who you are, Mr. Brodie," she had gently smiled. "And who might this young man be?"

She nodded when he introduced Rory, then sent one of the young lads to the field to summon his father.

No questions were asked when young Brimley returned to the stone cottage with his oldest son.

"You seem to make a habit of rescuing young lads," he commented. "We've room enough, and he'll be good to have around for the young ones," he assured Brodie.

"The son of a *relative* as far as anyone needs to know," he then added, the story that would eventually make its way around the nearby village.

"Yer leavin'?" Rory said, fighting back the tears when it came time to go.

"There are things I must do." Brodie assured him that these were good people, and he must tell no one about what happened in London.

"I need you to be brave, as brave as yer mother would want. Do ye ken?"

Rory slowly nodded. "Ye'll come back?"

"Aye," he had promised, then turned the cart back toward the village.

Four

LONDON

I HAD LEARNED a great deal from Brodie over the past two years in the various inquiry cases we'd had taken.

One: Assume that anyone might be the criminal in an investigation.

Two: It is quite often the innocent bystander who saw something important they weren't even aware of.

Three: Always be aware of my surroundings.

Four: Trust no one—except for Brodie of course.

They were lessons that he'd learned on the streets as a boy and then in his time with the MET and during our private inquiry cases. Lessons to live by, as he put it somewhat grimly at the time.

And then there were the aspects of every case that must be determined:

Who had the motive for murder?

That might be anyone. A family member, someone wronged by the victim, greed for either wealth or power. Then there were the cases of foreign espionage, someone killed passing information or someone else determined to topple the government.

Who had the means?

Most usually it was someone in a position known to the victim beforehand, someone trusted, an acquaintance, or someone who moved in certain circles that brought them into contact with the victim and might never be suspected.

And who had the opportunity? Often someone who seemed unlikely, perhaps even innocent, however, they had the means and the motive, and then created the opportunity.

Motive, means, and opportunity. I found it all fascinating.

Brodie, of course, called it something different—morbid curiosity about the darker aspects of human nature that I had been studying for some time. He suggested that it was a dark aspect of my nature.

Women, ladies in particular, according to his experience, simply weren't supposed to be interested in such things.

Yes, well, I had my opinion on that!

It was very possible that accounted for the fact that Brodie and I worked so well together...that and other things.

This was something very different. There was a warrant out for Brodie's arrest for murder. Not that I thought for a moment that he had killed that poor woman.

I knew exactly where this came from—Chief Inspector Abberline, his illusions of promotion even now, ten years later —and that previous case where Brodie chose to protect the woman rather than feed her to the wolves, as the saying goes.

And then there was revenge.

Now, a young woman was dead.

I refused to believe that Brodie had anything to do with that, even though there was very obviously a history there. I knew him. He might be capable of many things, but murder wasn't one of them.

Knowing him as I did, he would be determined to find who had killed her. And I was equally determined to help in that.

Abberline was an ambitious man. He was completely self-absorbed and considered himself superior to anyone else.

He used people for his own advancement. Case in point: that previous murder Brodie had investigated while with the MET. And now, ten years later, it was obvious that Abberline was more determined than ever.

Not only in the matter of the woman's death, but undoubtedly in an effort to resolve that old case, something that he undoubtedly saw as his way to long-overdue promotion.

I did hope that Brodie would contact me. I wanted to help him with this. Two were far more likely to resolve an issue than one person on their own.

I knew that Munro's warning in that regard was undoubtedly correct. That simple wedding ceremony in Scotland was not a widely known fact. However, once more, I put nothing past Abberline.

It was very possible that he was more than aware that Brodie and I were now husband and wife. If so, he would undoubtedly attempt to use that to get to Brodie.

But not if I had anything to say about it.

I was not about to sit idly by, waiting for Abberline to slither up to my doorstep—and that was a perfect description of him.

Therefore, I intended to begin my own inquiries, beginning with the scene of the murder, once I was certain the police had completed their business there.

It wouldn't be difficult to determine precisely where the woman had lived in Charing Cross.

I was aware that I would need to take precautions.

I dressed in clothes I used from time to time when out and about London that included a sturdy walking skirt Templeton brought me from one of her tours, shirtwaist, jacket, and boots.

Downstairs I gathered my bag that included my notebook and that revealing patch of wool cloth, then prepared to depart. Rupert met me at the door.

"I fed him earlier," Mrs. Ryan announced. "He likes bacon."

Imagine that!

"He seemed quite upset about something last night," she added. "And you were up quite late as well. A new inquiry case, miss?"

"Some matters I need to look into...." I left it at that. "Will you be going out today?" I then asked, with a thought to that '*something*' the night before she had mentioned.

"The market for your supper and some bake goods that are almost gone."

Her biscuits and scones. Rupert would be pleased with that.

"Anything you or Mr. Brodie might want, miss?"

There wasn't, of course, with his whereabouts unknown. I reminded her to set the locks on both doors when she left.

"Of course, miss. I always do."

That left the subject of Rupert who waited at the door as the cab I had called for earlier had arrived. He had most definitely earned his supper and breakfast the night before.

He shot out the door when I opened it, then proceeded to

take care of some morning business before planting himself at the kerb.

I recognized the driver from previous occasions.

"The Strand, miss?" he asked as I climbed aboard and Rupert followed.

Instead, I gave him the address in Holborn where I hoped to find someone.

A person who might be able to provide information about that case ten years earlier.

Mr. Conner had been with the MET for very near thirty years, then was forced to retire because of an injury.

He lived on a small pension due to that injury, other income including work from Brodie, and additional work that Brodie described as *'assistance'* for others. That frequently included security work at the docks and *'other things'* that he didn't explain and I didn't ask about.

A fellow Scot, he knew the streets as only one who had walked them for many years and had encountered all sorts of criminals. He lived alone and frequented a tavern near where he kept a flat.

He was gruff and could be as hard as the streets of the East End, but he was loyal to Brodie and I liked him very much. With his connections, it was very likely he already knew about the warrant Abberline had put out for Brodie's arrest. Very possibly he knew about that old case, and might well know where Brodie was.

I could have sent a message round by one of the messenger services, but it might not have been delivered for some time. He didn't have a telephone. Consequently, the only way to find him was to go there.

It was very near midday when I arrived in Holborn. There was no answer at his flat. A man who occupied the flat next door informed me that Mr. Conner had been out most of the night, which might mean anything.

"You might ask at the Black Bull, across the way."

The Black Bull Tavern was in a narrow space between a dry goods shop and an engraver's. I might have missed it, except for the sign over the door, that of a black bull.

I stepped inside. The musty smell of cigarette smoke, along with stale beer and equally stale bodies filled the room, along with an enthusiastic shout over the sound of dice being slammed down at a table. Tables lined one side of the tavern with the bar at the back.

I was not unfamiliar with the inside of taverns and pubs—in fact I had been in my fair share in our past inquiries. Unfortunately, I often drew unwanted attention. I suppose part of it might have been the sight of the hound.

That enthusiastic uproar of drink and gambling immediately fell silent, a dozen or more faces staring at me, including the one I was looking for.

Mr. Conner was tall, with close-cropped white hair, his brown eyes staring back at me from one of those tables.

He spoke to his companion, then rose, and approached me.

"Miss Forsythe, yer not something this sort usually sees in here," he commented in that unmistakable Scot accent. "I won't say that I'm not pleased."

He could be quite engaging. "I trust ye've come about the arrest warrant Abberline has out for Brodie."

It seemed that he was indeed well informed. "I do need to speak with you about it."

He nodded. "Not here. These fellows can't keep something private to save themselves, and all they know how to do is gape at a pretty young woman.

"We'll go down the way to the public house. They won't be

crowded yet this time of the late morning. And I suppose we must include that filthy creature." He looked down at Rupert.

The '*filthy creature*' merely grinned.

The public house where one might find a meal was much like the one across from the office on the Strand.

"The filthy beast is with me, Mr. Finlay," Mr. Conner told the man behind the counter as we entered. "He won't bother."

Mr. Finlay nodded. "Keepin' strange company are ye nowadays?"

Mr. Conner ordered coffee, then escorted me to a table in the back, some distance apart from the only other customer.

He waited until Mr. Finlay brought the coffee.

"Will you be having a bit to eat?" he asked.

I shook my head.

"Not this mornin'," Mr. Conner told him.

"You know about the arrest warrant that Abberline has for Brodie."

He nodded. "I heard about it last night from one of the lads I keep in contact with. We raise a pint or two from time to time." He gave me a long look. "This situation is most serious."

"I want to help but I have no idea where he is."

"Ye've not seen him since ye learned about this?"

"Not since two days ago. With the death of the young woman, I'm certain he's determined to find whoever murdered her."

I knew that he and Brodie were extremely close from the time they worked together at the MET, perhaps including that particular case ten years earlier. They had a mutual respect, as well as mutual dislike of the Chief Inspector.

"I cannot help him if I don't know everything about this," I told him.

"Has it occurred to ye that he doesn't want you involved?"

There was no need to reply to that. My presence there was answer enough.

He swore under his breath. "I knew ye could be stubborn..." The rest went unspoken. He shook his head.

"Brodie'll not take kindly to my telling ye what I know, or allowing ye to involve yerself."

I waited. He swore again, then began with a question of his own.

"What do ye know about the reason he left the MET?"

"I know that it was over a case where a woman witnessed a murder that he was investigating. It seems that she was threatened because of what she saw. The Chief Inspector demanded that he turn the woman over to the police. When Brodie refused, Abberline threatened to have charges brought against him. He left the MET shortly after.

"She had returned to London and was living under another name," I told him what I had learned. "And apparently there is a child, a boy Brodie was seen leaving the woman's flat with the night she was killed."

"You know a great deal," he replied.

"Munro was able to provide me with some information. "But there is obviously a great deal more that I don't know about all of this."

I retrieved the cloth from my bag and handed it to him.

His gaze narrowed. "Where did you get this?"

"The *beast*, as you called him." I then explained the encounter the previous night. "He returned to the town house with this piece of cloth."

The frown deepened. "Has Abberline called on ye?"

"Not yet. However, I would imagine that is only a matter of time."

He was clearly trying to decide what to tell me. He shook his head.

"Nothing has changed about the man," he replied, then paused as Mr. Finlay appeared to fill our coffee mugs. When he had returned to the counter, Mr. Conner handed the cloth back to me.

"It would seem that Mr. Abberline has already sent someone to watch yer place with the hope of finding Brodie."

"When was the last time you spoke with him?" I then asked.

He took a long sip of coffee, holding the mug between both hands.

"Some days before. He had asked me to inquire through people I know about counterfeit money that has been found about London. He was hoping to find a connection..." He shook his head. "Not since then."

"What do you know about the woman who was murdered?"

He seemed to have come to some sort of a decision as he set the mug back on the table, then sat back in his chair.

"She was hardly more than a girl when she showed up at Covent Garden, selling fresh produce. According to the story she told, the woman her father kept with threw her out of where they lived.

"It's difficult enough to make it at the Garden if ye own the stall and work it yerself, but a young thing like that..."

He shook his head. "She was near starvin' to death when she was accused of stealin'.

"Brodie stepped in the middle of the situation when she might have been arrested, and paid the vendor what he claimed he was out. Comin' from where he had, he felt sorry for her, and found her a place where she could stay, along with work at a public house that paid better than what she could make at the Garden.

"She made the acquaintance of a woman there who worked in one of the private men's clubs, one of those fancy places where they go to drink, gamble, and..." He hesitated and looked at me.

"I quite understand," I told him. "Please continue."

"She was a pretty little thing and eventually became acquainted exclusively with one of the young men. She made far more money there in one night than a month at the public house."

It wasn't difficult to know what that had included.

"The young man promised to take care of her," I replied.

"Aye, with fancy clothes, her own flat verra near the club, and a good amount of coin in the bargain," he continued.

"She witnessed a murder." I also knew that much.

He nodded. "The young man she had been with was killed. She saw the man who did it. She was terrified and went to Brodie. He promised to help her. Abberline had other thoughts in the matter.

"He needed a witness in order to solve the crime. However, she was threatened if she ever revealed what she had seen."

I knew the rest of it. "And Brodie helped her to leave London for some place safe.

"Aye, as far from Abberline as possible and under a different name," Mr. Conner replied.

"She returned and apparently found work at the Brown Hotel,"

He nodded. "That was just over a year ago."

"Why did she return?"

"That, I do not know, miss. I only know that Brodie was aware of it."

As much as he was Brodie's friend, and would undoubtedly say anything to protect him, I did believe that Conner didn't know the reason she had returned.

"He was seen leaving her flat with a boy," I then told him. "Do you know anything about that?

I thought I saw something in the expression on Mr. Conner's face, perhaps a thought, something he might have said, then decided against.

"Mr. Brodie might be able to tell ye more about that," he replied.

"If I knew where to find him," I pointed out. "Do you know where he is?"

He shook his head. "There are many places for a man to go when he knows the streets. I've already put the word out to contacts I have," he said. "There's a man I'm to meet later who may be able to tell me something."

I nodded, then caught that sharp look.

"The man is known to frequent an establishment in Whitechapel on the high street," he continued. "He sells information, and I've used him in the past. But it's no place for a lady, and Brodie would have none of yer goin' there, with the killings of those women."

A series of murders that were still unsolved by the police.

"You will tell me what you learn from the man?"

He nodded. "If ye'll give me yer word that ye'll stay away from there. The man has enough to worry about out there."

I knew he was referring to Brodie.

I agreed. "And you'll tell me if you hear from him?"

He nodded. "Aye."

He paid for our coffee and then escorted me from the Public House, out onto the street. I caught that thorough look down one end of the street, then the other before we continued to the corner. He waited with me until a cabman appeared, that gaze watchful.

I climbed aboard the cab and the hound followed. Mr. Conner paused as he closed the gate.

"Do not underestimate Abberline," he cautioned. "He's waited a long time, and he will use everything at his disposal to get to our *friend*." He glanced down at the beast.

"And as much as the animal smells and has disgusting habits, keep that creature with ye at all times, and see that ye have protection."

I assured him that I would.

Five

WHILE I HAD PROMISED that I would not attempt to follow Mr. Conner into Whitechapel for his meeting with the man who might be able to provide information about Brodie, that did not mean that I was going to sit idly by.

I needed to know more if I was going to help Brodie. With Mr. Conner's warning about Abberline, not to mention the incident the night before, it seemed that I was being watched. And perhaps followed as well. That required extra measures, and Templeton was the one who might be able to assist with that.

Visiting my friend was always an adventure in the unusual, to say the least.

She was a highly acclaimed actress, had traveled widely in numerous productions, was rumored to have had an affair with the Prince of Wales—something she would never come right out and admit but used to her advantage from time to time. And she had a most unusual companion—Ziggy.

Ziggy was a four-and-a-half-foot-long iguana from South America, presented to Templeton as a gift from an *'admirer'* with whom she had spent some time on one of her tours. When she left Buenos Aires on her return to London, Ziggy had accompanied her.

He had resided in the London Zoo for a time. He had rejoined her at the theater more recently after she discovered that he wasn't eating and had lost considerable color.

Not having any knowledge about iguanas, I could only assume the matter had become quite serious.

At the theater, he usually had the run of the place until curtain time. In his wanderings about, usually in search of food —he was an herbivore according to Templeton—he had periodically terrorized stage workers, fellow actors, and members of the orchestra.

With that in mind, I arrived at the Drury and kept a watchful eye out as I stepped into the foyer of the theater. There I was met by another acquaintance of my friend—an imposing, life-like statue of William Shakespeare.

Templeton claimed, and with some evidence to support it, that she communicated regularly with Sir William, who happened to have been dead for very near three hundred years.

Not that I doubted her...the evidence had been information he had supposedly provided on more than one occasion in our inquiry cases.

Brodie was convinced that she was quite insane. I preferred *eccentric*. If she thought that she communicated with William Shakespeare, who was I to question it? I had experienced far more unusual things in my travels.

Templeton arrived at the entrance in attire far different from her costume for the play, a riding habit, along with a crop. Most unusual for someone who was not inclined to go riding on a horse.

According to her, they were unpredictable, prone to

running off unexpectedly, and relieved themselves at the most inopportune moments.

This from a woman who kept a pet iguana that was quite unpredictable, and had the habit of running off and causing havoc throughout the theater.

I had no idea about the rest of it, except that I had gotten in the habit of checking the bottom of my boots after a visit with her.

She was quite excited now as she clasped both my hands.

"He said you would be paying a visit," she excitedly announced. "How wonderful!"

There was no one else in the foyer, no attendant that early in the afternoon. Only that statue...as I was saying, but who was I to doubt her.

She looped her arm through mine as we walked together toward the adjacent hallway that led to her dressing room.

"I thought it might be Lily at first," she continued. "I decided that couldn't be, as she is undoubtedly at her studies most of the day. The girl is quite marvelous. She has spoken of becoming an actress?"

In addition to her musical skills and solving codes.

Templeton leaned in and whispered. "Wills thinks she is quite marvelous as well. He has a particular play in mind for her. I did explain that she is quite young and that you might have a say in it."

"I do appreciate that," I replied.

"And what is this nasty business about Brodie?" she asked.

She was not in the habit of reading the dailies or keeping company with officers of the MET.

"You've spoken with Munro?" I asked.

They had a history, as they say, and had spent a great deal of time together—that was probably the most discreet way of describing it. And that had included Templeton being accused of murder, along with a rather graphic piece of artwork.

There had been a *'separation,'* as she called it, when she left for performances in France and Italy, Munro declaring that she was impossible, unpredictable, and he would not take place in line with other rumored lovers.

"I haven't seen him," she replied with something that could have been a bit of sadness in someone I had never known to have regrets over a man.

"He is being quite impossible, unpredictable, and there is that whole Scottish thing. He can be stubborn, domineering, and he does have a temper."

All things that I recognized from first-hand experience.

"It was Wills who told me the news," she said then. "And he is most distressed about it. That is the reason he knew you would be coming to see me."

Of course.

"So, tell me, what is to be done to assist Brodie?"

I did feel a bit like *Alice*, who had fallen down a rabbit hole. I then explained how I thought best to go about investigating the situation.

Templeton nodded. "Yes, a costume is in order. We must simply find the right one for you. There are dozens upon dozens in the costume room. I'm certain that we will be able to find something.

"This is going to be such fun!" she announced as we reached her dressing room and she explained to Mrs. Finch what was needed.

The adventure began in the room in the theater where the costumes of her fellow actors were kept. She went among the rows of racks hung with costumes as if shopping at Harrods, emerging with several items of clothing over her arm.

"We'll start with these," she said as we returned to her dressing room.

I had to admit that the transformation was quite amazing in spite of the fact that I had declined both the wig and makeup.

When finished, I thought it might be best to disguise myself as a man particularly due to my height, with trousers, a threadbare jacket, stained shirt, and a cap with my hair tucked up.

The entire ensemble made me look like a character from one of Mr. Dickens' novels, and I wasn't certain that I would have recognized myself.

"Some smudge to the face and it will be perfect!" Templeton announced where she sat at her dressing table. Then a much different expression crossed her face.

"No one will recognize you, and Wills agrees," she announced. "Still, he cautions that you must be very careful and not forget the weapon you always carry."

Of course he would know about that.

"Oh, I do wish that I was going with you."

That might very well have included Ziggy, and I wasn't at all certain that the streets of London were ready for him.

"When will you begin?" she asked.

"Tonight."

I wanted to go to Charing Cross as soon as possible to see what I might be able to learn from the place where Ellie Sutton was murdered.

"Where will you stay while you investigate this nasty business? You can hardly return to the town house. Abberline has quite the reputation when pursuing things."

Yes, I was aware. I had shared with her about Rupert's midnight adventure.

"Wait..." she suddenly said.

A message from Wills? She did have that look about her, as if staring off at something over my shoulder.

"You absolutely cannot stay at the office either. Wills is most adamant about it."

Oh dear. Not that I believed it. I wasn't one to call the man a liar. And the truth was that the office might very well be on Abberline's list of places to look for Brodie. It made sense.

"I know the perfect place," Templeton announced. "It's nearby, a flat used by one of the actresses who usually appears in the afternoon short plays.

It seemed that the young woman was presently away for a time.

"A man she has been seeing proposed to her," she continued. "He wants her to give up the theater. They had a falling-out over the issue and she decided some time away was called for. She left for Paris and the flat is empty. No one would ever think to look for you there.

"The landlady is quite used to theater people coming and going so there should be no difficulty from that quarter. And I'm certain there is no problem having the hound with you." She retrieved a key from her dressing room table and handed it to me.

"Sophie left this with me in case she should need me to send her anything she might have forgotten, or decides to stay longer in Paris."

That certainly did not bode well for the marriage proposal.

Templeton provided a carpet bag for the clothes. I quickly stowed them away. She hugged me as I thanked her and stood to leave.

"You must be very careful," she warned.

"Of course," I replied.

I found a cab for the short ride to the office on the Strand.

Mr. Cavendish paddled out from the alcove, a club in his hand. He lowered a club he had been holding when he saw Rupert and then myself.

Brodie had not returned. Still, there were others who had been there, just as Wills had predicted. Score one more for the bard.

"The bloody peelers," Mr. Cavendish said. "Kicked in the door and had their way with the place while I was out and about. The office is a mess. Miss Effie came over earlier and cleaned up a bit, and I had a man in to repair the lock." He grinned.

"Somethin' new for him—he's usually breaking into a place, not locking up. He left a new key." He handed it to me.

"They're lookin' for Mr. Brodie and anything or anyone that might tell them where he is. You need to be careful, miss."

It was amazing how diligent Abberline could be when it served his own purposes.

I was aware that in the past Mr. Cavendish might perhaps have done some things that could possibly put him afoul of the police. Minor issues to be certain, but I reminded him that he needed to be careful as well.

He nodded. "I'll be stayin' at the Public House for now. The owner has a particular dislike for the police."

And perhaps with Miss Effie, I thought. There did seem to be something there, as she was always providing him and Rupert with food, and made certain the door to the storage room at the back of the Public House was open for them when the weather set in.

"Whatever Mr. Brodie is about, that one is determined to

find him. And he wouldn't hesitate to use you as well, if you get my meanin'."

I did.

Before leaving, I went up to the office. It was obvious that it had been searched quite thoroughly.

Files had been pulled from the file cabinet, and were stacked atop the desk in piles that had spilled over onto the floor. A bottle of my aunt's very fine whisky was still there. I put it in my bag. I was not about to leave it for one of Abberline's men, should they return.

The blackboard had been pushed against the far wall, obviously in Abberline's search for something that might tell him where he might find Brodie. There was some satisfaction that he didn't find anything there.

The telephone line was still intact. I placed a call to the town house. Mrs. Ryan eventually answered.

"*Praise the saints that yer safe,*" she said, then proceeded to tell me that Abberline's men had been there as well after I left that morning.

The Chief Inspector and his men had indeed been busy. They had an official paper signed by the magistrate allowing them to search the town house.

"*Irish trash, the man was!*" she exclaimed, which was quite a statement, as Mrs. Ryan was Irish as well.

There was more—however, the connection crackled, went silent for a moment, then she was there again.

"*...gave them a piece of my mind, I did!*" I caught part of the rest of it. "*Said they were lookin' for Mr. Brodie. I told them he hadn't been here in days, but that wasn't good enough. Then, they began to tear the place apart. I wish the hound had been here!*"

I explained that I would be away for a few days, but didn't

say more, or where. The less she knew, the safer it was for her. I then told her that she should go to Sussex Square.

I knew that she would be safe there. There were boundaries even Abberline dared not cross, unless he wished to find himself sweeping the streets in his next position, which was an entertaining thought.

And there was Munro, of course. A confrontation with Abberline's men would not end well for any of them if the Chief Inspector was foolish enough to go there and attempt what he had done at the office and the town house.

I didn't leave a note for Brodie if he should return. Best not to let anyone know that I had been there if Abberline should return. I then locked the door behind me, obviously not that it would stop anyone.

Mr. Cavendish was on the sidewalk when I reached the street below. Rupert lay at the entrance to the alcove. After his behavior the night before, I was confident that if there was anyone lurking about now, he would have let us know.

We accompanied Mr. Cavendish to the Public House. I ordered supper, though I had little appetite. My thoughts churned over what I had learned, dozens of questions, and the matter of what to do next.

This part of the case was where I would usually have exchanged ideas, thoughts, and those questions with Brodie. At present, I was very much on my own.

It was an odd feeling, still I was determined to continue. I could only hope that he was aware of the warrant, and either Mr. Conner or Munro would find him. I was confident that he could elude the police until the murderer was found. He had, after all, once been one of them, and with the additional experience of living on the street.

"Is the food not to yer likin', miss?" Miss Effie asked, of the meat pies she had served.

I realized that I had barely touched mine, while Mr. Cavendish and the hound had finished theirs.

"It's excellent, as usual," I replied. "I seem to have no appetite."

"I can well understand." She exchanged a look with Mr. Cavendish. "I'll put it in a tin to send along with you."

When she returned, I paid for the meal and we left the Public House.

"Where can I reach you, miss, if I should hear from Mr. Brodie?" Mr. Cavendish asked.

I could have explained about my temporary lodging at the flat on Drury Lane, but decided against it.

He had once been severely injured in a past inquiry because of information he had. With the incident at the office, I would not take that risk that he might be injured, or worse, if Abberline returned.

"I do think the hound should remain with you," I told him out of concern. "I can take care of myself."

He shook his head. "Mr. Brodie would have none of that. Besides, you have the extra meat pie. The hound gets hungry late of the night. And he'll just follow you."

It was a poor excuse. It was obvious he wouldn't be persuaded.

"If you learn something, you might pass it on to Mr. Conner." That seemed the best.

He nodded. "Be careful, miss."

Then I set off, the tin with the meat pie in one hand, Templeton's carpet bag—somewhat heavier with the bottle of Old Lodge whisky in it—over my shoulder, and the hound at my side. It occurred to me that we were an odd sight, as I watched the street and the alcoves near the front of shops as I crossed the Strand.

Drury Lane was not far; I could have easily walked there. However, something Brodie had taught me came to mind, that it was best to let others think one thing while doing something different.

Case in point, we had once hired a cab and had the driver deliver us to one location, then found a second driver to take us to our intended destination, thereby eluding anyone who might have followed. And I wanted to make certain we were not followed, even though I was confident Rupert would have alerted me to anyone who lingered, followed, or suddenly approached.

I waved down a cab and we climbed aboard. I had the driver let us off several blocks away, then secured another cab and had the driver take us to the theater, going back round the way we had just come.

Those attending the evening performance had begun to gather. I then slipped through the crowd, continued down the street to Drury Lane, then circled round to the back of the building where Templeton's friend Sophie had her flat.

With Rupert beside me, I made my way through the back entrance to the flat where the young actress had lived before fleeing her lover.

I turned on the electric, a single fixture glowing on the wall beside the door. The flat was small, with a bedroom off the main room, an overstuffed chair, quite worn in several places, a coal stove, and a small table and chairs. I put the tin with the supper I had not eaten in the food box on the counter.

A shadow suddenly scurried away, the remnants of a moldy loaf of bread scattered about. I looked down at Rupert, who sat on the rug.

"I do expect you to take care of that sort of thing," I informed him. He merely lay down and stared up at me with large soulful eyes that seemed to say that rats were not his favorite fare.

The flat was quite cold. I set pieces of coal in the stove and lit the fire. It gradually grew, glowing across the rough wood floor and a simple but adequate rug, illuminating a half-dozen or more handbills tacked to the wall announcing forthcoming plays.

A pull-cord to a light fixture over the table, hung over a vase of crumbling roses. No doubt remnants of that marriage proposal.

The bedroom was nothing more than a narrow bed pushed against the wall with a small table and washstand. More handbills and posters decorated the walls, including one that featured Templeton. Bedcovers had been neatly folded. It seemed that Sophie was confident she wouldn't need them.

With a thought to the other occupant of the flat that I had discovered fleeing the breadbox, I did wonder if there might be other occupants in the bed. It was not uncommon in parts of London.

Until I had the opportunity to make further inspections, the overstuffed chair in the outer room would have to do.

I made notes in my notebook, including the hound's encounter with Abberline's constable the night before, and the fact that the police had come calling at both the office and the town house.

I then put more coal on the fire, and checked that the lock on the door was secure. Pouring myself a bit of my aunt's very fine whisky, I settled myself in that chair before the coal stove, with Rupert at my feet.

Unfortunately, sleep was long in coming, even with a

second dram of whisky. It was well past midnight when I last checked the watch pinned to my shirtwaist, questions stirring my thoughts.

Who was murdered ten years earlier? Who was the man who had supported Ellie Sutton for a while? Someone high-placed? Whom had she seen the night that she was forced to leave London? Supposedly she'd fled a threat? But from whom?

I hoped to learn some of the answers the next morning.

Mayfair

The night air was cold, mist slipping along the rooftops and across the sidewalks.

No light shone from inside the town house—no late fire gleaming from the fireplace in the front parlor, no light spilling out from the tall windows that lined the street.

Nor had there been anyone at the office on the Strand, although there were signs someone had been—the splintered wood around the door frame, a new lock, and other things seen through the glass panes in that door—files stacked atop the desk, the chalkboard wiped clean.

And below? Neither the Mudger, nor the hound. Both were gone.

Brodie made his way down from the office, and then to Mayfair.

It was the same, not even a light at the servants' entrance.

Slipping through the shadows, he caught a sudden movement across the way just beyond the circle of light from the street lamp.

Someone returning from a late-night engagement? Perhaps one of the residents out for a walk? Or, someone else...?

Then the flare of a match, followed by a stream of cigarette smoke in the cold night air, and a shadow. A man, stocky, hiding there, watching the street. Watching the town house?

The thought went no further than the obvious—Abberline!

No stone unturned, Brodie thought grimly. Anything and everything to feed the man's ambition.

No matter the harm it caused. No matter the truth.

He watched until the glow of the cigarette was crushed out and only that shadow shifting against the cold night air remained, watching, waiting.

He glanced again at the darkened windows of the town house.

Where was Mikaela? What had happened?

Had Abberline already been there?

He cursed—Abberline and his ambitions, his schemes, and Ellie's foolishness that had cost her life, and now this! If Mikaela was harmed in any way...

The thought went no further. She was too intelligent, resourceful, and stubborn. Then there was the next thought—what would she do?

He cursed again. He didn't like this part, the two of them off in different directions, apart, when what he wanted...was to make certain Mikaela was safe, to be with her. It didn't matter where as long as they were together.

When had she become so important to him?

From the beginning, he supposed, when she had walked

into the office on the Strand and both aggravated and fascinated him.

And now? She was a part of him. She had somehow slipped inside him, just there when he took a deep breath, when she was finally near. But she wasn't.

He moved through the shadows at the side of the town house, back past that darkened servants' entrance, and disappeared into the night.

Six

DRURY LANE

THE EARLY MORNING sounds in the building wakened me—the creak of floorboards overhead, voices, then the slam of a door. Usual morning sounds that moved past the door, followed by silence as others in the tenement left for the day.

And then there was the hound, staring up at me, a paw on my arm as I struggled out from what little sleep I had managed after dozing off in the chair.

Waking up in a different place was always a bit confusing, those first moments as the brain gradually stirs disorienting. On my travels, my brain had quickly adjusted to different surroundings, with curiosity and energy to start the day and explore.

This morning my brain seemed to be somewhere else, possibly due to those two drams of whisky. I required another stroke of Rupert's paw to rouse me from the past few hours in the chair.

I sat up, wincing at the pain in my back from the chair and

a dull headache. First things first, as Rupert went to the door of the flat and whined. I was much of the same opinion.

I checked the hallway, then went to the rear entrance to let him out.

"If you're not back in good time, I'm leaving you here," I told him as if I expected an answer. I opened the door and he bolted out into the alley.

When I would have returned to the flat, I encountered a stout woman with a stained apron. Her frown was surrounded by a faint mustache of the sort older women tend to acquire, and she clutched a broom in both hands.

"What 'ave we 'ere?" she demanded.

It is always best to stay as close to the truth as possible when conducting our investigations. Therefore, I explained that I would be staying in Sophie's flat while she was away. The larger truth was that I had no idea how long I would need to be there.

"Sent by one of the theater people?" she asked with a narrowed gaze beneath one long eyebrow where two should have been.

She would have made a great character in one of my novels.

I nodded, the headache beginning to throb.

"What might be yer name?"

Considering everything that had happened, it was obviously unwise, perhaps even dangerous, to give my real name. Nor was I willing to involve Templeton by mentioning her name.

"Emma," I replied.

After all, Emma Fortescue, the character in my novels, was my other self, according to my sister Linny, who declared that she had no idea why I bothered to disguise the fact that Emma was me.

"I'm Mrs. Peabody, the landlady 'ere," the woman announced, "and the rents are due on the first."

I couldn't help it. It might have been the headache, too little sleep or the leftover effects of the whisky. My thought just naturally wondered if there was a Mr. Peabody?

I wondered if he had a mustache. Or possibly he was merely a figment of her imagination as I had discovered in our inquiries. The title 'Mrs' was often used to create the illusion of respectability, or possibly keep unwanted men away. Although that didn't seem as if it would have been a problem in this case.

"The flat is paid up 'til the first." She gestured to Sophie's door. "I know you theater people...I was once in theater meself."

That conjured up images of the roles she might have played, Dogberry from *Much Ado*, for instance. I glanced at that mustache, no makeup required for the part.

My upper lip twitched. I forced a smile, and thanked her for the information.

"This building is all I have," she continued as I returned to the flat. "If yer one day late, the door will be nailed shut and yer belongings in the street. And I don't abide creatures in the building."

She had obviously noticed Rupert as I turned him out. I thought of the other *creature* I had encountered the night before in the breadbox, and thought it best not to mention it, and gave the excuse, ridiculous as it was, that the hound had a part in the current play.

"A dog? In a play?" she replied. "You don't say. Does he do tricks?"

There was, of course, his ability to steal food, retrieve various body parts of a carcass, and attack unsavory characters, that included stalking police constables. I merely nodded.

"I s'pose there's no harm then," Mrs. Peabody continued. "As long as there's no mess and he doesn't frighten the other tenants. That will be an extra two shillings a month," she added.

So much for concern about any mess, as long as there was payment in it.

I assured her that I would pay the additional amount, then escaped back to the flat. I would very definitely use the character of Mrs. Peabody in my next novel, mustache included.

I had donned more suitable clothes that I had brought from the office on the Strand, then read back over the notes I had made the night before.

The hound had not yet returned as I was ready to leave, however, the warehouse for the Times newspaper was not far. I locked the door of the flat behind me and set off.

I had researched newspaper archives previously and hoped that I might find information about the murder of Stephen Matthews ten years earlier, that Abby Sutton had witnessed and had put her life in danger. Anything that might provide information that could be useful, since it was very obvious the two murders were somehow linked.

I hadn't worn the costume Templeton and Mrs. Finch had provided. I thought the disguise of a common laborer, and a man at that, might be a bit suspicious at the Times warehouse. Not to mention it would draw unwanted attention. I then left the building on Drury Lane, and kept a watchful eye on the street.

The Times archives were kept in the same building where the dailies were printed, and not far from the Strand. With the usual traffic on the street, it was far quicker to walk than wait for a cab, and less likely to draw attention.

I arrived at the main floor entrance to the Times, and *Emma Fortescue* signed in. I then took the elevator to the third floor, where the newspaper archives were kept. The newspaper '*morgue*,' as it was called, a somewhat morbid name—but oddly appropriate to the case.

As I knew well, the newspaper had begun storing archives of past issues as far back as 1785 on microfilm. More recent issues had yet to be preserved on film, including issues from ten years earlier. These daily issues were stored in catalogue boxes.

Alex Sinclair had provided the date of the murder. I gave it to the clerk along with a request for the crime sheet from that same date and several subsequent issues. It was possible more articles would have appeared as the investigation continued into that previous murder.

The clerk eventually returned and handed me a pair of gloves to protect the pages as I read through the dailies. I went to a nearby desk, pulled on the gloves, and opened the issue from the date after the murder.

In the way that sensational crimes involving well-known or high-placed persons often made the front page as well, I found the complete article that had appeared in the daily about the murder reported on the crime sheet.

THE TIMES
11 January 1880

Members of the Metropolitan Police were summoned to the Clarendon Sports Club in the late evening hours, where the body of a prominent member was discovered in one of the gaming rooms.

The victim has been identified as Stephen Matthews, of St. James's, Westminster, and his death under suspicious circumstances is being investigated as murder.

Officers of the Metropolitan Police who arrived at the location of the victim's death, included Inspectors Angus Brodie and William Morrissey.

Those in the company of the victim throughout the evening were questioned, with reports of a witness to the murder. As the investigation continues, the name of the witness has not been provided to this journalist.

Others questioned at the club that provides a wide variety of sports, gambling, and social companions, include the club manager, as well as several prominent members who were present during the evening.

Stephen Matthews was the son of the Sir Edward Matthews, and heir to Argosy Trading Company.

Chief Inspector Abberline of the Metropolitan Police is in charge of the investigation and has vowed to find those responsible.

T. Burke

That original article provided valuable information including the name of the journalist who wrote the article, T. Burke.

None other than Theodolphus Burke, who had established

himself as somewhat of an expert on criminal activities, including the more recent Whitechapel murders.

I had made his acquaintance when he attended my first book signing.

It was obvious from the outset of the event that '*Teddy*,' a name that better suited him, had considered coverage of a book-signing beneath his journalistic talent. Particularly a book written by a woman.

Then there was the comment I'd overheard in his conversation with a customer, that referred to me as the '*author of fluff and nonsense.*'

He had then mistakenly, or perhaps deliberately, referred to me as *Emma,* the protagonist of my travel novels. I might have excused it as an oversight.

Still, at the end of the afternoon, he dismissed me with a condescending smile, as '*My dear,*' along with the announcement that he was going to write a book one day about his own adventures, turning the conversation around to himself.

At that point I had seriously considered telling him precisely what he could do with his opinion of my book, his pretentious name, and his pathetic journalistic skills.

The only reason I had not was my consideration for the bookstore owner who had exclaimed that it was his best day ever for book sales.

Revenge was sweet with the success of that book and the others that followed. However, *Teddy* might be able to tell me more about that old murder that was never solved.

The next article I found provided information Burke received from someone within the police—most interesting—who was to '*remain anonymous,*' according to the article. That person had apparently informed him that the witness to the murder had suddenly disappeared.

In that article, *Teddy* had gone on to speculate the reason, then added that Inspector A. Brodie was being questioned in the matter.

'*It is this journalist's opinion that there is more to this horrible situation that has not yet been discovered. It is well known that there are those within the ranks of the police who have found themselves in questionable circumstances previously, and now possibly once more.*'

It had continued:

'*An innocent man has been murdered. The family is now in the depths of grief and despair. One can only hope that the witness will be found and justice will prevail. At this time, Inspector A. Brodie has been removed from the case. Inspector William Morrissey will continue the investigation.*'

As I already knew, the 'witness' was not found, and Brodie had been threatened with formal charges for obstructing the case. Instead he chose to resign when Abberline was unable to make a case against him.

I requested the next several issues of the Times, but found nothing more regarding the case.

I reluctantly added *Teddy's* name to my notes. If he was able to provide more information from that old case, I was willing to endure the man's condescending arrogance. I also wrote down the name of William Morrissey, the investigator who had continued with the case.

Mr. Conner might know him, and then there was also the possibility that I might be able to speak with the Matthews family.

Questioning a family after a tragedy was always a delicate matter, even ten years later. I knew of some who continued to mourn long after a loss. They might see my questions as an intrusion, or they might simply refuse to meet with me.

And then there was the private men's club where the murder occurred. Even though it had been a decade since the murder, there might still be someone among the staff who remembered something that was heard or seen.

I assumed that everyone who was at the club that night had been questioned. Still, something might have been forgotten at the time, then remembered later, in that way that the memory works.

I returned the past issues of the dailies to the clerk at the desk, then took the lift back to the ground floor.

The journalists who wrote for the Times worked at another location, at the newspaper offices near London Bridge. If I was to speak with Mr. Burke regarding that old murder, I would need to go there.

Two murders, ten years apart. A coincidence?

In the inquiry cases I had assisted Brodie, there were no coincidences, most particularly when it came to murder.

What had the woman who called herself Ellie Sutton seen the night Stephen Matthews was killed? The murderer?

Who would threaten her? And why?

She disappeared and had lived anonymously for almost ten years—why had she returned? And who had killed her?

I refused to believe that Brodie had anything to do with her death. Yet that raised the question, what was he doing at the scene of Ellie Sutton's murder? I pushed back other questions that came with that.

The hound was waiting for me as I left the building and grinned up at me from the sidewalk. I shouldn't have been surprised. He had proven himself to have remarkable tracking skills in the past.

A headache reminded me that I hadn't eaten since breakfast the day before. I supposed that food was in order. Rupert needed no persuasion as we found a street vendor nearby who provided sandwiches on long rolls of bread with slices of ham and cheese.

The hound finished his in two bites, then the rest of mine.

According to the information Munro had provided, Ellie Sutton had worked at Brown's Hotel, which was very near Mayfair.

I had passed it often, with that imposing Georgian façade on Albemarle Street that was actually eleven town houses that also included employee rooms. Just a year ago, it had been connected to the St. George's hotel at the back, with a throughway between the two buildings.

I assumed that officers of the MET and perhaps even Abberline himself had already been there after the woman's death. I wasn't certain what I might learn. It was a place to start with my own inquiries.

I waved down a cab and climbed aboard. I didn't wait for the cabman to inform me that he didn't take animals. I simply handed him the full fare with additional for the hound and gave him the name of the hotel.

Many of the finer hotels about London provided rooms for their maids and clerks, so that they were always available when their work day, or night, started. However, Ellie Sutton had lived apart.

Perhaps her position as floor manager was that above a maid or clerk, and had allowed her to afford her own flat. And then, of course, there was the boy Lucy Penworth had spoken of. It was doubtful that children were allowed in the employees' quarters at the hotel.

Another complication was the fact that I was not dressed in the manner the hotel was undoubtedly accustomed to seeing in their guests—visiting dignitaries, and those of society that included visiting royalty.

The clothes I wore were far more practical, since our inquiry cases might take us anywhere about London or beyond. And there was the issue of not wanting to draw attention to myself.

It was obvious that Abberline had sent the constable to have me watched. Perhaps to apprehend Brodie if he had gone to the town house? I wanted to know where Brodie was as well, still I was not about to make finding him any easier for Abberline.

And it did seem that my best hope to learn something about Ellie Sutton would be with the maids and other staff she had worked with.

I had the driver continue around to Dover Street when we reached the hotel, where I hoped to find a service entrance where I might enter the hotel. He pulled up at a carriage park where other cabs and coaches waited for their next fare from the hotel.

I made certain there were no constables patrolling about the park or Dover Street, then stepped down from the cab. I gave the hound instructions to stay at the carriage park, then crossed the street.

CARLA SIMPSON

Luck was with me. A row of delivery vans sat waiting to be unloaded at the service entrance.

I had found a way inside the hotel and had stepped into the middle of a shift change for hotel staff. Wait staff, maids, clerks emerged from an adjacent hallway and moved past me as another group arrived from the previous shift.

They were a variety of ages, from young maids in uniforms to men in shirts and trousers with the hotel logo, chatting each other up with an occasional mention of sore feet or an aching back.

"There was just meself, and the gentleman wanted me to hoist the trunk into the lift..." followed by an invitation to one of the young women who was dressed in a simple but fine-quality dark blue gown, to join him at the local pub.

"That's two straight shifts for me today," she replied, "what with being short-staffed after what happened to Mrs. Sutton. I'm going straight to bed."

"There was gossip up on the third floor about that..." a maid commented. "Poor thing."

"Mr. Prewitt was in another meeting with the MET today..." another young man commented. "I took tea into 'em. Heard one of the constables ask about any men who might have come round asking for her..."

"I don't think there were any men," another woman replied. "Kept to herself, she did. And I don't believe for a minute that she was married. There was never a word about a husband."

"She might have been a widow," another commented.

"I heard there was a boy," I commented as I removed my hat and joined the conversation. In for a penny, in for a pound as the saying goes.

"And who might you be?" the young woman who had worked two shifts asked.

"Emma Fortescue," I replied.

"You're the new one," she replied.

I smiled in return.

"You're a day early."

There was obviously a new employee expected.

"I wanted to get settled in before I start," I replied.

"Yer a tall one, ain't you. Mrs. Mayweather will have a bit of work with the uniform. I'm Maisy. Come along then, you'll be sharin' a room with me." She turned and headed down an adjacent hallway.

"You don't snore, do ya?"

Not according to the person who would know that, I thought, as I followed her.

"Where's yer bag?" she asked as we reached the room.

"There's just this," I indicated the carpet bag.

"Well, come on, then," she opened the door. "That poor woman, Mrs. Sutton. And I heard she had a boy?"

"It was in the dailies..." I replied.

"Gossip, and there's plenty o' that around here. Some didn't like her 'cause she kept to herself. Not one to talk yer head off, but she was kind. She didn't stay here. Had a room some other place," Maisy continued.

"But we got along. She was the floor matron in this building, although I gotta admit, she seemed a bit young. But she had the experience for the job from some other place." She pointed past me.

"That will be your bed over there," she continued, indicating the one against the wall. "And the bottom two drawers in the chest as well. The loo is down the hall. We share it with the rest of the girls."

"I imagine the police were here," I commented.

She nodded. "I heard they were, but not interested in the likes of me or the other girls that worked under her. I heard they met for several hours with the hotel manager."

"How long had she worked here?" I asked, since Maisy seemed to be the talkative sort.

She was thoughtful for a moment. "Must be goin' on two years now. She arrived about the same time I came here."

"Did she say where she was from?"

"Not outright, but London for sure. I could hear it in the way she talked. You can tell them that are from outside London. Not like yerself, of course. You talk real proper."

I set my bag on the bed with the pretense of staying.

"It's sad about the boy," I commented. "Did she speak of him?"

Maisy shook her head. "She was real secretive about him. The only way I knew anything, she was late one morning and upset. Said it was on accounta the boy was sick and she had to leave him alone."

"What about the boy's father?"

She shook her head. "She never talked about no one. I got the feeling he wasn't around. As far as any other men," she shrugged.

"There might have been someone before, but not now. And she was real dodgy lately about someone who came round. She took to having one of the lads at the dock in the alley check before she left of a night, like she thought someone might be there waitin' for her. Maisy frowned. "And I got the feelin' she was afraid."

"Did she say who that man was?"

She shook her head. "Like I said, she kept to herself."

"What about the man? Did she say what he looked like? If

he should come back," I added. "The other girls should be warned."

Maisy didn't seem to think anything unusual about my curiosity.

"The way she described him, he weren't no fancy high-class dresser like some of the guests that have too much of the drink and then return to the hotel of an evenin'. But fine enough, more than you and me. She said he wore a plaid jacket, trousers, and boots, like one of those City gents.

"I saw 'im once, then he disappeared. He wore one of those hats that City gents wear," she added. "Round and funny lookin', if you ask me. And he had a piece of paper tucked in the band, like those who go to the betting parlors."

"A bowler hat?" I suggested.

"That's it, and he smoked cigarettes—lots of them. Them brown ones that have a sharp smell. I saw a half dozen or more crushed out by the fence at the carriage park across the way one night, where the drivers wait to be called round for a guest."

A description that might be found on any street in London, I thought. A man with a bowler hat with a piece of paper tucked in the band.

"Was she able to see his face?"

"She said he had a full beard, and he was the short burly sort. The top of his hat reached just over the top of the fence at the yard."

I went over the description in my head. Stocky of build, a full beard. A man of some means, with a penchant for bowler hats, though not a fancy dresser. He smoked cigarettes, Turkish blend perhaps, by the description.

I thought of that aromatic fragrance that engulfed the office on the Strand when Brodie lit his pipe.

I came back around to the present as she asked, "Where did you work before?"

"Privately," I replied. That seemed the best answer.

Not that I had performed a maid's duties other than picking up the paperwork at the office on the Strand after Brodie had scattered it about, or swept chunks of mud left by his boots, or brought him coffee, or...

How was it that I missed the small things between a man and woman—his clothes scattered about, the touch of his hand on my cheek, the sound of his voice no more than a sleepy mumble early of a morning... *'Come here, lass.'*

Good heavens, I was beginning to think like some pathetic, dithering female who had lost all sense. I pulled my thoughts back to the matter at hand as Maisy moved about the small room. She had undressed down to her shift and drawers. She hung her uniform on a hook on the wall.

"I get first go at the loo," she said with a cheerful smile. "If ye hurry, ye might get there before the other girls who just came off shift. You have to move right quick before the hot water runs out." Then she was out the door and headed down the hallway.

Maisy had been an enormous help with the information she had provided. I now had a description of a man who had apparently been stalking Ellie Sutton. But I needed more if I was going to be able to help Brodie.

The shift-change over, I slipped out into the empty hallway, then left the hotel. I walked across to the carriage park where the man whose appearance she had described had been seen on more than one occasion.

Someone who had frightened Ellie Sutton. And then murdered her?

Seven

MAISY HAD DESCRIBED the man she had seen as barely taller than the fence where drivers waited to be called for hotel guests.

That would put him at no more than five-and-a-half feet tall, but quite muscular. *Burly*, she had described him, and apparently someone who dressed well enough to wear that bowler hat.

Yet, I needed to know more. I needed to know who the man was and what, if anything, it had to do with Ellie Sutton's murder.

It was very near evening, but there was another place I wanted to go. Best under the cover of darkness, along with a disguise in case I should encounter anyone.

Rupert suddenly appeared with the remnants of a paper bakery sack hanging from his mouth. He did have a fondness for cakes and scones. I only hoped that the person who had been attached to the sack hadn't been injured.

I returned to Drury Lane. When I left some time later, I

had to admit that I wouldn't have recognized myself in my disguise. It was somewhat reassuring.

For his part, Rupert refused to come near me until he was satisfied, with that keen sense of smell, that I was there underneath the clothes.

I checked the street as I left Drury Lane. The only glance that passed our way was from the cabman, obviously not used to having what appeared to be a dustman or common laborer for a passenger. Then there was the hound of course—extra fare required, and we set off.

I had been to Charing Cross on a past inquiry case. It was a part of London where entire streets of dilapidated tenement buildings, some near three hundred years old, were being torn down to make away for new housing as part of the government's efforts to address poverty and homelessness.

According to the information Alex Sinclair had provided, the address where Ellie Sutton had lived was at the edge of Charing Cross, a part of the area where factory workers, tradesmen, and others with skills that earned a steady wage, lived with their families in some of the less rundown tenements.

I had the driver let me off at the street just over from Craven Street where Ellie Sutton had lived, the hound falling into step beside me.

There was a street light at the corner, the rest of the street dark and filled with shadows, except for the occasional glow of light from a ground floor window of one of the tenements.

I had no idea what I might find at the flat where Ellie Sutton had lived. Nevertheless, I had learned from Brodie there was always something, some small detail that might be important, that was often overlooked. I was hoping there was something that might tell me something important about her and the night she died.

The police had already searched the premises after her body was discovered by the woman who collected the rents. I could only hope there was some detail they missed.

I approached the tenement directly behind the one on Craven Street. It had a narrow alley alongside it, most often used by dustmen who collected rubbish. I certainly looked the part.

In this part of London, rubbish was often left to rot piled at the kerb or in a bin at the back of a house, where it drew rats. It had obviously been some time since the refuse had been picked up here by the look of the piled garbage and those who scavenged among it.

I started down that alley toward the tenement at Craven Street where Ellie Sutton had lived. As I approached the front of the building the sound of voices quite near stopped me. I hid in the shadows and listened. It appeared that the tenement was being guarded by officers from the MET.

"It's been two days now, and not a sign of 'im," one of the constables commented.

"The orders came straight from the Chief Inspector," came the reply at the street in front of the tenement.

"He wants one of us here day and night. He knows the man and he's certain he'll come back."

"Fine enough for him to say. He's not the one workin' double shifts and standin' out here freezin' his bollocks off."

Abberline! No stone unturned.

But their complaints told me far more. As of yet, the police had no idea where Brodie was.

I heard that familiar rumble from the hound beside me. I managed to grab the ruff of fur about his neck and whispered one of the few commands he understood, or chose to understand, before he charged off.

It wouldn't do to have him attack one of the constables and possibly expose the fact that I was there.

"*Did ye hear somethin'?*" One of the constables commented.

"*Probably some animal rummaging about in the garbage,*" his companion responded. There was another comment, and a curse at the cold.

"*Best get on with our rounds. Wouldn't want Abberline to think we were not doing our job.*"

I listened as they moved down the street until the sound of their bootsteps faded. Satisfied that they were gone for now, I quickly went to the entrance of the tenement.

From previous experience, I knew there were usually six flats to a floor in these old tenement buildings, with someone who collected the rents occupying a ground floor flat, where they could watch the comings and goings of the tenants.

Rupert was presently nose-deep into a rubbish pile at the kerb, the police constables forgotten for now. I told him to *stay*. It would be difficult to explain his presence if he were to follow me inside.

There was a light in the window beside the main entrance of the tenement. My guess was that was where the landlady lived, and then a light that flickered overhead from the second-floor landing. I hid in the shadows at the main entrance and listened to the sounds of the building.

There were footsteps overhead then the slam of a door along with bits of conversation behind the door of that ground floor flat. The door suddenly opened, and a bag of trash was dumped into the hallway.

"*I told ya, I can't rent out 2-C until the bloody peelers is through with their investigation,*" a woman explained.

"*As it is, I'll be lucky to find anyone t' take it, with what happened there. All that blood that needs to be cleaned up. There is already word about the murder on the street. No family will want to rent the place."* The door slammed shut once more.

Flat 2-C. It appeared that I now knew which flat Ellie Sutton had lived in.

The next part was going to be a bit more difficult—getting inside. I had considered that as well before setting out, and I had come prepared.

I waited and listened as the sounds in the building settled once more. When no one else appeared I quickly made my way to the stairs. At the second-floor landing, I moved down the hall to flat 2-C.

I tried the latch. The door was locked, no doubt after the police removed Ellie Sutton's body. I needed to work quickly if I was to get inside without being seen.

My work with Brodie had provided me with a few new skills that were useful from time to time. After watching him pick a lock, I had insisted that he teach me how it was done.

There had been some argument over that, of course, however, in the end I had persuaded him to show me his methods. I had then practiced on the lock on the door to the office.

"Ye have a natural feel for it," he had announced at the time, when I successfully picked the lock on the third attempt. Yet, not in a complimentary manner.

"I willna have ye go around picking locks unless I'm there, in case there should be any trouble."

In this instance, he was not here and I needed to get inside the flat.

I made a bend in the tip of one hairpin that I pulled from my hair tucked under the cap, then another in the closed end of the second hairpin so that it formed an angle for a lever.

I then inserted the first one into the lock and used the

second one to move that one carefully back and forth as I listened for the telltale click of the inner parts of the lock.

Of course, all of it was dependent on the type of lock, as Brodie had explained it. Those found in most upper-class residences as well as business establishments might be more difficult, or there might even be a second locking mechanism such as a dead bolt. But not here.

I carefully applied a bit of pressure to the hairpin that was the lever and heard a distinctive click as the pin inside clicked back as it would have with a key. I smiled to myself, retrieved the hairpin, and entered the darkened flat.

I closed the door behind me and was immediately seized from the back of my jacket, my cap jarred loose from my head with a muffled curse.

I prepared to defend myself as I caught the vague scent of cinnamon, followed by another curse. And then something muttered in Gaelic, equally offensive by the sound of it.

A ghost, Munro had called him, speaking as one who shared that experience when they were lads in Edinburgh. *He could hide and no one would ever find him. Or...find him in the most unlikely place.*

It seemed that I had found my '*ghost.*'

"Good evening," I greeted Brodie, which brought another curse. "It is good to see you again."

I heard a faint click and the flat was suddenly illuminated by the beam of a hand-held light that he rudely flashed in my face.

"What the devil are ye doin' here?" he demanded.

I pushed the lamp aside. "I might ask you the same question," I replied and rubbed my scalp where the cap had been so rudely removed along with several more pins and a few strands of hair.

"Isn't it a bit dangerous for you to be here?" I added.

"And what is this?" He waved the cap at me.

I snatched it back. "Part of the disguise that Templeton provided so that I might go about without being followed."

"No wart on yer chin?" he commented. There was no mistaking the sarcasm.

He was in a temper, and being particularly peevish with a reminder of a previous disguise I had worn in that first inquiry case.

"I only needed something to get past the constables if I should encounter them."

"Good God, Mikaela! Have ye no sense?"

"Present company excluded, I have remarkable sense."

"We made a bargain when we left Edinburgh," he reminded me. "Ye promised that ye wouldna endanger yerself."

He did have a convenient memory, edited for the purpose of his own argument.

"I promised that I wouldn't endanger myself unless it was absolutely necessary," I corrected him, struggling to keep to a whisper.

"It *is* absolutely necessary. And I will not sit idly by while you're in danger of being arrested and possibly imprisoned."

That dark gaze narrowed on me. There was undoubtedly more he wanted to say, there usually was. However, under the circumstances, this was not the time or the place. Then, a sound from the hallway put an end to it.

We both went completely still.

"*I told you it wasn't nothin'. Yer hearin' things,*" a man's voice came from across the hall.

Brodie pulled me behind him, then switched off the lamp.

The door nearby, possibly just across the hall, slammed shut once more. I slowly let out the breath I was holding.

"How did ye know I wasna some thief or the landlady?" he demanded. "Ye would have been in a fine situation then."

He switched the lamp back on. So that I could see how angry he was?

"In the first place, the landlady didn't hear me, and you're the one making all the noise, bellowing for all the building to hear," I pointed out.

"And in the second place, a thief wouldn't have locked the door behind him. He would have left it unlocked to make it easy for him to escape." I gave him a long look. "You locked it behind yourself...?"

"So that no one would come in while I was here without some warning."

It made sense—no surprises, such as the neighbor across the hall.

"I wasna expecting someone to pick the lock. It is clear that it was a mistake to teach ye such things."

Of course, dear, I thought, then asked, "What are you doing here? Didn't you think that it might be dangerous to come back?"

"I had no opportunity to look for anything that night that might provide a clue who murdered Ellie...the young woman. Wot are ye doin' here and dressed like a common worker?"

"The very same," I hissed back at him. "Since you disappeared and I refuse to believe that you had anything to do with her murder."

"Ye try a man's soul, Mikaela Forsythe. It's not as if there isna enough to worry about."

"Then I suggest, we get started before someone overhears you. Now, what are we looking for?" I asked.

It was obvious that the constables who were first called to

the building the night Ellie Sutton was murdered would have found a weapon, if one was found and taken in for evidence.

"Anything that might tell me who did this," Brodie replied. "A letter, or note she might have received, anything out of the ordinary.

There was something in his voice, something almost sad.

"It wasn't your fault, you know," I pointed out and thought of what Alex Sinclair had shared with me.

Ellie Sutton had apparently made the decision to return to London even knowing the risk. But for what reason?

"I couldna protect her."

There was more. I heard it in his voice, but he didn't say anything more about that night. Or before.

"What about the boy?" I asked.

He looked at me then with more than a little surprise.

"It was in the article in the daily about the murder."

He eventually nodded. "He's safe."

Just those two words as he started to search the flat with the meticulous attention to detail of the investigator looking for clues. It was obvious that he wasn't going to share anything more.

Anything out of the ordinary.

I moved about the main room of the flat at the edge of light from the hand-held as Brodie swept it back and forth, and reminded myself to bring my own the next time I was in a similar situation.

Shadows appeared then disappeared in the darkened room. I caught a glimpse of something, lost it, then glimpsed it again —a small glass tumbler on the table, the sort that Brodie and I had in the office on the Strand when we shared a dram of whisky.

That seemed odd. Particularly for a woman who had just returned from work and then was attacked and murdered.

Was it simply left from the day before the murder? Had she shared a drink with someone? Still, there was only the one glass.

The image of Ellie Sutton drinking alone didn't fit with the few details I had learned about her.

"What have ye there?"

"A glass tumbler. I wonder if Ellie Sutton was in the habit of drinking at the end of the day. It might be able to tell us something if there are prints on the glass," I suggested.

The murderer perhaps? That did seem highly unlikely. I couldn't imagine someone sitting there either before or after, and drinking. Or had it been someone else?

"She didn't drink," he replied, as if that was the end of the discussion about the glass.

Still...no stone unturned.

I found a cloth on the floor. I carefully wrapped the tumbler and put it in the pocket of my jacket.

I then continued my search, but found nothing more, other than a child's toy on the counter beside a small cupboard. It was a toy locomotive. Not surprising considering a young boy had lived there until...

What might that tell us?

I put it in my other pocket as Brodie suddenly crouched to the floor and aimed the beam of the hand-held over a dark stain.

I joined him. It was blood. Not surprising under the circumstances. However there was some sort of mark in the dried blood.

That 'something' appeared to be an imprint made by a boot. I looked up at Brodie.

"Yours?" I asked, since he had been there that night.

He shook his head. "Not made by a common work boot."

Upon further inspection with the hand-held, the toe of the boot print appeared, faint, as I imagined the murderer had stood there, and what he had done after killing Ellie Sutton. It was almost as if...

"What is it?" Brodie asked.

I wasn't at all certain what it was, an impression more than anything.

"It's almost as if the murderer paused here," I added.

He stared at that stain. "Perhaps."

But if so, what did that tell us?

Before leaving Drury Lane, I had pocketed the revolver along with my notebook and pen. I took those out and made a drawing of that imprint in the blood. I had no idea what it might tell us—something, anything, nothing.

The sketch was crude. I was not the artist in the family, but it was good enough. I then rose and continued my search of the flat as Brodie continued his.

It was suddenly interrupted by a loud baying sound, the sort of sound that might be made by a hound.

Brodie looked over at me. "What the devil?"

"Rupert," I whispered.

He swore under his breath.

"You did insist that I take him with me when I was out and about on my own," I pointed out, as more baying came from the street at the front of the tenement.

Rupert had a particular dislike of the police. It seemed very likely the two constables had returned. It also seemed that our search was at an end.

Brodie shut off the hand-held light and went to the door. He cracked it open and peered out into the hallway.

He nodded to me and I followed as we left the flat then made our way to the stairs. He flattened me against the wall of the stairwell with his arm as I heard voices from the entryway below.

"It's nothin' but the bloody peelers," the man I had heard earlier in that ground floor flat. *"Some sort of ruckus, most likely a stray in the trash. Hope the animal takes a bite outta 'em."*

That was very likely, I thought. In the very least, I hoped that Rupert was able to keep the police occupied while we made our escape.

When neither the man nor his companion appeared, Brodie grabbed me by the hand and we escaped down those stairs to the entryway.

He opened the door, we slipped out the entrance, then down that alley toward the street behind the tenement.

The hound was right behind us.

We stopped at the end of the alley, where Brodie checked to make certain there were no constables about. He looked down at me.

"Ye would drive a man crazy, Mikaela Brodie. Nevertheless, I'll keep ye." He pulled me against him in a quick fierce embrace.

"If ye go off again on yer own..."

A familiar threat. I reached up and pushed my hand back through that thick mane of hair.

"Promises, promises..." I replied.

Eight

I SAT in at the threadbare overstuffed chair in the flat in Drury Lane, and studied my new notes after our adventure at Charing Cross.

We had purchased food from a street vendor who had set up his cart near the theater, and brought it back to the flat.

The hound was quite content, asleep at my feet after all the excitement and devouring a sandwich of his own, then the remnants of mine.

Brodie sat across from me in the wood chair at the table, glass in hand. I had poured us both a dram of my aunt's very fine whisky that I had brought to the flat earlier.

"I know a man who might be able to tell me about that mark from the boot heel," Brodie commented.

Me? As in himself, as if he was the only person involved in this now. The man could be most irritating.

I took another swallow of whisky and, for now, chose not to comment on that.

I had explained Rupert's encounter the previous night at

the town house. Brodie listened, unusually quiet, his mane of dark hair still wet after making thorough use of the washbasin, a cloth, and the soap he found there

"Aye," he commented. "Abberline, havin' ye watched."

There was a weariness about him I had not noticed before, in the way he pushed a hand back through his overlong hair. I caught a glimpse of grey among the dark waves.

Now, he took another sip of whisky, stroking that piece of dark blue wool between thumb and forefinger, thoughts hidden behind that dark gaze.

"Tell me about the boy," I said then.

That dark gaze met mine as I paused at the notes I was making.

He didn't reply right away, and I saw the shift of expression on his face, the frown line between those dark brows deepening. He took another drink.

"I received a telephone call from her that night from the hotel where she worked. She was about to leave after her shift and saw a man waiting...she had seen him before and after everything that happened years ago, it frightened her."

"Ellie Sutton," I commented. He nodded.

"I told her to stay at the hotel, but she refused because of the boy. He was alone at the flat on Charing Cross."

He continued to explain that he had gone there, but arrived too late. Ellie Sutton was already dead. And the boy?

"It had just happened, the police hadn't arrived yet. He was hiding there."

I tried to imagine what that was like for the boy, the horror of what he must have seen.

"I needed a safe place for him, and took him with me," he continued.

I waited, yet he didn't say where that safe place was. He seemed to know my thoughts.

"It's best ye not know, lass." He fingered that piece of wool. "Ye can see that Abberline willna stop to get at me, even through you. Not even you can stop him. Where the boy is now, even if I shouldna return for him, he will be safe enough."

That could have only one meaning—if he was unable to return.

"And his mother?" I asked.

"She was verra young when I first encountered her on the streets, near Lily's age," he continued.

"There was a difficulty with her father, and the mother turned her out." The frown deepened. "Not uncommon on the streets," he added, then paused.

"A woman I knew took her in, then found her work in one of the taverns."

According to Brodie, that same woman worked in one of the private gentleman's clubs—the Clarendon Sports Club. Ellie Sutton soon went to work there.

In the way that a pretty young girl might quickly be noticed, it was not long before she came to the attention of one of the club's prominent members, Stephen Matthews.

"I didn't see her for some time, and then she appeared at the flat that I had at the time." He stared into his glass as he swirled the whisky.

"There had been some difficulty with the young man, and she was forced to leave the club. She had a little money, but no place to go. She stayed for a while, then I returned from my shift one night and found a note.

"The young man had come for her with the promise of marriage."

"Stephen Matthews," I replied and explained the article about the first murder that I had found, written by Mr. Burke.

As I had learned from our inquiries such promises rarely came to pass, particularly if the young man was from a wealthy family, and the young woman was not. The scandals of the rich were swept under the carpet. She had returned with him to his private apartment at the club with devastating consequences.

She had witnessed his murder and fled, terrified. She went to the one person who had helped her before. She swore that she had nothing to do with Matthews' death, however she had seen the man who had murdered him.

Brodie was called in to investigate the murder. There were employees of the club who saw Ellie flee that night.

Rumors and speculation mounted. There was no other suspect. It was obvious that Ellie Sutton was going to be arrested.

Brodie needed time to find the murderer. He knew only too well what she would face if she was jailed.

"And she was going to have a child." I concluded the obvious.

"Aye."

Brodie refused to give her up to the police and helped her leave London. He left the MET shortly thereafter, amid accusations that he had tampered with evidence, namely the only person who saw what happened that night. Equally important, Abberline's efforts to solve the case and receive that coveted promotion disappeared as well.

"What about Inspector Morrissey, who was also part of the case?" I asked of the name I had read in the archives.

"Was he able to learn anything more after you left?"

"A good man." He poured himself more whisky. "With a family." He looked at me.

"When a man has a family, those he cares about, it changes things."

Was it possible that Inspector Morrissey had been threatened as well?

"He left the MET some time after and went to work with his wife's brother at a tobacco shop near Piccadilly Circus. I havena spoken with him since. I thought it best to leave the man be."

"Why did Ellie return after all this time when she was safe?" I asked.

He hesitated, then tossed back the rest of the whisky in his glass.

"There was no life for her where she was, and she felt it was important for the boy to know his family, though I warned her against it."

I sensed there was something more he might have said, but then decided not to speak of it. He picked up that piece of dark blue wool again and studied it.

"The hound?" he commented.

"He does have a particular dislike for the police. My guess would be there is a constable with a sizeable wound that needed a bandage," I replied.

Rupert was presently on the floor beside the chair, snoring. Although there was twitching and a sudden movement of the legs as if he was chasing down some victim in his sleep.

"There was someone else at the townhouse after ye left," Brodie said.

"I saw him across the way. I couldn't see him clearly, but enough to know it was not the police. He wore a suit with a bowler hat, and he was there long enough to smoke several cigarettes."

A description that might have been anyone, except that it also fit the description of the man Maisy told me about.

Sent by Abberline after the encounter of one of his men with Rupert? Or, by someone else?

I made a note of that.

"I want to speak with the writer for the Times who wrote the original newspaper article about Stephen Matthews' murder ten years ago," I said then. "There might be something that he learned afterward, or some piece of gossip from that night that could be useful now."

Before he could object, I continued. "Might Sir Avery be able to intervene in the matter now? So that you're not arrested?"

He shook his head. "I willna involve him or the Agency."

I tried again. "What about staff at the club? Other guests that night," I suggested. I assumed they were questioned at the time as well.

"I spoke with them at the time," he replied. "And as for other guests..."

I knew the answer to that. Most would have responded as far as it didn't involve them in the scandal of the young man's murder.

"Did Ellie describe the person she saw that night after Stephen Matthews was murdered?"

"No. She was young, terrified by what happened, as if she was in shock when she found me."

There was more I wanted to ask. Where had he been the past days? Where was he staying at night, was anyone helping him? How could I reach him if I found something important...?

All of that had to wait as Rupert suddenly leapt up, fur up on his back, his head cocked, as he went to the door.

When I would have said something, Brodie warned me to silence as he came out of the chair and followed the hound to the door.

"What did ye tell the landlady when ye came here?" he whispered.

"Nothing...I gave her a false name."

"Wot name?"

"Emma Fortescue." Perhaps not a good idea, as I now thought about it. Yet, I hadn't wanted to use to my real name, which would only have brought undue attention

"Emma...?"

Then he nodded. "Aye, and it seems that she must have said something to someone...the police are here. We need to leave!"

Wherever he had been, he was exhausted. We both were. None of it mattered as I grabbed the jacket and my bag.

Brodie continued to listen at the door. He shook his head, then glanced past me to the bedroom and the window in the far wall that faced out to the back of the building.

"This way," he whispered. I followed with the hound right behind me.

He was able to force the window open, check the alley, then grabbed my hand. He gave me a leg up and I was scrambling out the opening with Brodie immediately after. Then he grabbed my hand. I caught a glimpse of Rupert as he leapt out the window and followed as we ran down the alley.

I did hate that we had to leave what was left of my aunt's very fine whisky.

Just beyond the theater, Brodie waved down a coach.

"Do ye have the fare?"

I nodded and he pulled the door open as the coach pulled alongside. I climbed inside, the hound just behind me. However, Brodie did not follow.

"Where are you going?" I asked.

He shook his head, he would not say.

"Ye need to go—you know where," he said then, that dark gaze intense. "And dinna give the driver the address until yer well past the district."

I did know where—Sussex Square, and very badly wanted him to come with me. We would find a way through this together. But I knew just as well that he would not.

"How do I find you if I should learn something important?"

Again he shook his head, then reached for my hand. His was warm, while mine was icy cold. I was afraid and I hated being afraid. Not for myself, but for him.

"I will find ye. Trust me." He gave a signal to the driver and the coach lurched away from the kerb.

Damn bloody stubborn Scot!

I knew exactly his meaning when we parted, he wanted me to go to Sussex Square.

I had not wanted to involve my great-aunt. Still, I knew that he was right. Sussex Square was almost a fortress, occupied by a woman whose ancestors included one of the first kings of Britain. And in spite of her age, she was quite formidable. If one of her own was threatened, I would not have put it past her to meet the 'enemy' at the gate with a sword.

It was late in the evening when I arrived, the driver slowing to a stop at those massive gates.

"Are ye certain, sir?" he called down from atop the coach.

Sir? I almost laughed, and then assured him that this was the address. He then swung the coach through those gates and up the drive to the front entrance.

Sussex Square had been our childhood home for my sister and me after the deaths of both parents. To say being raised by our great-aunt was somewhat unconventional was a mild understatement.

My sister and I were provided with the finest of private educations, a year in Paris, summers at Old Lodge in the north of Scotland, as well as winters at our great-aunt's chateau in the south of France.

In between, there were the adventures that included hunting in the woods; masquerading as pirates, complete with a pirate ship on the green at Sussex Square; horse-back riding; and participating in our great-aunt's somewhat eccentric adventures. Those had included card readings and séances, with an odd assortment of friends and acquaintances that included several peers of the realm, the Queen's favorite cousin, and a notable admiral or two.

We thought it all quite normal. Didn't everyone have a pirate ship in the garden?

As a result I had learned long ago to expect almost anything when returning to Sussex Square.

That included her preparations for safari, which she was embarking on the following month.

As a young girl, our aunt had also lived for a time in the West Indies, as her father had been appointed governor of one of the islands for a time. There had been countless stories of her adventures on the island. Hence the pirate ship from our own childhood.

She had been ridiculed for it in one of the dailies, called *eccentric*, which I thought was a compliment. She didn't care a fig what other people thought. As Brodie had pointed out, that was undoubtedly where my view of certain things came from. I took that as a compliment as well.

My aunt's head butler, Mr. Symons, greeted me at the entrance to Sussex Square.

His stoic gaze took in my trousers, shirt, and jacket, and then the hound. There was only the slightest lift of one eyebrow.

"I will be staying for a few days," I informed him.

"Of course, miss," Mr. Symons said with a nod. "I will inform the staff to prepare a room."

That was hardly necessary.

"Saints preserve us!" greeted us as Rupert followed me into the great hall. If it involved saints, it could only be Mrs. Ryan.

She had appeared at the sound of my arrival—unusual for that time of the night, along with several servants, Munro, and my aunt.

"Hello, dear!" My aunt greeted me with a kiss on the cheek, as if she took no notice of my clothing. "It is always good to see you."

As if this was a social call for afternoon tea, cards, or perhaps a séance with her medium.

She glanced down at my bag and immediately told one of the servants to take it to the guest room in the west wing.

"Have you eaten, dear? We had a splendid bit of roast partridge for supper. And what of Brodie?"

What indeed?

The less everyone knew the better. Except for Munro. I did keep my answer brief.

"He is quite well, and off on a new aspect of a case."

That seemed to satisfy Munro. He nodded to me, then told my aunt that he would make certain the front gate was secure. I did notice then that he was carrying a rifle, the sort of weapon that might be used for hunting animals.

"Come along, dear," my aunt told me. "You look

exhausted. I'll send up one of the girls with a nightcap. You do look as if you could use it. A bit of the whisky will help you sleep."

It was going to take a great deal of it, I thought. Tired as I was and worried about Brodie, I needed to think what was to be done next, if I was to help solve Ellie Sutton's murder and prevent him going to prison.

Nine

AS CHILDREN, after coming to live with our great-aunt, we often wakened to a new adventure. It seemed that she was determined to make up for our mother's death, our father's preference for gambling over raising his daughters, and then his untimely death.

It was quite common to waken and find some special event had been arranged that inevitably took us away from our tutors and daily lessons. I had wholeheartedly embraced such truancy, while Linnie had worried that we might somehow miss something important in our education.

There was the occasion when our great-aunt arranged for our own private zoo, with animals brought to Sussex Square and allowed to roam about the grounds much to the fear of the servants, although it had not included any predatory beasts.

Never at a loss for imagination we had wakened one morning on another occasion to find a circus in the gardens behind the manor, complete with performers, elephants, horses, camels, and a dancing bear.

It is possible that my aunt's somewhat different approach

to her newfound parenthood accounted for my fascination for adventure, and then travel to some of the places where those various creatures had come from.

I listened to an unusual sound, my eyes still closed. Possibly a dream.

However, the sound persisted, then fading only to return quite loud. I opened both eyes, the awareness of where I was slowly returning.

I glanced at the bed beside me. I was decidedly alone and threw back the covers, then swung my feet to the floor and dressed in clothes I had worn before I went off to Charing Cross the night before.

The other details of the night before returned as I splashed water on my face and brushed my hair. I then went in search of my great-aunt, Munro, and coffee. Not in that order.

Coffee came first. I had followed the smell of it rather than wait for one of the servants to bring it up to the room, as I knew my aunt would have requested. I didn't have time for that.

In the kitchens, I was directed to the gardens behind the manor as Cook set a new pot to brew.

"You need only follow the clouds of steam," she informed me.

Steam? And that sound.

Oh dear. As I was saying, one might expect anything.

The gardens of Sussex Square were considered on a par with those at St. James's Park and Kensington. They wrapped around the manor within those stone walls and rolled out to the private forest that held many adventures for my sister and me as children. And they contained flowers, shrubs, and trees of every variety imaginable, brought by other Montgomery ancestors from the far corners of the empire.

The sound that had wakened me grew louder as I reached the back entrance and then stepped out onto the flagstone veranda. And there were clouds of steam puffing into the cold morning air at the far side of the gardens nearest the forest.

As the clouds of steam momentarily cleared, I caught sight of my aunt seated atop a motor carriage as she circumnavigated the pony cart path.

"Good heavens!" I exclaimed.

There was a single comment from the man beside me. "Aye."

"When did this happen?"

"Yesterday, and the place has been in chaos ever since," Munro replied. "Ye might want to stand to the side where it's safe. She missed a turn earlier."

Oh dear.

"How did she come by the thing?" I then asked as I watched her weaving somewhat unsteadily along the cart path in the distance.

"She made an investment with a German fellow she met at the embassy. A man by the name of Benz. He's been working on the contraptions for a good many years, and had the bloody thing shipped over so that she might see what her money was invested in."

I watched as the *'contraption'* putted along quite efficiently around the track, except for a handful of minor corrections on the part of the operator, and discovered there were two persons in the motor carriage. Lily was seated beside my aunt.

"I'm prepared to rescue them if there's a stramash," he continued.

That was an interesting choice of words, I thought, as my aunt had rounded the back of the track and gradually made their way back toward the manor. A Scottish word that I had learned might mean anything from a street fight to some other sort of chaos.

"Ye were out and about last night," he said. "Ye have seen him then."

I nodded. "We came upon some information that might be helpful in finding who killed Ellie Sutton. And he's going to speak with the man he worked with before the murder at the gentlemen's club."

"Morrissey."

"You know him?"

He nodded. "Know of."

I waited for more and was forced to ask the obvious question. Munro was much like Brodie in that he shared only as much as necessary. Never let it be said that either man would talk you to death.

"You didn't like him?" I presumed.

Munro stared off as my aunt gradually approached the manor.

"He was...careful," he eventually replied.

I thought his reply was somewhat *careful*. Perhaps more than he wanted to say? I wanted to know more.

"In what way?"

"He looked to himself first. Others afterward. Particularly when there was compensation in it."

Compensation?

"Do you mean that he took bribes from people?"

"He lived well enough, and still does, if ye get me meanin'."

I glanced over at Munro, that blue gaze sharp as it met mine.

"He took money for favors?"

Bribes were not unusual, I had learned from Brodie. The MET had been plagued with rumors of it over the years.

Money slipped from one hand to another, to simply look the other way over a contraband cargo that reached the port of London. Someone of importance who paid to keep an affair secret. An incriminating report that conveniently disappeared to avoid charges.

Had that somehow affected the investigation into Stephen Matthews' murder? Someone paid to simply look the other way? Or was it something else?

"Was Brodie aware?"

"Aye, and he was always watching his back."

"Did he think that Morrissey might know something that he wasn't sharing about the murder that night?"

"As I said, Morrissey was careful."

Brodie hoped to question a man who had secrets, perhaps secrets that might cost him more than he was ever paid?

"Ye need to be most careful, in this," Munro cautioned then. "Desperate men will do desperate things."

I felt that gaze watching me.

"What will ye do next?"

"I want to speak with the man at the Times who wrote the article for the dailies about that murder ten years ago, Theodolphus Burke. There might be something that I can learn there."

He made that sound I had heard Brodie make hundreds of times, that might have been acknowledgement or disapproval. It seemed to be something Scots were prone to. I thought it might be disapproval of my aunt at the helm of the motor carriage.

"Is there danger?" I then asked as the contraption chugged toward us.

He didn't answer, which I realized was an answer in itself, and very likely not about the motor carriage, as he went down the steps as Lily and my aunt arrived with a lurch and a belch of steam—from the invention, not my aunt.

"What do you think of my new motor carriage?" my aunt greeted me. "It is most exhilarating. Mr. Munro calls it *the beast*." She giggled.

Aside from the fact that all manner of persons and animals might be endangered from said beast?

Point of fact, Rupert, who was no stranger to all manner of conveyances on the streets of London, had appeared from the forest beyond and circled warily as the equipage spat another cloud of steam like a dragon, and then shuddered.

I was not a stranger to motor carriages, or automobiles, as the Americans called them, courtesy of my friend Templeton's tours. She always returned with news of this or that which was popular among *the colonials*, as some still referred to them.

And there had been speculation that before too many more years, such things would replace coaches and carriages altogether, not to mention horse-drawn trams.

It did seem as if Herr Benz might have a successful invention, as my aunt stepped down from the motor carriage with assistance from Munro.

"Ain't it grand!" Lily exclaimed excitedly as she bounded around from the other side. "I drove it earlier."

Both of them wore goggles, leather caps, and gloves that extended the length of their arms. While my aunt was dressed in the latest riding costume in a shade of deep purple that she was quite fond of, Lily was dressed in a split skirt and jacket.

My aunt smiled at me from behind the goggles which were a bit too large as Munro assisted her out of the beast. They made her look like a bug.

"I had Madame make the driving costume for me," she announced. "She has suggested that I might need a coat worn over when taking the thing out about London. There is so much debris and mud."

The '*beast*' seemed to be an appropriate description as the motor carriage shuddered again like a dying creature, and then went completely silent.

"Some lessons are in order, perhaps?" I suggested to my aunt as delicately as possible out of concern over what I had just witnessed.

She waved off the suggestion. "It's not at all complicated. You flip a lever here, another one there, and a battery ignites an electric charge that starts the motor, according to Herr Benz's instructions. And then you're off! You simply aim it where you want to go."

That was the part that concerned me—aiming it through the streets of London.

"It's not like you to be a Nervous Nellie," she added. Something I had never considered myself to be.

"I'm just concerned for your safety." I thought it best not to point out that she was almost eighty-six years old...

"You needn't worry, dear. If anything should happen all the arrangements have been made for my send-off."

Her '*send-off*,' much like the one I had planned, was a glorious Viking funeral complete with a sailboat that was an exact replica of those ancient sailing crafts, sent out in a blaze of glory.

"I do have the stone slab in the family crypt," she continued, "if there should be any question of my existence."

I had seen it as a child, installed years before by her father, Lord Montgomery, just prior to his death. He had not been of the Viking persuasion for such things.

The slab noted her full name and title, along with the date of her birth to make things official, she had explained.

There was what I considered a peculiar engraving in the slab—*"Do not look for me, for I am not here!"*

It did, of course, reference that Viking send-off that she intended.

"It will be up to you and your sister, along with Mr. Brodie, of course, to see the rest of it taken care of," she added pragmatically. "I certainly do not want someone prying the slab open and inspecting my bones some years hence. It is so very rude."

Of course. We'd had the conversation previously, and I had promised to fulfill her wishes. Although I was of the opinion that she might outlive me.

She was off, giving instructions right and left. First order was to see that the Benz mobile was sufficiently prepared for her next foray. She intended to take it out on the streets.

I thought an out-rider might be called for, someone astride to go ahead and make way through the usual traffic. I made a mental note to speak with Munro about it before I left to speak with Mr. Burke at the Times.

Lily had removed her goggles.

"Have ye ridden in a motor carriage before? It's almost as fast as Mr. Hamby's team," she added of my aunt's driver and the team of matched bays that usually transported her about London.

"Her ladyship says we need to know how to handle one before we leave on safari," she commented as we returned to the manor.

I had no idea how that was related to their plans for safari. I was almost afraid to ask. I had visions of my aunt attempting to run down a water buffalo or perhaps a giraffe. Almost as terrifying as imagining her atop a camel, the means by which I had traversed that wild plain.

"Are ye working a new inquiry case?" Lily asked, pulling me back from my terrifying musings.

"I'm making some inquiries regarding a woman who was found dead." I chose that description rather than...

"A new murder case? Will Mr. Brodie be joining you?"

So much for attempting to gloss over things, or avoid them altogether. After our previous inquiry case, I had insisted that she focus on her lessons, which I hoped might provide her a good beginning in life, rather than the position of a maid in a brothel.

"How are you coming along with your studies?" I asked, moving the conversation in a different direction as we climbed the stairs toward the bedrooms on the second floor. I saw the face she made.

"Mr. Clark says my reading is much improved," she replied of the fifth or possibly sixth tutor we had retained for her. I had lost count. The previous ones had each lasted a very short time.

"I've started one of yer books," she added quite excited. "Miss Lenore says that those adventures are from yer travels. Have ye really done all those things?"

Oh dear, I did need to have a conversation with my sister about divulging too much to Lily about those adventures, most particularly the one that took me to the Greek Islands.

"I had to sneak it from her ladyship's library, but Miss Lenore is hardly here, wot with keepin' company with Mr. Warren," she continued. "Wot is the inquiry case yer investigating?" she then asked as we reached the guest room.

She was most curious and observant, and had contributed valuable skill in a previous investigation. Still, I had already seen the lengths that some persons—namely the Chief Inspector—were willing to go in our present case.

I refused to expose her or anyone else to the man's almost

insane obsession to prove Brodie was somehow involved in Ellie Sutton's murder.

"A young woman was found dead and I am assisting in trying to find those responsible," I explained.

"How do you go about finding who killed her?"

I explained that it required tracking down those who had contact with her and speaking with them, if they could be found.

I didn't go into the details of the murder that Ellie Sutton had witnessed ten years earlier, as I only had the information from that older newspaper article. I was hopeful that Mr. Burke might be able to tell me more.

"What about Mr. Brodie? Is he out following clues as well?" she then asked.

I simply nodded but didn't explain. However, quick minds...

"Is there some danger? Is that the reason yer here? And Mrs. Ryan as well? She refused to say anything."

As I was saying...

"There is repair work being done to the office..." I didn't go into further explanation on that and didn't explain about the further incident at the town house.

"Wot is this?" Lily asked with her usual sharp-eyed observation as she stood at the writing desk. "A locomotive?"

It was the toy I had retrieved from Ellie Sutton's flat. At the time, I had a thought that it might tell us something. I needed to call on Mr. Brimley in that regard. I had added that to my list as well.

"It belongs to a person involved in our current inquiry case. I need to see someone who may be able to tell me something about it."

"And this?" she held up the piece of dark blue wool that I

had taken from my bag. "It looks the same as the police uniforms."

I could have explained that it was merely something that Rupert had picked up. Still, there was that old saying about one lie needing another and then another, until one was caught up by them. And I reminded myself that Lily was indeed very intelligent and clever, and thought how I would feel if our positions were reversed.

The answer, of course, was that I would have pestered until I had the answer.

"It's from a police constable's uniform," I finally replied. I saw the way her brows drew together, another question forming.

"And it might be important to the case?"

"Perhaps."

"Mr. Clark says the same thing when he doesn't want to explain something to me because he thinks I canna understand."

My aunt insisted that I take breakfast with her and Lily, and then further insisted that I have her driver take me to my meeting. She would take the motor carriage if she needed to venture out into London.

And she was off to continue practicing her *'driving skills,'* even though I had explained to her that a safari caravan did not require driving machines since there were no paved roads as in London.

"One can never be too prepared," she cheerfully replied.

I cautioned Mr. Symons to not let her go out alone in the motor carriage. He reminded me that he had been with her for over thirty years and had not yet had to send anyone to rescue her.

When I pointed out that thirty years ago, she was not

eighty-six years old, he simply reminded me that she had proven herself quite resourceful.

"Much as yourself, miss."

Conversation ended.

If I was a religious person, I would have uttered a prayer on her behalf. As I was not, I said nothing more. I merely wrapped several biscuits in a napkin for the hound, placed my notebook and pen in my bag, and prepared to leave.

Lily made a face when I explained where I was going and whom I was hoping to meet with.

"His mother must not have liked him. Who would name a child Theodolphus?"

I was of the same opinion.

"I need to return these to her ladyship," Lily said then of the goggles. "She misplaced the other pair earlier. She might need them."

A butler announced that my great-aunt's driver had pulled round to the front entrance as I arrived at the entrance hall. Rupert had re-appeared from the general direction of the kitchens, his muzzle covered with cake crumbs. I saw Mrs. Ryan's hand in this.

He reeked of some overpowering perfume fragrance that reminded me think of the brothel in Edinburgh. That could explain his sheepish demeanor, head down, refusing to look at me.

"Mrs. Hastings did make a comment earlier that she refused to have him in the place smelling like...I believe she described it as a piss-pot," Mr. Symons explained. "Beggin' your pardon, miss."

I wasn't certain which was worse, Rupert's usual aroma, which I had become accustomed to, somewhat. Or his new scent.

My aunt's driver, Mr. Hastings, opened the coach door. I climbed inside, Rupert behind me as if escaping an inferno, and we were off.

No sooner had we departed than Mr. Hastings unexpectedly drew the team to a lurching halt. The coach door was pulled open and Lily climbed inside.

"I thought ye might need help," she explained with a grin, then called up to him to proceed.

Ten

I HAD no objections to Lily accompanying me—not that there was much choice in the matter. As for any danger, I was confident that I could protect us both. And I was reminded that she could be most persistent when she was determined about something.

It did seem good experience to have her venture somewhere about London besides the office on the Strand, Sussex Square, and the theater while she was away from her studies. I understood completely that she found them boring. And I did enjoy her company.

I was not concerned that she might meet Theo Burke in spite of his reputation about the city for being...shall we say difficult in the least, condescending toward women, and devious when it came to 'getting the story,' as they say.

After all, Lily had grown up on the streets of Edinburgh, not exactly a provincial hamlet, and had been employed in a brothel.

I had wondered in that previous inquiry case if any of the

'customers' of the Church had thoughts that their activities there might be looked upon by the Almighty.

Where Lily was concerned, as I said, she reminded me of me. And I had to admit that I had also been thoroughly bored with my studies that included Latin—I couldn't understand how that might be of any use to me—a smattering of science at the time, fed by my avid curiosity of the inventions I saw at the Exhibition, and the classics in literature.

I looked across at Lily now as we arrived at the Times offices, her gaze fixed out the side window, with a particular *glint* in them. That was the only word for it.

Dear girl, what adventures will you have? I could only imagine.

Traversing London was always an adventure of itself. There were new buildings being built, the congestion of traffic on the streets that included all sorts of conveyances—I did look for my aunt, however I did not spot her motor carriage.

There was also signage on the sides of trams and omnibuses that advertised everything from hair tonics for men and ladies' soaps, to the premium cigars from Cuba available at smoke shops. I was grateful Brodie preferred the occasional pipe tobacco.

We were only a matter of a few miles from Sussex Square, when I thought how much more convenient it might be if one traversed above the streets in a balloon.

It was very near eleven in the morning when we arrived at the Times office building. We stepped down from the coach and were immediately accosted by a woman who thrust a pamphlet into my hands.

"There's a meeting Wednesday next," she informed. "You and your daughter should attend. We need to fight for our rights!" And she was off to spread the word. Not my first encounter with that determined group of women.

"Rights?" Lily frowned. "What sort of rights?"

"The right to vote," I explained as we went to the entrance of that red brick building with the peak roof line that included the Times logo.

"Vote?" she eagerly replied. "Women will be allowed to vote?"

"I suspect that it will be an uphill battle," I explained. "I do feel that if those such as Lady Antonia and myself are expected to pay taxes, then we should be able to vote for the representatives who determine what those taxes are spent for."

"I get wot yer talkin' about," she replied as we entered the Times building.

Lily was appropriately dressed in a traveling costume. Then there was the hound and his new 'fragrance,' not the usual guest at the newspaper office. I was reminded of that by the clerk at a desk.

"I'm sorry, miss. Animals are not allowed."

I thought that most amusing considering the clerk closely resembled a hedgehog—short-cropped hair bristled on his head, beady eyes looking as if he was constantly surprised.

"His name is Rupert," Lily indignantly replied, then added, "He's famous."

Which was highly debatable, but creative, I thought.

"He does tricks. Mr. Burke is doing a story about him," she continued.

The girl did have an imagination and the trick hound was presently sniffing the *hedgehog's* trousers, something that usually preceded a sampling of one's leg.

"Tricks?"

Lily smiled. "And Lady Forsythe does have an appointment

with Mr. Burke," she put in, to my surprise, as I had never discussed my family connection. Nor was there an appointment, as I had decided that it was best to take my chances and stop in unannounced. I had discovered in the past that it was easier to achieve what I was after when I caught someone off-guard.

"Of course," the clerk exclaimed as he attempted to put distance between himself and Rupert.

He directed us to the third floor. "The lift is at the end of the hall."

"An appointment?" I commented to Lily as we entered the lift and proceeded to the third floor.

"It worked, didn't it?" Lily replied. "Like the ones the men used to make at the *'Church.'*"

Theodolphus Burke. Once again, I wondered just who had given him that name. Perhaps himself? It was pretentious and not something that one would forget.

Burke had acquired a reputation for being somewhat theatrical in his work. His articles were often quite over the top and read like something William Shakespeare might have written, with a penchant for an opinion. He had gained quite a following.

No insult to Mr. Shakespeare, in the event he was drifting about near the newspaper offices this afternoon.

It had also been noted that his particular style had been labeled *'sensationalism'* by some of the more staid news publications. That, along with his ability to acquire information about a crime that his competitors frequently failed to learn, substantially increased the readership of the Times.

We eventually arrived at the third floor and I cautioned Lily to allow me to ask the questions. Mr. Burke also had a reputation with regard to women, and not in a positive way.

I gave my name to the woman at the desk, who was somewhat plain-faced, in a grey gown, with grey hair pulled back in a bun, a sallow complexion and grey eyes. Rupert sat on the floor beside Lily, ears flattened. Usually a sign that he was about to attack.

"I'll see if he will meet with you," the woman announced.

"Is this about the murder of that woman, Ellie Sutton?" Lily asked as we waited.

She was indeed well informed. I doubted that she had heard it from Munro. He never revealed anything about Brodie's work.

It seemed unlikely that it could have come from my great-aunt. She was far too preoccupied with leaving the following month for her safari. I most certainly hadn't discussed it with her.

She was very clever. A word here, a word there might have sparked that curiosity. And the truth was that Brodie and I were frequently off on a new inquiry case. That left the possibility that Mrs. Ryan might have mentioned something, yet she only knew that there was a new case, not the nature of it.

"I read about it in the daily, written by Mr. Burke. Her ladyship said as how I could improve my reading skills. The article said it was an old case that Mr. Brodie had investigated."

"I'm attempting to help him find who killed her," I explained.

"I don't like what he wrote about Mr. Brodie."

Hmmm. Her first experience with journalism for the sake of selling newspapers no matter what the truth might be.

"And the woman had a boy?" she asked. "What will happen to him now?"

I hadn't thought that far beyond the need to find who had murdered his mother and to clear Brodie.

Of course, there was the possibility that the boy would remain safely tucked away. Or there might be other family. However, if that was the case, wouldn't Brodie have taken him to them?

Lily obviously had no regard for Theodolphus Burke. I was inclined to agree, still I did want to find out what he had learned from that earlier murder that Ellie Sutton had witnessed.

The attendant had returned with a somewhat disdainful look down her nose at both Ellie and the hound, and announced that Mr. Burke would see me now.

"I'll wait here," Lily said. "To make certain the hound don't attack no one." She glanced over at the attendant.

"Lady Forsythe." I was greeted as Burke rose from behind a desk that at a glance was buried in hand-written notes he had apparently dashed off, possibly about a forthcoming story, a few odd copies of other newspapers—the competition, no doubt—and a badly stained coffee cup.

He was shorter than I remembered from a past encounter, with a short coat over a shirt and brocade vest that I also remembered and that was glaringly out of place.

And his greeting was gratuitous. He had written previously with obvious disdain for me upon the conclusion of the first case I had taken with Brodie:

'Lady Forsythe has now ventured into the world of crime. Something to amuse herself, no doubt. One can only hope that she won't muddy her white gloves.'

I didn't give a fig about any of that. I accepted Burke for the weasel that he was. Still, I might learn something that could be useful.

"And how is former detective Angus Brodie this fine spring morning?"

I smiled past the colorful curse I would have preferred to use as I took the chair across the desk from him.

"Someone with your vast resources would know better than myself," I replied.

"And always a pleasure to see you," he commented with a self-satisfied expression. "But alas I have no word on his whereabouts. And he is most resourceful." That expression sharpened. "I have no information that I can share that would be useful."

I thought of the revolver that I now carried. I suppose being arrested for murder might not be useful to the situation.

Where bantering caustic innuendos back and forth only proved how despicable the man was, perhaps a bit of flattery might work. The man was known to be quite impressed with himself and his journalistic abilities.

"I read your articles regarding the murder of Stephen Matthews ten years ago."

"Looking for material for a new novel, perhaps?" he asked, in that irritating nasal tone, as if the words were stuffed up his nose.

"It did seem as if Chief Inspector Abberline was quite determined to ignore information that you felt might be important," I continued.

He returned to his chair at the desk. "I am aware of the difficulty between Abberline and Angus Brodie in the matter. And I believe that you have had some disagreement with the Chief Inspector in the past as well, regarding your sister's disappearance." He sat back at his chair and studied me.

"I believe that I am not speaking out of turn when I say the man is the epitome of a fool. He is concerned only with feathering his own nest and perhaps willing to overlook certain facts, as he's demonstrated on more than one occasion."

I was forced to agree with him on that. "Indeed," I replied.

"To what do I owe the pleasure of this visit then, Lady Forsythe?"

I refused to let him goad me into a confrontation when I would have liked to drop him to the floor.

"In a follow-up article that you wrote after the murder at the Clarendon Club, you mentioned a comment made by one of the staff. That someone was seen leaving the club that night just before the body of Stephen Matthews was found," I began. "And then in subsequent issues of the newspaper, there was no further mention. Did you ever learn who that might have been? It does seem that it might have been important."

His gaze narrowed. "Very observant, Lady Forsythe. I believe that you're the first person who noticed that."

His use of my title had grown irritating, particularly since he had written several articles under a *nom de plume* for the newspaper—satire it was called—that were highly critical of anyone with a title and their affectations of importance. Affectations which I would have informed him that I did not have.

That would have to wait for another day. There were far more important matters at hand.

Burke, being the clever, despicable sort, might respond to something offered that would be to his advantage.

And I very much wanted the name of the club employee who had seen that person leaving just before Matthews' murder was discovered.

"That information might have been helpful in finding the murderer," I continued. "A potential coup for yourself, if you were able to provide the name from your source."

"It seems that Ellie Sutton was the only one who knew who the murderer was. And now the poor soul is dead," he added.

"It's possible that this staff member might have seen her killer. But of course, Angus Brodie was there as well. And now the boy has gone missing," he continued. "It seems that once more Brodie is in the middle of it, and may very well find himself charged with murder. There was a witness of course."

"Merely someone who saw him leave with the boy." I reminded him of what he had already written about in the daily. "You know as well as I, that does not make Brodie the murderer."

"Most interesting," he replied then. "I do understand your professional interest in this, considering your collaboration on past cases. I wonder if there is another reason, Lady Forsythe, something that my readers would be interested in perhaps?"

The man was walking on thin ice, I could already hear the cracks forming with his persistent probing for information. Nevertheless, I did want information from him and chose to ignore the question. I then dangled the bait that I was fairly certain he would not be able to ignore.

"In the interest of solving the current murder," I reminded him. "It appears that Chief Inspector Abberline is at somewhat of an impasse as before. He is, after all, a man consumed with ambition. And he does have a reputation for coming up short, as they say," I added.

Those weasel eyes sharpened. "You perhaps have a proposal to make, Lady Forsythe?"

"Quid pro quo, Mr. Burke," I replied. "A term you might be familiar with."

"Something for something?" he replied.

"Precisely."

"Please continue."

"The opportunity for an exclusive for the Times when we expose the murderer in the present case, in exchange now for the information you had in the original murder, including the name of the club employee who saw that person leaving just before Stephen Matthews' body was discovered."

That gaze narrowed. "That is providing that you and Angus Brodie are able to solve this new murder. I might be able to do that myself. I am not without skills and my own resources."

Crack, crack, crack...

"Perhaps, however you do not have the additional clues that we now have in the matter of Ellie Sutton's murder. And if we are able to solve the crime before you do, we would be in a position to ensure that other publications carry the story."

"What might those clues be that the police have not yet discovered?"

"I am not at liberty to discuss those at this time," I replied. "Suffice it to say that we have information that the police do not have. I must leave it at that so as not to jeopardize our investigation. Still, you must admit that an exclusive article would be highly prized by the Times," I pointed out. "Not to mention additional material for the book you intend to write."

I caught the new interest in his gaze. Not that it was a secret. He had mentioned in a handful of articles that the *public would no doubt eagerly await a book should he decide to write one about his adventures in journalism.*

"And perhaps an introduction to a well-known London publisher by someone who has been very successful?" He suggested the obvious.

I would rather have had a fingernail ripped off. Still...

"That might be arranged," I replied.

"As well as an endorsement of my book." He added yet another requirement.

"Perhaps. Yet, it would depend on the publisher's final say in the matter."

A slow smile followed. "Do we need a contract between us, Lady Forsythe?" he suggested. "Something in writing perhaps."

And something he could use in a newspaper article should I renege? I would sooner have made a pact with the devil.

"You have my word, Mr. Burke."

"The word of a well-placed lady. I will remember that," he replied.

He then opened a drawer and pulled out a file. The man did seem to be well organized. Detestable but organized.

He opened the file which I noted was labeled *Matthews Murder,' 11 June, 1881.*

"The employee in question was an usher for gentlemen attending the club of an evening, a man by the name of Thomas Iverson. I spoke with him, but he remembered little about the man he saw."

Or perhaps chose to remember little, I thought?

"Do you know where I might find him?" I asked

That slow smile again. "He might still be employed at the club. If not, you have proven yourself to be resourceful in the past. I'm certain you will be able to locate him."

"Were you able to speak with Mr. and Mrs. Matthews afterward?" I then asked. "Something that Mr. Matthews might have remembered from that night, since he was also there."

Burke shook his head. "I sent round a request, but it was declined. I was given the excuse that Mr. Matthews needed to attend to business and Mrs. Matthews was not available."

She might have taken herself off to get away from it all, I thought

"I did inquire after the appropriate mourning period and

attempted to speak with them after the service at Highgate, where young Matthews was buried. It seems that business took precedence even over the burial of his son."

"Mr. Matthews didn't attend?" I asked, as that did seem odd.

"I thought it strange as well, but Matthews has the reputation of putting business ahead of everything else, according to those I spoke with at the time."

He stood then, our meeting obviously at an end. "I look forward to writing that exclusive article when you solve the young woman's murder," he said with great humor.

When pigs fly, I thought. I just might write it myself.

I now had the name of the man at the club the night Stephen Matthews was murdered. It was possible that he had seen the murderer as well.

Or was *he* the murderer over some matter at the club? It was most definitely something to check up on.

I returned to the ground floor where Lily and the hound waited. There was someone else I wanted to call on before returning to Sussex Square.

Lily had previously met Mr. Brimley and found his samples in glass jars—severed hands, eyeballs, and other gruesome collections—fascinating.

She was about to be fascinated again, and I could only imagine what ideas stirred in her head.

Eleven

THE RIDE across London to Mr. Brimley's shop took considerable time as it was after the noon hour and the streets were filled with trams, cabs, delivery vans, and all sorts of carts.

I thought of each of them replaced by a motor carriage of some sort and the prospect was daunting, with steam filling the air along with smoke from the coal fires of winter. Add to that the industrial smoke from the outer parts of the city.

The street traffic changed noticeably as we turned off the main thoroughfare and into the district very near the Strand, were Mr. Brimley had his shop. I asked our driver to wait as he pulled to the kerb outside the chemist's shop.

The hound was the first to exit and bounded off down the street. This was a familiar area for him, with exciting places to explore, no doubt. Lily followed me into the shop where we were greeted by his assistant.

"Good day, Miss Forsythe. If you're wantin' to see Mr. Brimley, he's in back." She made a face. "He has a body back there wot the hospital sent over last night. He's been at it ever since. Reminds me of that story I heard about a body being used to create a monster that went about terrifying people."

Ah, the novel *Frankenstein*, written by Mary Shelley. I hadn't made that comparison in the past. Most certainly Mr. Brimley didn't resemble in the slightest the scientist who created the monster in the novel.

Studying eyeballs and hands was one thing, however, an entire body? I suppose there was a great deal to learn, so long as the *'body'* didn't come off the table and start terrorizing all of London.

I continued to the back of the shop which had a long counter against one wall with microscopes. His photo-imaging machine and all sorts of tools of the trade for a chemist, including pill-making machines, were there as well. Shelves behind were lined with jars of powders and other medicines that included laudanum, morphine, and opium.

In the past, I had found Mr. Brimley to be most knowledgeable in all things related to injuries and medicines. And more than once he had come to my personal aid with surgical skills that were most useful at the time. Bullets could be nasty business, as I had learned in our first inquiry case.

In the time since, he had provided assistance on more than one occasion. Brodie had known him for several years and had helped him with a situation in the past that I was not familiar with, only that it had created a deep bond of friendship in that way of those who go through things together.

As for his medical skills, Mr. Brimley had attended King's College, but left short of receiving his certificate, for reasons that weren't explained. As a result, he set up his shop in one of the poorer areas of London, providing care to those who often could not afford it and might have died if not for his skills in medicine.

He looked up as I entered the back of the shop and came face-to-face with the man in full-length apron with rubber gloves, enormous glasses, and a headband with a cord attached, a light gleaming from his forehead.

Then I caught a glimpse of the *'patient'* laid out before him. He was obviously quite dead, with a greyish pallor, and his chest cavity gaping open.

Mr. Brimley blinked, his eyes enormous behind thick lenses. "Miss Forsythe. A pleasant surprise."

I could not say the same for the corpse.

"A new specimen?" I commented. "I hope I'm not interrupting."

"A project that I've undertaken to better understand the human body with the hope that I might be able to better serve people here in the East End," he explained as he laid aside what appeared to be a surgical instrument, then removed the head lamp. He stripped off thick rubber gloves.

"I do have only a short amount of time to make my observations..." he added, "before the body begins to decay. The poor man was found outside a tavern. My guess would be heart failure, but as the man had no known family..." He gestured to the table. "Tell me, what brings you here? Not a personal injury or malady, I hope."

"I do need your expertise in the matter of a case I am assisting Brodie with."

"Hmmm. Yes." he replied.

I wasn't certain what that was supposed to mean, but I dismissed it as Brimley being distracted with his latest *'project.'*

"I have brought an item that I would like you to look at. It may be able to provide a clue." I glanced at the body. "I don't wish to disturb you." Body decay and all that, I thought.

"No, no, quite all right. I just need to pack the body."

Pack? I thought of packing one's travel bag or...

Mr. Brimley then pulled several leather pouches from a nearby bucket and placed them inside and about the body cavity.

"They're filled with ice," he explained. "I don't have a cold box for storage. I have to improvise."

Indeed.

"How may I assist you?" he asked as he pulled a sheet up over the *'project.'*

From my bag I removed the small glass tumbler that I'd found at Ellie Sutton's flat at Charing Cross.

"I need to know what you can tell me about this, if there are fingerprints." I had wrapped it in a handkerchief before leaving Sussex Square, to preserve any marks.

"Hmmm," he commented again. "Part of a new inquiry case that you're pursuing?"

"A young woman who was murdered," I replied. "It's most complicated."

"Let us see what we can see," he said then as he went to the long counter.

He set the tumbler on the counter and then retrieved a container of gun powder. I had learned in the past it could be used as quite an ingenious method of detecting, since the gun powder that would stick to anything that contained an oily substance...such as a person's fingerprints.

He brushed off the excess gunpowder then held the glass up to the overhead light.

"There appear to be two prints, both somewhat large," he announced, as I went to the counter to observe that he had discovered.

He took the tumbler now smudged with gun powder and

carefully pressed a piece of tissue paper against the powdered glass.

"Now let us see what these prints tell us under the microscope." He then laid the tissue paper with those marks on the glass and turned on the electric light attached to the microscope.

"I would say most definitely a man's fingerprints," he said, looking through the eyepiece. "The curve at the edge of the thumb and the second finger." He stood back and I stepped up to the microscope.

The print of the thumb was obvious. It was the print of the second finger that he'd retrieved from the glass tumbler that revealed something most interesting. There was a clear line that extended from the tip of the finger to the joint.

"A scar?"

"So it would seem," Mr. Brimley replied.

And very definitely a man's hand had held the glass. "Might I keep the paper?" I asked, not certain at the moment what that might be able to tell me.

"What can you tell me about any residue inside the glass?" I then asked.

He held the glass up to the overhead light. "There is a bit of stain dried at the bottom of the tumbler." He set it on the counter and went to a floor cabinet much like a physician's, then took out a large glass jar.

"Water purified with a ceramic and carbon filter," he explained. "The water one finds around the city is filled with all sorts of filthy elements." He returned with the jar and poured a small portion of the purified water into the tumbler and slowly swirled it about.

"Hmmm," he made that sound again as he smelled the water in the tumbler. "Chloroform smells a great deal like ether, and cyanide has a distinct almond smell. I don't find either. My guess from what I do smell would be brandy."

Brandy, and a man's fingerprints.

As if Ellie Sutton might have been entertaining someone?

Brodie had been insistent that she kept to herself. And she was terrified that night when she called him. Then, only a short time later, she was dead.

Or?

My next thought was ridiculous in the extreme, and quite chilling.

Was it possible that the murderer sat at the table in her flat and poured himself a drink afterward? To steady himself after such a horrific deed? Or was it something else? I shuddered at the thought.

"There is something else that I would have you look at," I told him. I retrieved the toy locomotive and set it on the counter.

"A child's toy," he commented as he again picked up the magnifying glass and began to inspect the object.

Then he brushed the sides with gun powder as he had the glass tumbler, and pressed tissue paper against the long part of the locomotive. The imprint was smudged and much smaller than the ones found on the glass tumbler.

"A child's print, to be certain," he commented. "No surprise there."

I was disappointed although not surprised.

"It's not the usual sort of toy one finds in the East End," he commented. "Most toys are cloth dolls and carved wood objects easily made from scraps. This is made of steel, and very finely detailed," he continued as he wiped it with a cloth.

"It's the sort of toy that might be found in the possession of a boy of some position, not one of the street urchins here and about. I suppose it might have been stolen. That is more likely."

It might have been stolen. I knew so little about Ellie Sutton or the boy.

"How did you come by it?" Mr. Brimley asked.

"In Charing Cross in the matter of inquiries I'm making. I was hoping that it might provide some information."

He continued to study the toy, turning it over and over in those hands that had been fingers-deep in the cavity of a man's body. Ever the scientist, he looked at such things in a detached way, much like a student hoping to learn something.

"There is a number stamped into the metal at the bottom, usually the work of the craftsman who made it," he added. "There are people who might be able to tell you more about it —Hamley's toy shop for instance," he added. "If it was purchased there, they might have a record of the person it was sold to. That way, it can be returned, if the purchaser has a mind to."

I thanked him for the information. As before when I first arrived, he seemed preoccupied about something and looked at me as if he would have shared something more.

"What is it?"

"Would this be in the matter of the woman who was murdered over in Charing Cross?" he asked.

"Yes, I'm assisting Brodie in the case."

There was something quite odd then in his expression and something that I sensed.

"Be careful, Miss Forsythe."

That seemed somewhat odd for him to say, knowing nothing about the case. Or did he know something?

"Is there something more?" I asked.

It was one of those intuitive feelings that Brodie had been

known to tease me about. Brimley's comment and the expression on his face might have been nothing more than preoccupation, his wish to return to the cadaver after I had interrupted him. Obviously, there was a limited amount of time to make his observations, even with the body packed in ice.

Mr. Brimley shook his head.

"Please be careful," he repeated.

Hamley's on Regent Street was well known across the whole of London. And while my memories from childhood were filled with adventures rather than dolls, there were still ample toys about Sussex Square when my sister and I were children. Particularly at the Christmas holiday.

Our great-aunt went overboard with giving gifts, of course. And they were not limited to dolls for Linnie, but included game sets, stuffed animals, and an amazing wind-up bird in a golden cage that I remembered quite well. It moved and emitted a warbling sound when the mechanism on the bottom of the case was wound up.

"It sang? Like real birds in the gardens at Sussex Square?" Lily asked, her mouth pinched at one corner as if she didn't believe me as I described it.

"Really quite simple," I replied. "Like a wind-up music box." Her expression was doubtful.

"I'll show you when we reach the toy shop," I replied as the driver arrived at our destination.

As he stepped down from the driver's seat atop the coach, Mr. Hastings handed me a folded piece of paper.

"A man brought this round for you, miss, while you were in the chemist's shop. Odd man, he was, rolling around on a wood platform. He liked to spook the horses when he rounded the corner off the street."

I hadn't told anyone that we would be going to Mr. Brimley's shop before leaving Sussex Square. However, there was one person who would know to leave a message for me with Mr. Cavendish, and who might also know that I would visit the chemist. He had said that he would find me.

I opened the note written in that way of someone most familiar with writing reports, the words brief, to the point, in a brisk hand. I could almost imagine him writing it in some place where he wouldn't be noticed, perhaps impatient that he had to write it at all, after telling me in no uncertain terms that he didn't want me involved.

'The boot was made by a man named Greene with a shop near St. James's. I will then call on Morrissey...'

The pencil had stopped there as if he had another thought, but hadn't written it.

Greene was well known across London for well-made leather boots that were worn by those among the officers in the military. Was it possible that Brodie might be able to learn who had purchased those boots?

As for Morrissey, what might he know or be willing to share now, after the recent murder of Ellie Sutton, who had witnessed that original murder?

Rupert had returned. I could only guess that he might have followed Mr. Cavendish when he had delivered that note. He jumped into the coach and I followed.

To say that Hamley's was an adventure in itself was a mild understatement.

It was multiple floors of a large building that looked out onto Regent Street, with windowfront displays filled with all manner of toys and entertainments to draw the customer inside.

I asked Mr. Hastings to return in an hour as we arrived and told Rupert to *stay*. Lily and I then entered the store.

It was late afternoon and there were only a few customers on the main floor. Still, the abundance and variety of toys, games, and at least a half-dozen mechanical miniature trains rolling on tracks set about was impressive.

It was a child's paradise, along with those who had grown up but still persisted in playing with toys. I knew only too well the husband of one of my aunt's acquaintances had the entire final battle of Waterloo in miniature in his library.

It included ships making that historic landing, mounted English soldiers riding to the charge, and a field of French cannon and infantry, along with a miniature Napoleon.

There was a similar battle set up in an alcove of the toy store. This one was set on a seascape, and if my memory of history lessons served me, it was the defeat of the Spanish Armada under the reign of Elizabeth.

Lily was fascinated with it all.

"Good afternoon. How may we serve you?" a voice very near asked.

"Bloody hell! What is that?" she exclaimed, drawing the attention of a nearby customer and clerk.

That was an automaton as I had seen before in a previous inquiry, a movable doll powered by electricity. My particular experience had been a life-size replica of man in full evening attire who nodded, bowed, and then held out his hand.

This one was a golden-haired, blue-eyed doll with a permanently fixed smile as her head was turned toward us and she spoke. It did seem as if Mr. Edison's invention of recording voices had now made it into the world of toys.

"Good afternoon," a more human voice greeted us as a man in a suit appeared. "Priscilla is quite fascinating, isn't she," he asked. Apparently, that was the doll's name.

"I can think of another word," Lily commented, and I thought it best to step into the conversation.

"I am looking for information about a toy locomotive that I've come across," I explained. "I was hoping there might be someone who could tell me about it."

"That would be Mr. Ambrose Hamley. He's the store manager and our authority on our mechanical trains," he replied.

"Is he available?"

We were directed to a series of glass display cases that contained all manner of miniature train pieces, including locomotives much like the one I had found in Charing Cross. I was introduced to Mr. David Hamley, a great nephew of one of the original Hamley brothers.

He was quite boyish in appearance and wore spectacles, the sleeves of his white shirt presently rolled back. He held a train car in one hand and a small paint brush in the other.

The clerk explained my request. Young Mr. Hamley smiled.

"Of course, whatever way I can be of assistance."

Although admittedly the enthusiasm was meant for Lily. I could have sworn her eyes rolled back in her head. She immediately made her escape into an adjacent part of the store.

"Just a few repairs I'm making for a customer," he went on to explain. "The trains are my specialty. It seems the lad this was purchased for dropped this train car and it was badly scraped and lost a door. I'm making the repairs for them," he went on to explain.

"Now, let me see the piece that you have."

I removed the miniature train engine from my bag and set it on the counter.

"There is a number stamped into the bottom of the piece," I added.

He was careful as he picked it up, turning it over in his hands like a rare jewel. "I do remember this piece," he eventually said. "One of the more intricately made ones for detail. Very exact. As I recall, it was purchased as a first piece, with others to be added to complete the set just as one would see it at the rail station."

"Can you tell me who purchased it?"

"We do keep a record of this sort of purchase, so that we can provide the additional pieces as the customer purchases others," he explained and then went into a room behind the counter.

He returned, leafing through the pages of a ledger book, talking to himself as he read through the entries, turned a page, then another one.

"Here it is. A locomotive with that registration number was purchased on 4 December, the past year, by Mrs. Adelaide Matthews. No doubt a gift for the coming Christmas."

If there was more, I failed to hear it except for that name.

Adelaide Matthews had purchased the locomotive. And had then given it to Ellie's son? It was the only possibly answer!

"Are you certain?" I asked.

"Yes, it's right here. There were additional purchases made

as well. Quite remarkable, as the pieces are quite expensive—twelve in all. There are entries for each one along with their registration numbers. It appears that Mrs. Matthews hasn't yet returned for the other pieces to the set.

"Look at this!" Lily exclaimed as she returned with something in hand. "It's full of all sorts of colors and patterns. You look through here, and then turn the cylinder..."

She was as excited as a child, then her expression fell when she saw my face. "Have I done something wrong? I didn't mean any harm." She handed me the kaleidoscope.

I forced myself past what I had just learned.

"Not at all," I assured her. "And they are quite marvelous, aren't they?" I could only imagine what this was like for her, having spent so many years working in a brothel, her childhood stolen from her.

"We will take the kaleidoscope," I told Mr. Hamley.

"Shall I have it wrapped for you?"

"Not at all, and I would like a list of those other pieces if it's not too much trouble."

What did it mean? And did Brodie know who had purchased the toy locomotive for Ellie Sutton's son?

Twelve

MOST OF THE streetlamps across the city had been lit by the time Mr. Hastings turned back toward Sussex Square.

I had the list of the additional pieces of the train set that had been purchased by Adelaide Matthews, and could only assume that she had bought the pieces for Ellie Sutton's son—her grandson. Yet, Ellie and the boy had lived in Charing Cross, a part of London populated by lower-class working families. And nothing that I had seen in that brief visit to the flat hinted at any contact she had from the Matthews family. Except for that toy locomotive.

She'd been afraid of someone. If she had reached out for help to anyone other than Brodie, I would have expected it to be the boy's grandparents. Then she had been brutally murdered.

It was a sad and confusing situation that made no sense, as Mr. Hastings wound his way through the streets. He did so with the expertise of one who had done this many times, thereby shortening the journey that could easily have taken the better part of an hour.

I thought again of the motor carriage and wondered if the journey would have been any quicker. Lily was most entertaining with her questions about the kaleidoscope.

How did it work? How did they get all those colors and shapes into the tube? Unfortunately, I lacked an inventor's explanation about light refraction, though I was certain Mr. Brimley would have been able to explain.

"I never had such a thing before," she exclaimed, and thanked me for what had to be the dozenth time as we wound our way through the streets of London. I couldn't help but feel sadness for her. For all intents and purposes, as far as anyone knew, she'd had no childhood.

Not unlike Brodie, forced to fend for himself on the streets of London, doing God knows what, to survive.

I knew bits and pieces that he had shared with me, yet I was not naïve. There was undoubtedly a great part more of it that he had not shared.

I was certain that explained his support of my decision to take Lily as my ward—someone who had no family, no future, except perhaps as a housemaid, or worse, as I had seen at the 'Church' in Edinburgh.

And what now of Ellie Sutton's son?

His situation seemed very different. The Matthews family was considered quite affluent with the Argosy Company interests in shipping.

In my search of the articles I had found regarding that previous murder case, apparently Stephen Matthew had been the only child. No others were mentioned. Surely the Matthews would want to provide for their grandchild...

The coach swung into the drive at Sussex Square and then abruptly stopped.

"Look at all the lights in the manor," Lily said as she leaned out the window. "Is her ladyship having a celebration?"

Not that I was aware of, and if she was, everyone would have been made aware. She did love a party. I leaned out the other window.

"Mr. Hastings?" I called out.

"The gates are closed, miss. And the way blocked."

Closed? The gates were never closed, particularly when someone was out and about. It was then that the coach door was pulled open and a face loomed through the shadows of the thin light from the lanterns on the coach—a face with a policeman's hat atop his head.

Rupert lunged. It took some effort, but Lily was able to restrain him. The officer reared back from the door opening, and I did wonder by the look on his face if he might be the same one Rupert had encountered at the town house. There did seem to be a strong dislike.

"Is there something wrong?" I asked.

"Not at all, miss. Official business, we have orders to check everyone arriving."

"For what reason?" I demanded.

"The Chief Inspector can provide that information, miss."

Abberline!

I looked to the manor, well lit, all about the front and down that long driveway. Several feelings rose at once, not the least was anger that Abberline had taken it upon himself to come here.

Had something happened? Had Brodie been found and arrested? Or was it something else?

Brodie had mentioned that Abberline would try to find him through me. That was not going to happen, nor was I going to be intimidated or allow anyone to intimidate my great-aunt.

"I am Lady Montgomery's niece and this is my ward. Unless you have ambitions to be collecting garbage on the streets—I assure you that can be arranged—you *will* let us pass now."

He nodded and immediately stepped back from the coach then called to another constable positioned at the gate. At a signal, the gates were opened and we were allowed to proceed.

As we passed by one of the lamp posts along the driveway, I caught the expression on Lily's face. Her eyes were as large as saucers, and she grinned.

"I thought for a minute that ye might take that revolver ye carry and shoot him."

I didn't tell her that for just a minute I had considered it. If he thought a dog bite might be painful…

Of course, there is no doubt that would have immediately sent me to jail.

My first instinct as the coach drew to a stop before the steps to the manor was to find my aunt. At eighty-six years of age, she had outlived a great many people. She was for the most part hale and hearty, and was planning to depart for safari the following month.

However…

I raced up the steps with Lily and the hound behind me, and encountered Mr. Symons at the entrance.

"Miss Forsythe," he greeted me in a quiet tone.

"My aunt?"

"Oh, quite all right. And yourself?"

I was better now.

"We do have guests," he continued with a glance toward to the front parlor.

"Yes, I encountered two at the gates."

"A word of caution, miss?"

I nodded. "Noted, Mr. Symons," I replied as Mrs. Ryan appeared.

"Mr. Abberline arrived some time ago," she informed me. Her eyes narrowed and lips thinned with disapproval, no doubt remembering his lack of interest when her daughter, Mary, had gone missing and was then found murdered.

"He has taken it upon himself to question her ladyship quite thoroughly."

"How is she doing?" I asked as I heard some of the conversation from the parlor—Abberline's insistence.

And my aunt's calm response.

"I have no idea what you are speaking of, Mr. Abberline. As I have said, my niece is here to visit as she frequently does. I know nothing about this other business."

Mrs. Ryan smiled. "She has him talking in circles. He is here to speak with you as well. The man is most abominable—a word of warning."

Not that I was not aware of that. I glanced at Lily, who stood nearby along with the hound.

"Lily might do with a bit of supper," I told her.

"I ain't hungry..." she started to protest.

"We shall remedy that," Mrs. Ryan assured me. "And the hound? A bit of Mr. Abberline's trousers, perhaps?"

"Something for the hound as well, other than that," I replied, then asked, "Is Mr. Munro about?"

"He is with her ladyship and Mr. Abberline. To make certain the Chief Inspector doesn't overstep himself."

Lily protested again about being sent off. I convinced her that she was needed to make certain Rupert didn't attack one of my aunt's *'guests.'*

"I'll go along," she finally replied. "But I've had experience with the constables when they used to come round the house in Edinburgh."

I could only imagine, still I thanked her for her care of Rupert. When they were off to the kitchens with Mrs. Ryan, I turned toward the front parlor.

My aunt was seated in her usual chair. She wore a satin gown in a deep shade of blue that I had seen when she hosted her annual Christmas party attended by the Prince of Wales, his wife, and other titled acquaintances this past season.

Her ensemble included an enormous number of jewels on her wrists, fingers, and about her neck that were almost obscene, along with the wooden staff she held before her. An heirloom, set with the blue sapphire the size of a goose egg from that original ancestor from France—William the Conqueror, according to family legend.

She looked as if she was holding court, and meant to put Abberline in his place. Never let it be said that Lady Antonia Montgomery didn't have her moments.

Munro stood beside her chair, dressed in his usual black trousers and short coat, arms folded behind his back. He looked very much the part of the dutiful servant. However, I knew better, as I glimpsed the faint outline of something tucked beneath his coat, the dutiful expression on his face failing to disguise that sharp blue gaze.

I smothered back a smile and replaced it with an expression of mock surprise as my aunt greeted me.

"Here you are, my dear," my aunt exclaimed. "I do hope your appointment at the dressmaker's was successful." And then almost as an afterthought, "We have visitors."

"Yes, quite successful," I replied, keeping with her ruse as I crossed the parlor and kissed her cheek.

She gestured to the Chief Inspector and the constable that stood apart before the hearth in the fireplace.

"Do forgive me, I have forgotten your name. The afflictions of age, you see," she made the excuse, efficiently putting the Chief Inspector in his place.

Age, my foot, I thought as I watched a performance that would have rivaled any that Templeton would have performed on the stage. Not that it was a total surprise.

This was a woman who had stared down a half-dozen suitors, a list of foreign diplomats, and a king or two over a lifetime with that cool smile and even cooler gaze.

"Chief Inspector Abberline, your ladyship," he replied through tight lips.

"Oh, yes, of course," my aunt replied with another dismissive wave of her hand. "He has questions about something or another..." she added in that same vague manner that she performed so well.

Abberline stood now and turned to me in acknowledgment. "Good evening, Miss Forsythe. I do have questions, in the matter of a recent inquiry case that you and Mr. Brodie have undertaken."

I calmly met that beady, weasel-like gaze and half expected his nose to twitch. I was reminded that weasels are clever, persistent, and could be dangerous.

"It is of great importance to the Metropolitan Police," he continued.

Did weasels chatter much like a squirrel, I thought? Definitely a squeaky, chirping sound...

"There has been a murder, and it would seem that Mr. Brodie may be involved," he then explained. "In the matter of the death of a young woman."

A young woman of little means who would not have

mattered in the past, I thought. Not unlike Mrs. Ryan's daughter, Mary, in that first inquiry case. But this was far more important, and there was only one reason—Brodie.

The Chief Inspector was determined to connect him to the murder, hence the warrant that now had Brodie in hiding. A means for having the revenge over that old case that had denied his advancement?

Weasel indeed. And he no doubt took me for some feather-brained fool who could be intimidated.

Not likely, I thought. When dealing with a weasel it was necessary to respond appropriately.

"Someone has died?" I replied with mock surprise. "How very dreadful. That would seem somewhat extreme over the matter." I added with no small amount of sarcasm. "Although I suppose there are some who will go to all lengths to prevent being discovered."

"You misunderstand," he replied with a twitch of irritation at his cheek. "It is the murder we are investigating."

I smiled again. "Sir Avery mentioned nothing about a murder," I added.

"Sir Avery?" he frowned.

"You asked about the case we are investigating," I reminded him. "The matter of a case that he has asked us to investigate."

"You know very well what I am referring to, Miss Forsythe."

Was he going to mention that I had been followed and then watched at the town house? Another smile, although I was rapidly running out of them.

"I am certain you understand that I am not at liberty to discuss the case. That information would have to be authorized by Sir Avery of the Special Services as it is of a serious issue for the Crown."

"Miss Forsythe, I must insist you cooperate!"

I wasn't certain if it was his threatening tone or the fact that the Chief Inspector took a step toward me. There was a sudden distinct growl from the entrance to the parlor. It seemed that the hound had returned.

"Sir?" the constable standing behind him cautioned.

The man's color had faded noticeably. Was it possible that he had a wound on his leg?

"I repeat that I must insist that you tell me everything you know about the murder of Ellie Sutton!" Abberline repeated.

There was no need to look down, as I detected the faint aroma that accompanied the hound, now standing at my side. I rested my hand on his head.

"Our case is confidential," I repeated. "Sir Avery would have to approve any information that I divulge."

The possibility of apoplexy was most fascinating as Abberline's face flushed with color. A vein stood out on his forehead and threatened to pop, and his cheek twitched repeatedly.

"You are reminded, Miss Forsythe...!"

This, said with raised hand, immediately brought another snarl from the hound and cut off the rest of Abberline's words.

"You must forgive Rupert," my aunt interjected. "He is most protective of my niece. It is in the blood you know. These animals have been protecting royalty since the Middle Ages."

She was off on another tale of her own and most serious. "The breed is quite ancient, you know, used for...hunting by my ancestors. Rupert won the award as *best hound* at Crufts the past year, over the hound presented by the Prince of Wales. His Highness is quite the admirer."

Abberline's face drained several shades. "I see. And your memory seems quite lacking, Miss Forsythe. A malady that it is hoped will soon pass."

His meaning was clear. It was also quite clear that my aunt had managed to bring the questioning to an end.

"There is more that I will learn in this matter, I assure you," he then said in parting. "And to make certain that your household is well protected," he added, turning to my aunt. "I will see that my men are positioned at the gate if anyone should attempt to enter."

"So good of you," Aunt Antonia replied as she rose from her chair and tapped her staff with authority.

"Mr. Munro will show you out. Good evening, Mr. Abberline."

The Chief Inspector turned to Mr. Hughes and nodded. They both passed by in the company of Munro on their way to the front entrance. Mr. Hughes walked a wide path around the hound.

I let out the breath I had been holding as Munro returned.

"Good job, Mr. Munro," my aunt announced. "For a moment I was afraid that you might send the man out in another manner."

Munro and I exchanged a look. I knew quite well he could have done precisely that.

"Crufts dog show?" I commented of the tale she had told Abberline.

"I'm certain that he would do quite well," my aunt replied. "You must consider it for next year."

I looked down at Rupert and wondered if there were points deducted for the aroma of the dog. He would most certainly take first prize for skill in protection.

"With that, I am retiring for the night," she announced. "Please have the servants put out the lights, and do be careful, my dear."

"The beast doesna care for the Chief Inspector," Munro commented.

"He is not the only one," I replied, stroking the hound's ears.

"The man will not be satisfied until he has Brodie in prison," Munro added when my aunt had gone, tap, tapping her way to the lift with her staff.

"He must be warned about Abberline's visit," I replied.

"I'll see to it."

"You know where he is?" I asked. The answer came as he opened the front of his coat and took out the revolver I was certain I had seen there.

"I need to know what he's learned about the murder. I'm going with you," I replied.

"Yer going to warn Mr. Brodie?"

I looked up, Lily standing at the entrance to the parlor.

"I don't like that man, the one wot was here. I can help."

"No!" Quite adamant, the meaning clear, as Munro strode purposefully past me to the hallway.

"I can!" she insisted, her blue eyes snapping with fire. "Mr. Brodie is not a criminal!"

It was one thing for me to go with Munro to a destination unknown. And it wasn't as if Lily hadn't encountered the unsavory side of the streets before, but there was something inside me that simply couldn't allow that. Possibly some protective instinct...

"My aunt is quite elderly," I pointed out. "She often thinks that she is much stronger than she is. At her age..."

"What about the safari?"

"Going about on safari is quite leisurely, and will be restful for her," I lied. It seemed that I was accumulating several of those. "Still, this business can be most distressing, and I would not want to risk any harm coming to her." I continued.

Lily's blue eyes narrowed with suspicion.

"I need you to stay here, should the Chief Inspector return. You have become quite skilled with the rapier," I reminded her. "It would be your responsibility to make certain that she is not harmed."

"I canna see anyone harmin' her."

I would have placed a bet on my great-aunt over anyone as well. After all, she was descended from William the Conqueror. And there was a houseful of servants.

"I need your promise that you will see that she is well protected."

"All right," she grumbled, a sound not unlike the hound. "But only because she has been good to me."

Victory. A small one, but I would take it.

I went to find Munro as Lily went to the lift, no doubt on her way to the Sword Room. I almost wished that Abberline would return.

I was not inclined to have Lily imprisoned for assaulting the Chief Inspector.

Still, it would have been most enjoyable to watch.

I found Munro coming out of his room adjacent to the servants' quarters. He had changed his trousers and coat for clothes I might see on the streets of the East End with a cap pulled low over that sharp gaze.

"I am going with you," I insisted.

"He would not want it," he replied with that strong Gaelic accent that reminded me of Brodie. "Where I have to go, I canna be seen with a woman."

"Nevertheless," I replied.

And something else that reminded me of Brodie, a curse in Gaelic.

"I have heard that before," I commented. "I have information for him that is important. He would want to know."

He did not attempt to leave without me, however, there was another curse.

I found the clothes I'd arrived in the night before. They had been cleaned as best as possible, no doubt by my aunt's servants.

I quickly dressed in the trousers, shirt, and jacket, then pulled on my boots, grabbed the carpet bag and tucked it beneath my arm. I returned to the kitchen where Munro waited.

"Ye think that will keep others from knowin' there is a woman under yer clothes?" he snapped.

I did wonder how Templeton had ever gotten on with him. Yet, there had been the proof in that mural painted above the headboard of her bed...

"It has worked before," I pointed out, then asked, "How do you propose to get past the police at the front gate?"

"That is what the Chief Inspector would expect," he replied.

Thirteen

IT WAS important to remember that I was with someone who had made a career of eluding the police along with Brodie as we slipped out the back of the manor.

There were no lamp posts or torches to light the way, only the hint of a moon and the faint crunch of our boot steps as I followed Munro to the green, following along the track my aunt had used earlier with her motor carriage.

We then passed the stables, with a faint nickering sound from the horses within, then beyond to the line of the forest I had explored countless afternoons as a child.

Munro switched on a hand-held light and guided the way through the twist and snarl of old trees and undergrowth that might have tangled around our ankles as we moved deeper through the wood.

As a branch scraped my cheek, I was thankful that I had changed into the trousers and jacket Templeton had provided.

I had ventured into the forest as a child but never this far, often returning from my adventures covered with mud, burrs, and scratches from brambles. However, it did seem that Munro knew precisely where he was going.

That ancient stone wall that surrounded the wood and the manor suddenly loomed up in front of us in the beam of the hand-held.

I had heard the stories about the manor and that ancient wall from my great-aunt. The original stone fortress had been built by none other than the Conqueror as a place to get away from the main fortress that became the Tower of London. Here, he could undoubtedly consort with all sorts, hunt, undoubtedly with debauchery included. The sort of things past kings had been known for.

The manor had been rebuilt with the original stones some centuries later by another ancestor. Yet, the wall that had been built to keep certain people out and others in, remained and provided those great adventures for me as a child.

It was impressive in height, well over ten feet, much taller here where the centuries had hidden it and others had not removed the top rows of stones over time, as they had done with the wall near the front gates.

The edges of the stones had been worn over time. There wasn't a foot-hold to be found. There didn't appear to be any way to climb up and then over it.

"Is there some other place?"

He shook his head and then moved low-hanging branches away from the wall to reveal a large iron ring embedded in a stone. He took hold of the iron ring and pulled. A portion of the wall slowly moved and then opened a gap in the wall.

"The smuggler's gate," he said, standing back from the portion of the wall that he had just opened.

I had heard stories from my aunt and had visions of swarthy adventurers in tricorn hats, brandishing flintlock pistols to anyone who might have discovered them, and could only wonder what those smugglers—no doubt an ancestor or two—might have taken through the gate.

Whisky perhaps?

"Where does this go?"

He said nothing, but stepped into that opening. I followed the beam of his light and stepped out onto what appeared to be a carriage path. Light from the sliver of a moon gleamed on an expanse of green on the other side of the path.

I had seen an old map that my aunt's father had made that included Sussex Square and a handful of estates that surrounded it in this part of London. Unless I was mistaken, the carriage path lay between the boundaries of Sussex Square and the estate of the Earl of Rossmore.

From past holiday events, I remembered the present Earl of Rossmore as a craggy old fool with bad teeth, who once thought to combine the two estates through marriage to my great-aunt. She was the one who called him a fool.

"As if I had need of someone who merely wanted the family fortune," she once said. *"And the old fool has bad teeth. Nevertheless, I feel sorry for him at Christmas holiday. He has no family left. I believe they all fled in spite of his money. I wonder why?"*

The Rossmore residence sat in darkened shadows, like an old woman. At the thought of those bad teeth, I shuddered, most appreciative that Brodie had excellent teeth.

"There doesna seem to be anyone about, and the roadway is just beyond," Munro said in lowered voice. He then looked up at the sky and that crescent moon still quite low. "We should be able to find a cabman there."

I nodded and we set off. It was obvious that he knew the way quite well.

The roadway led to the main thoroughfare that I had taken countless times to Sussex Square and then to the town house, and farther on to the office on the Strand.

We eventually were able to find a cabman.

"St. Giles," Munro told him.

"That's out of me way," the driver replied.

"There will be extra coin in it," Munro told him, and we climbed aboard.

St. Giles was the perfect place for someone who wanted to disappear. So dangerous even the police dared not patrol its streets.

It was a place of crumbling tenements side-by-side with doss houses, a beer hall, and any number of taverns where numbers were run and other transactions made by women with no other way to support themselves.

Munro jerked my cap even lower over my face.

"Keep yer head down, speak to no one, and stay close. Do ye ken?"

I nodded.

How we could possibly find Brodie here, among the shadows of buildings and other shadows that moved here— men, women, even children who appeared with thin grimy faces in the flickering light from a tavern, then disappeared just as quickly as we passed?

Then a hand clamped over my shoulder. Munro was there, even as I slipped my hand to my pocket and the revolver I'd slipped in there before leaving Sussex Square.

"Leave off!" he threatened, and the light from the tavern glinted off the blade of the knife in his hand.

Just as quickly as the man had appeared, he disappeared once more into the shadows.

"Come along," Munro said in a low voice. "And keep to the street, away from the buildings."

I nodded as we continued toward the glow of lights from a tall building at the end of the street. Laughter, music, and wild shouts spilled out onto the street in front of a beer hall, the lights inside hazy with smoke.

Munro climbed the steps and I followed. A man of equal size with a badly scarred face immediately blocked our way.

"That will be a quid to go inside," he informed Munro, then added, "Each." He held out his hand.

Munro shoved that hand aside, even as I saw the blade in his other hand, held low at his side.

"I'm here to see MacGregor."

"Who's here to see 'im?"

"Munro, with a friend. Stand aside, or I'll cut ye from yer bollocks to yer gizzard."

The man grunted. "I've heard that name, along with another."

"Then, ye know well enough to stand aside," Munro replied.

"Wot is the trouble here?" another man asked as he came up behind the man at the door.

"This one says that he knows you. Don't know about the other one." He gestured to me.

"I know 'im." The second man nodded to Munro. "Let 'im pass, the other one too," he added with a look in my direction.

The beer hall was loud, raucous, and teeming with customers as we followed MacGregor to a long bar where he shouldered his way through, then stepped behind the counter.

"He's not about yet. What will you be havin'?" he asked Munro.

Munro nodded. "Beer."

I shook my head at the look the man then gave me.

Whether or not he saw through the disguise of my clothes, I had no way of knowing. There was no comment made. MacGregor, a fellow Scot by the name, simply accepted it.

"He's been gone since before noon. No way of knowin' when he will return," he informed Munro as he returned with a stout mug of beer.

"Anyone else about askin' for 'im?"

MacGregor shook his head. "Only one of the gals wot has her eye on him." There was another look in my direction. "Not that it done her any good, if ye get my meanin'. He's only come back for a couple of hours each night in one of the rooms upstairs."

This with a glance toward a door which I assumed led to a stairway.

"Then off again, and with a look o' the devil about him. Not that Miss Mabel is put off, ye ken?"

Munro angled a look at me, then told him, "We'll wait."

"Another pint?" MacGregor asked with a glance at the one that was now half empty.

"Aye."

As we waited, I kept the brim of my cap low, and looked about the crowded hall. Was Miss Mabel there, waiting for Brodie's return? I hoped not, and forced back the twinge of anger at the thought.

That brought the next question—would he return that night, or remain somewhere out on the street, following yet another clue in the search for Ellie Sutton's killer?

I caught the rap of knuckles on the bar in front of Munro. MacGregor then angled a look toward the entrance.

Brodie. His head was down, his jacket buttoned to his throat as he made his way into the hall, past the man we had encountered. I then caught a sudden streak of movement toward him.

The woman was shorter than myself, with light brown hair piled atop her head. She wore a long gabardine skirt, stained about the hem, and a shirtwaist that was too small, with sleeves rolled back to her elbows.

There was obvious familiarity as she greeted Brodie with a hand laid against the front of his coat. His expression was one I had seen dozens of times when encountering someone on the streets—intense, a quick nod, then the brush aside of her hand, and the obvious disappointment at her face.

Miss Mabel, no doubt. And truth be known, I could hardly blame her for trying. Brodie was handsome, those dark eyes, the dark beard, and that intense look that gave him the appearance of someone who might be dangerous. His dark gaze fastened on Munro, and then me beside him.

To say that intense expression suddenly changed is an understatement. There was surprise, followed by what could only be described as anger as he recognized me with my coat and cap pulled low.

"What the devil?" The question aimed at Munro. "Have ye lost yer mind bringin' her here? And you!" he snapped, glaring at me.

"Best not here," Munro calmly replied with a jerk of his head in Mabel's direction. "Before there are too many questions."

It took all of Brodie's control not to say something, most

likely very colorful. But there was something else there, something behind the anger.

"I have information," I told him, cutting off any further comment that would most likely have been a curse.

With a look about, he nodded. "This way."

We followed him to that door just off the bar. It opened into a short hallway, another door that possibly led to a storeroom, and a dimly lit staircase.

Brodie moved ahead, shielding me as a man passed by, adjusting his clothes. At the landing we heard muffled sounds and encountered a man and woman in the shadows who hadn't waited to reach a room. We quickly moved past to the stairs that led to the next floor.

He stopped at a room, unlocked it, and removed a sliver of paper that had been lodged between the edge of the door and the door frame. A clever precaution. If it fell, he would know that someone had entered while he was gone.

The room was dark and musty with a small window so badly smudged that a curtain wouldn't have been necessary. I heard the sound of him moving about, then the slow glow of a single electric light over a scarred table and a bed in the corner.

"I'll wait downstairs." Munro stood in the doorway behind me.

"I'll hear the reason ye brought her here," Brodie snapped.

"I made him bring me." As soon as the words were out, I realized how ridiculous that was. I doubted anyone had made Munro do anything.

He closed the door. "There are things she needs to tell ye, and other things ye need to know."

It was said in a way, with a certain sharpness, undertones I was certain had been formed years before by two young boys.

Brodie pulled a chair out from the table for me and I sat.

He shoved the other one toward Munro with a single word, "Talk."

This was someone I had glimpsed, but didn't fully know; someone hardened by the streets, loss, and the things that he had done, and that were done to him. I saw it in his expression and the sharpness in that dark gaze at a sudden noise on the other side of the door. Just as suddenly, the noise was gone.

And I wondered about the other Brodie, the one I had stood beside in that simple ceremony in Scotland, who had comforted me countless times, and challenged me. He had opened his heart a small piece, and I had stepped in, when I had never needed or wanted someone in that way.

I had seen him take down a criminal, and gentle an injured child on the streets. He had shared a glimpse of his past with me, what made him who he was. And I had wanted more.

He could be maddening, overbearing, impossible to reason with. At the same time, he had only to say that one thing to me —*"I will not have ye hurt, lass."*

How did he know precisely how that melted my own anger, stubbornness, and whatever point it was that I was trying to make him understand?

I felt the weight of the medallion he had given me, where it lay against my skin under my shirtwaist—a simple token that meant more to him than anything else—and I wondered, who was he now?

I was about to find out.

He knew that I intended to pay a visit to the newspaper archive, and then with the writer who had covered the story about Ellie Sutton's murder.

"I spoke to Theodolphus Burke," I began. "He wrote about the case ten years before as well. Burke gave me the name of a man who worked at the Clarendon Club the night that

Stephen Matthews was murdered. An usher by the name of Iverson. There is a possibility that he is still employed there. It will be simple enough to find out. It could be helpful to know if he saw anything the night Stephen Matthews was murdered that might be helpful now."

I paused, but Brodie said nothing.

"I then had Mr. Brimley inspect the tumbler I found in the flat in Charing Cross." I caught the sudden change in his expression, however I had no way of knowing what it meant.

"I also had him look at the toy locomotive that we found. He made several interesting observations—most particularly that the metal was stamped on the bottom. It seems that toys of that quality are often registered. I then went to Hamley's toy shop. The locomotive was purchased there and registered to the person who purchased it."

For the first time that dark gaze met mine.

"The entire train set of ten pieces, including the locomotive, was requested by Mrs. Adelaide Matthews—Stephen Matthews' mother. It would seem that she reached out to her grandson with that gift."

"Aye."

"Ellie Sutton was a witness the night Stephen Matthews was killed," I continued. "She left London to protect her child, then returned just over a year ago.

"It seems reasonable that after the death of their son and Ellie's disappearance, Mr. and Mrs. Matthews wanted a relationship with the child now that Ellie had returned to London. It's possible that she might have told them something. It could be useful to speak with them."

When I would have pursued it further, Munro asked, "What have ye learned about the man who was seen outside the town house in Mayfair?"

"I spoke with Dooley and Conner." Brodie shook his head. "They made inquiries with those they know who take on outside work from time to time. Men who provide private protection for those who want it."

"Whoever it was that I saw watching the town house isn't part of the MET."

Someone else then. But who? I thought. And what did it mean?

"What about that boot print we found at Charing Cross?" I asked.

"According to a bootmaker near the Strand, the boot is expensive, made of Italian leather. The sort usually worn by a gentleman or someone of means."

"What about Morrissey? Was he able to tell ye anything?" Munro asked of the former police inspector.

He shook his head. "I spoke with his wife. She was not pleased to see me, and she was scared. It seems that he had a visit from a man right after the news about Ellie's murder broke." He exchanged a look with Munro.

"He refused to discuss the man with her, only saying that it was regarding an old case."

"Did she see the man?" I asked. "Was she able to describe him?"

"She didna recognize him, but she did say that he wore a finely made suit and a bowler hat."

I thought about that. "Do you believe that he might have been sent by Abberline?"

That dark gaze narrowed on me, then went to Munro.

"Has something happened?"

"Abberline made a visit to Sussex Square earlier tonight," Munro told him.

Brodie was quiet, too quiet, watching me as Munro

explained the conversation that had taken place at Sussex Square.

"He left two of his men at the front gates to watch for anyone who might arrive or leave. I made certain we were not followed when we left."

Brodie looked at him. "How might ye have done that?"

"Her ladyship's family has a most interesting history."

"And her ladyship?" Brodie asked with a frown.

"If Abberline was smart, which he is not, he would have been concerned for his neck instead of concerned about his future. A *gowk* to be certain." There was a faint smile.

"I would not want to wager against Lady Montgomery in a fight," he continued. "There is steel, aye? Beneath the satin and fine manners—sharp steel," he added with a look over at me.

Brodie nodded. "Aye."

Another look passed between the friends.

"I think I need another beer and food, if there's any to be had," Munro commented as he went to the door.

"Abberline interrupted supper." He let himself out.

"*Gowk?*" I asked, the word Munro had used to describe Abberline. It was one I had not heard before.

"It means *fool*, a *simpleton*."

"That perfectly describes Abberline," I replied.

"Aye." He was thoughtful. "Ye shouldna have come here. Munro could have brought word about what ye learned."

"We had that conversation," I admitted.

"And ye still took a chance."

"Munro found another way to leave Sussex Square."

"Without climbin' over the wall, even though yer dressed for it?"

I had missed this, our discussion about clues in a case, the conversation that went with it, the sound of his voice. And the way he valued what I had to say, even if he didn't always agree with me.

"There is another way out," I continued to explain our escape. "Munro called it a *smuggler's gate*, at the edge of the property."

"Aye, used in the past to avoid the tax man, most usually over contraband whisky." He shook his head. "I am not surprised."

Nor was I, considering one of my aunt's most lucrative business ventures.

"And then ye come here." He shook his head as he reached out and removed my cap. My hair fell to my shoulders. He shook his head.

"*Mo lu uy*," he said in Gaelic, thoughtful as he took a length of my hair in his fingers and stroked it.

I looked at him in question.

"Ye shouldna have come here...this place. If ye had been followed, yer fate might be the same..."

"But we weren't followed. And I have been in worse places," I replied. "The *Church* and the Vaults in Edinburgh."

He nodded. "Ye seem to have a penchant for such things. But it's no place for ye."

And where was my place, if not with him?

"And the people here..." he continued.

"Such as Mr. MacGregor?" I suggested. "And the man at the door? We might have been more welcome if I had worn a gown."

"Not a welcome ye would care for. The women here..." He hesitated again.

"Like Mabel?" I suggested. "She did seem to be most welcoming when you arrived."

He shook his head. "She is a good soul, but not one that I fancy. Do ye ken?"

"What sort might that be?"

He tugged at that handful of hair. "One that argues and doesna listen to what I tell her; with her notes and crazy notions; one who takes risks enough to drive a man insane..." He tugged again, pulling me closer.

"Someone who is not shy about tellin' me when I'm wrong about something or bein' foolish; one who is honest, and true, and good-hearted most particularly when it comes to others..." His fingers brushed my cheek.

"A lass with red hair..."

Fourteen

I DID wish that I had my chalkboard as I tapped the pen on the notebook, trying to see what wasn't there as I went back over what we did know.

"Ellie Sutton saw something that night when Stephen Matthews was murdered. She shared an intimate relationship with him, and we have to assume that she saw something that night, very likely the killer. She came to you, and you arranged for her to leave London to protect her.

"There were others at the club that night," I continued. "Guests, Iverson, as well as other employees, and Mr. Matthews.

"Ellie went into hiding for her own safety and that of her child. The murderer was never caught. Ellie returned to London almost ten years later, where she found work to support herself and her child. She lived in that flat at Charing Cross with her son and worked at the Brown Hotel.

"It was there that she encountered someone she believed was following her. She was afraid and contacted you; she was followed to her flat and murdered.

"The question is...why? Was it random? A potential lover who was spurned and followed her? By all accounts she did not know the man, but was afraid of him. Who was he? And why was he following her?

"She lived quietly in that flat at Charing Cross. According to the young woman she worked with at the Brown Hotel, she kept to herself and was never seen with a man, and seemed genuinely afraid of the man she saw at the hotel—a man who wore a bowler hat. She contacted you and then rushed home out of fear for her son.

"There was no robbery, she had little of value, living from week to week on what she made at the hotel. The only other reason..." I approached the possibility hesitantly.

"I realize that you might not know, but there have been other instances of women being..." I thought of that series of murders in Whitechapel, still unsolved. Butchered was the word for those murders. Not that this one was the same. Still...

That dark gaze came up and met mine.

"It was not like that. There was only the knife wound, and her neck broken," Brodie replied. "All of it was very quick."

"Then she was murdered for some other reason, and by someone who left that imprint in blood and drank brandy after the deed was done." I saw the surprise on his face at something I had not mentioned earlier.

"There was a residue in the glass I took from her flat. I had Mr. Brimley examine it. There was no bottle that she might have had, and it seemed as if the murderer might have been the one to drink afterward, almost as if..."

"I get your meaning," Brodie replied. "As if it might have been a toast..."

Gruesome as that was, I had to admit that I'd had the same thought.

"Afterward," I continued. "Someone wearing a bowler hat is seen outside the town house, quite possibly the same man that followed Ellie Sutton.

"Motive, means, and opportunity." I repeated what he had reminded me of countless times. Look first at the means and opportunity, then look for the motive.

"The question is, of course, what was the motive?"

"Ye believe that her murder is connected to the murder that she witnessed ten years ago." He said aloud what I had been thinking.

"Someone still in London, afraid that she might tell you or the police what she saw that night..."

"Has anyone ever told ye that ye have a peculiar nature, Mikaela Forsythe Brodie?"

"I have heard that a time or two."

"Aye, curious, stubborn, and I wouldna have ye any other way."

With the memory of my own childhood experience that had left its mark, having seen my father take his own life, there was another possibility that I was hesitant to mention.

"Might the boy have seen something that night that could be important to finding the man who killed her?"

His reaction was immediate and intense.

"No! The boy has no part in this! He cannot!"

"But if there's a possibility that he knows something that could solve this..."

"Ye doona know what he's been through!"

My reaction to that was just as quick and intense. "I know exactly what he's been through! It's not something one forgets."

I had shared that experience of finding my father dead, when I was very near the age of Ellie Sutton's son. As I knew only too well, there were things that stayed with you, that would always be there, until they were no longer the first thing you thought of, or the second, or...

Ellie Sutton had been a strong young woman. She had done everything in her power to protect her son. Because of it, I had to believe that he had some of that grit from her, that he was just as strong as I had discovered I had to be.

The expression on Brodie's face told more than words, because he knew that it was true.

"I apologize...I shouldna have said wot I did. I know that ye understand."

I took his hand, sprinkled with dark hairs, in mine.

"There is someone who knows something. We just have to find them."

Not that that was going to be easy with the warrant Abberline had out for Brodie, and the man's certainty that Brodie was responsible. Judgment clouded by revenge and ambition? I was determined to learn more. I wanted very much to speak with Adelaide Matthews. She'd had contact with Ellie Sutton. It was possible that Ellie had shared something with her in the hope of resolving the past and providing a family for her son.

As I had learned very early, family was often tenuous at best, often fragile as glass that could be broken, only as durable as those who were strong and true. And I had found that in a most unlikely man.

I stayed the night with Brodie, something I added to my list of adventures, considering the sounds that came through the walls of the rooms on that second floor—quite interesting and most entertaining.

More than once, I wakened to a voice or a sound, Brodie beside me, his expression in the meager light that slipped under the door from the hallway one of either the desire to throttle someone—or embarrassment. It was difficult to tell.

"I've never heard that before..." I whispered, and then, "Is that even possible?"

"Curiosity can get ye into trouble, miss."

I thought that *'curiosity'* might be most...interesting, as long as it was with Brodie.

"What time is it?" I asked as he left the bed he'd occupied the last few nights and listened as he pulled on his trousers.

"Ye are the only woman I know who would wake in such a place and ask the time."

"Always good to know," I replied and pointed out, "...when deciding what to charge for the night, of course."

There followed a different sound as he moved quickly and I was immediately assaulted by a warm, half-dressed, demanding Scot, who smelled of cinnamon spice and...

The persistent knock at the door precluded anything more than that delicious taste.

Brodie went to the door, peered through the narrow opening, and Munro stepped inside the room.

I might have been embarrassed, however I had shared accommodations with an assortment of people on my travels to remote places where there wasn't even a word for modesty or embarrassment.

One either slept in their clothes or got on with the task of dressing as quickly and discreetly as possible.

I had not slept in my clothes. Therefore I quickly and discreetly pulled on the trousers and shirt I had worn the night before.

Munro on the other hand, didn't appear to have dressed quickly or discreetly, wherever it was that he had spent the night.

I thought of my friend Templeton, then dismissed it. Whatever their relationship was or was not, was definitely not for me to question or ponder.

I did briefly consider that it might have been advantageous to have Wills' insights. I had never had that connection. I would simply have to rely on instinct.

"A man Mac knows may have information on the man yer lookin' for," Munro quietly informed Brodie. "It seems there was someone—*spaideil,*" he said in obvious Gaelic. "The sort we've encountered on the streets that seems to fit the description."

He said something more in Gaelic. Brodie glanced over at me and I caught the frown amid that dark beard.

It was still dark beyond the window as I caught the rest of their conversation.

"Where?" Brodie asked.

"Tobacco Dock," Munro replied. "Mac will let us use his wagon."

"Aye."

Some other communication passed between them, one of those things that men shared—a look, a nod, obviously meant to exclude myself. Munro nodded, then left the room.

"What is it?" I asked. "And that word Munro used." I tried to say it, however failed quite miserably.

"*Spaideil,*" he repeated.

"What does it mean?"

"A fancy dresser."

"In the East End?"

"Aye. They're employed by others to handle...certain things."

Such as terrifying a young woman? And possibly murder? I thought.

"And the rest of it? I asked.

I gave him a long look, and waited.

"It seems the man wore a round hat with a narrow brim," he finally replied.

"A bowler hat?"

"Ye need to finish dressing," he said then. "And put yer hair up. There's no need to draw attention, even with few about this early in the day."

"Where are we going?"

"I need to find Morrissey and learn what he knows. Munro will see that ye get back to Sussex Square."

I ran my hand through my hair, loosening the tangles, then tucked it under the cap.

"I'm going with you."

I grabbed my jacket and left the room. I found Munro waiting at the bottom of the stairs. I caught his look over my shoulder as Brodie followed. I ignored both of them.

Hudson's on Regent Street was the tobacco shop where Brodie hoped to find Morrissey. The streets were empty for the most part as we arrived nearby, except for lamplighters, who extinguished the streetlamps as we passed.

Munro guided the horse around the end of the street and into a narrow alley that ran behind the shops that lined Regents Street, where we hoped to speak with Mr. Morrissey. Brodie had telephoned the shop earlier and set the meeting.

A wagon, with barrels still to be unloaded, sat in the alleyway behind the shop, and the back entrance was open. There was obviously someone inside the shop.

Munro stepped down as well. "Ye'll not go alone."

"Ye dinna trust the man," Brodie commented.

I wondered what was behind that comment. Munro simply nodded.

"Stay with the wagon," Brodie told me. There was a look as if he thought I might argue the matter. I didn't.

He knew Morrissey, and considering their history together and the event of that night ten years earlier, the man might have information he'd learned afterward that could be useful now.

I would only be in the way, not that I particularly cared to be relegated to the wagon. And Munro was with him. The two of them could be quite formidable. Still, there was Brodie's question and what wasn't said. Munro didn't trust Morrissey.

I had an uneasy feeling as I waited, questions racing through my thoughts.

It wasn't instinct or even a warning from the *'other world,'* as Templeton called it. It was the way the ears of the horses at the wagon suddenly perked up—a sound they picked up, a movement through the shadows at the other end of the alley, and a brief glimpse of a dark blue uniform. And then another.

I stepped down from the wagon and quickly entered the back of the shop. I found them there, with the man I assumed was Morrissey.

Munro was nearest as Brodie spoke with Morrissey. I caught only a few words, but an unmistakable undertone.

"I don't know anything," the man insisted. "After ten years? Did it occur to you that the woman killed the man? A lovers' quarrel, and her from the streets?"

"You walked away..." he added. "I have a family to protect."

Have a family to protect? Not *had*?

Did that mean that he had contacted the police after Brodie arranged to meet him?

"The police are here!" I warned as shadows moved along the front of the shop.

"Ye've betrayed me," Brodie accused Morrissey as he grabbed him by the neck of his shirt.

"I had no choice," Morrissey fired back. "Abberline threatened my family."

The glass in the door at the entrance to the tobacco shop shattered.

"We have to go," Munro shouted at Brodie.

"What do ye know!" Brodie demanded. "Who else was there that night?"

"It doesn't matter," Morrissey shouted. "The woman is dead and he'll have his pound of flesh."

I was certain he meant Abberline.

"Brodie..." I pleaded with him. He didn't seem to hear.

"What did ye learn afterward?" he demanded. "Why did someone want her dead?"

Morrissey simply shook his head and repeated what he had already said.

The door at the front of the shop shattered and was then kicked open as the police forced their way inside.

Brodie looked back at Munro. I had never before seen the expression I now saw on his face.

"Get her out of here!" he shouted to Munro.

Then, everything was in chaos. There were shouts from the police as a dozen or more charged inside as I was dragged to the back of the shop.

I yelled at Munro to let go. Unable to break his hold on my arm, I fought and kicked. If I wasn't being dragged behind him, I would have punched him in the face...

The sound of a gunshot stopped us. Munro glanced past me to the front of the shop as the shouts and chaos subsided.

"No...!" I cried.

Munro's hand tightened around my arm and I was dragged out the back of the tobacco shop.

Fifteen

"HE'S ALIVE."

I looked up as Munro came into the salon at Sussex Square.

"How do you know?" I finally managed.

"Those who still have connections into the MET," he replied. He came and knelt in front of where I sat now, in front of a roaring fire, trying to make the cold go away. He took hold of both my hands.

"Mr. Conner," he said then.

I nodded.

"No need to molly-coddle the girl," my aunt announced as she entered the salon with a maid in her wake. "Set the tray there, then you may leave, Tassy. And please close the doors after."

Then she poured three tumblers of her very fine whisky, and it wasn't even midday yet. She handed one to Munro, then one to me. My hands shook slightly.

"Of course he's alive," she announced. "I wouldn't have it any other way." She took a long sip from her own glass. "Drink up, my dear. We must discuss what is to be done next."

My aunt sat in her chair while Munro explained what had happened. She didn't interrupt him, but nodded from time to time.

"Morrissey is dead," he then announced with a look over at me.

That was the shot I had heard and had feared the worst. Now, the man who might have told Brodie more that he might have learned about the case was dead as well.

He had a family to protect! The words lay there like broken pieces of glass.

What about Ellie Sutton? What about her son? And Brodie, now imprisoned with charges of murder?

"I have contacted my lawyer and apprised him of the facts of the matter as well as the need for his services in seeing that these charges against Mr. Brodie are dropped," my aunt announced.

"It is not the first time that Abberline has run afoul of our family. This will not stand." She was like an admiral directing a military campaign.

"In the meantime," she continued, "what is to be done next to find this woman's murderer?"

I interrupted the campaign speech. "I want to see him."

"Of course, dear. In due time..."

"Today."

Sir Jamison Laughton, the Queen's Council and my aunt's lawyer as well, was able to make the arrangements.

"It required some persuasion on my part," he explained as my aunt and I met with him in his office at St. James's Park.

"I have been apprised of the charges against Mr. Brodie, as

well as the history of the events. It would seem there is a strong case against him in the matter of the murder of the woman, Ellie Sutton. Still," he continued, "given your relationship with Mr. Brodie, I have been able to obtain a time when you will be allowed to meet with him at Scotland Yard this afternoon."

Not the Tower? It did seem as if Abberline was reluctant to have Brodie anywhere near the Tower and Sir Avery. Most interesting, I thought.

"What else?" my great-aunt reminded him.

"I will have people I know make inquiries in the matter. Still, I can make no promises. You do understand?"

I nodded, my thoughts already turning toward that meeting to come.

"I will note that I have received communication from his Royal Highness, the Prince of Wales, as well," he continued. "That is the reason I have acted quickly in this. And of course, on behalf of Lady Montgomery." He nodded to my aunt.

He then handed me a folded note. "These are instructions to the warder at Scotland Yard, that will allow you to see the prisoner. You do understand that you must conduct yourself appropriately, so not to jeopardize Mr. Brodie's chances of vindication."

This was for my benefit, however, I was aware that he looked directly at my aunt when he said this.

I took the note, and nodded once more.

Munro accompanied me at the appointed time.

I had been to Scotland Yard in previous inquiry cases, yet not when so much hung in the balance.

I knew the Chief Inspector well enough to know that he would no doubt be gloating at having Brodie his prisoner.

Motive, means, and opportunity? It was a frequent topic of conversation when attempting to solve a murder. And now?

Abberline had proven that he had the means, and most certainly Brodie's determination to speak with Morrissey had provided the opportunity.

The Chief Inspector's motive? Ambition, no matter the cost, no matter the lives it destroyed.

I thought about Morrissey on that long coach ride to Scotland Yard. He had a family to protect! And it had cost him his life.

If I could have questioned him, I would have demanded to know if they were protected now! But I didn't have the gift of communicating with the dead like my friend Templeton.

The MET had recently moved from their original building at Whitehall Place into a new red-stone building with conical towers at the Victoria Embankment and was now called the New Scotland Yard. Featuring, no doubt, a new office for Chief Inspector Abberline.

I remembered a newspaper article some two years earlier that a dismembered woman's body was found during construction. It caused all sorts of speculation, and, to my knowledge, the woman's identity was never known.

I suggested that Munro wait in the coach rather than accompany me as we arrived at the arched granite entrance in the embankment.

"There are no charges against me, miss," he replied.

"Do you trust Abberline?" I asked.

"I see yer point, miss. If ye've not returned in a reasonable time, I will contact her ladyship."

"You are a good friend," I told him as Mr. Hastings appeared at the door.

"And ye as well, miss."

Friend. And then there was Brodie. Most certainly a friend in the beginning.

I had needed him to help find my sister—a man I could trust, my aunt had said of him at the time.

I stepped down from the coach and entered the New Scotland Yard, a massive four-story building. Brodie was somewhere inside.

I signed in at the ground floor desk, presented the note from Sir Laughton, and waited.

The constable at the desk returned, and I was escorted into the office of Chief Inspector Abberline. The note Sir Laughton had given me lay on the desk before him. He did not stand but indicated the chair across from him.

"Sir Laughton," he commented. "I should have known that you would use your name and title to persuade others to assist in your efforts. Not that it will do any good. The case against Angus Brodie is strong."

I had learned previously that it was pointless to argue with the man. That was not the reason I was there.

He studied me, chin resting on steepled fingers. "I have waited a long time for this," he said with a self-satisfied expression.

"If there is some irregularity with Sir Laughton's request, I will make a telephone call to his offices," I replied. "He did insist that I contact him once I've seen Mr. Brodie."

That gaze sharpened. Did I mention weasel?

"Yes, of course. A very thorough man, not that it will do any good. However, by all means you may proceed, Lady Forsythe. Or should I say, Mrs. Angus Brodie."

I waited, but did not respond. He eventually summoned one of his constables.

"You will escort Lady Forsythe to the holding area. There, she will be allowed to speak with the new prisoner—Brodie." He held up a hand as the constable waited at the door.

"She has been known to be most proficient with a firearm. You will see that she has no weapon."

"Yessir."

Not that I would have brought a weapon with me. Then again, I did experience a small moment of satisfaction that it was of some concern to Abberline.

Munro had seen to *'disarming'* me as we arrived.

"The man would like nothing better than to have a grievance against ye as well, miss. I know Brodie has seen that yer armed, as well as carrying the blade I gave ye when yer out and about on yer inquiry cases. I willna have my friend thinkin' that I sent ye in there like Daniel into the lion's den. Ye will give me both."

A quote from the Bible? That surprised me more than his insistence that I turn over both weapons to him. Who might have expected that? And when I commented on that?

"A woman I once kept company with was fond of the verses," he said with a frown. "She was far better at the verses than at..."

I had quickly handed both weapons over to him, before he went into greater detail.

Now, as I followed the constable to the door of Abberline's office, I said, "I assure you, if I had a weapon, you would already know of it."

The young constable stared at me as he finally understood my meaning.

"You may carry on," I told him and closed the door to Abberline's office rather sharply.

I had experience with someone incarcerated in the past— Templeton came to mind. It had been a somewhat bizarre experience. Detained in the matter of the dead Ambassador at the old Scotland Yard, she had proceeded to give a performance to the staff as Cleopatra—the play she was in at the time.

Then there was the situation with my sister's former husband, who made a series of catastrophic choices that ended his marriage, his career, and almost his life. He had been imprisoned for high crimes against the Crown. I emphasize the word *former.*

I had paid him a visit at Newgate in the course of our investigation, an experience never to be forgotten, with its dank stone walls and the certainty that the lives of those within were over. A place of the living dead, I had once heard it described.

But even those previous situations could not prepare me for what I saw as I was escorted into a part of the New Scotland Yard referred to as a 'holding area.'

I followed the young constable down a hallway at the ground floor, lined with a half-dozen rooms with stout doors and bars set into the small openings at each one.

"I will have to search you, miss," he announced politely enough.

I opened my bag to reveal that I carried no weapon. He nodded, then hesitated, his face coloring.

"The Chief Inspector did say that I was to search your person as well."

"And what precisely does that entail? As you can see," I turned about for his inspection. "There is hardly a place where I might conceal a weapon."

I had worn a gown and jacket from a previous stay at Sussex Square. The gown clung to me, while the jacket, when I opened it, left nothing to the imagination nor did it reveal any weapon.

"That is quite sufficient, miss," he stammered and promptly unlocked the door at cell number 1-B.

I stepped inside, and the door closed behind me with a startling finality.

It was quite dark inside the cell and almost suffocating with no outside window, in the event that a prisoner might attempt to claw and scrabble his way through thick stone walls, and then escape.

Furnishings were at a minimum, so as not to provide the prisoner in question anything that might be used as a weapon. What appeared to be a metal frame bed was attached at one wall, and was nothing more than a rack with a thin blanket that was still folded. A shallow basin had been attached at the opposite wall. Food, untouched, sat on a metal plate at the floor.

I caught the movement from that bed, and then a hoarse sound that I wouldn't have recognized if the constable hadn't checked the *'guest register'* as we arrived and confirmed that this was in fact where Brodie was being held.

I then heard the distinctive sound of chains...as he slowly emerged from the shadows in one corner of the cell.

Knowing Abberline...knowing his obsession with Brodie, I had tried to prepare myself for what I would find. Nothing I had imagined could have prepared me for what I saw.

He wore the trousers and shirt from the day before, however, the shirt was torn and stained with dried blood.

My first thought was that he must have been wounded as the police entered the smoke shop. There had been that one gunshot. But it seemed that it was Morrissey who was dead. Then I looked at his face.

His hair was tangled and matted, a cheek badly swollen and bloodied above the dark beard, and he shuffled forward in a way that had little to do with the chains on his ankles.

He moved like a very old man, bent and stooped, one arm held against his mid-section.

I had seen injured people before, even bodies in the course of our inquiry cases. But nothing compared to this. He had been beaten and quite savagely.

"Brodie...?" I almost didn't believe that it was him—didn't want to believe it.

"Wot...!" he said, in a thick rasping sound, "are ye doin' here!"

I gathered my thoughts and my emotions. It would have been so easy to become hysterical at what I saw...and I was not a hysterical person. But this was Brodie, and as with everything else about the man, everything I had known before went right out the window. Still...

It would do neither of us any good to give into what I was feeling, and I was fairly certain that he would have made some disparaging comment if I were to fall into a weeping fit.

It was ridiculous to ask how he was or how they were treating him. That was obvious.

"I'm here to see you..."

He cut off anything more I would have said.

"I dinna want ye here!"

"I can help you..."

"I dinna need yer help!"

"I might argue that...There are things that can be done, people who can assist. I've already contacted Sir Laughton..."

"No!"

There was something of the old Brodie in that angry response that brought on a fit of coughing. I held onto that, having dealt with it numerous times in the past.

"If you know anything that might be helpful, if Morrissey said anything before...a question you asked that he responded to before Abberline's men broke into the shop..."

"I dinna want ye part of this."

"That would seem moot at this point. I am part of it..."

"Mikaela!" The effort it took to speak brought on another spasm of coughing, and he looked as if he might drop to the floor.

All my resolve disappeared, and I went to him, holding onto him...holding him up. I didn't care about the blood or the bruises...

I could only imagine the strength it took as he pushed away from me. When I took a step toward him, he only shook his head.

"Abberline has waited ten years for this. I willna have ye part of it. Will ye once do as I say? Stay away!"

"Bloody hell, I will," I replied.

"I dinna want ye here!"

I had seen him angry countless times, at times directed at me, but never like this. When I reached out to touch him, he pulled away sharply.

"You need to trust me," I told him then. "I *will* find the man responsible for Ellie Sutton's murder." It was the only way to clear him, and seeing him bloodied and bruised for Abberline's cruel pleasure, perhaps save his life.

"I shouldna ha brought you into any of this..." he whispered.

He turned back to that corner of the room and slowly disappeared into the shadows.

"Trust me," I told him once more, then knocked at the door to let the constable know that I was ready to leave.

Munro took one look at me as I returned to the coach.

"Aye."

The rest of the trip back to Sussex Square was made in silence.

• • •

There is something to say regarding someone who knows you so well because they are very much like you.

At first, my great-aunt said nothing when we returned, waving away the servants as well as Lily and Mrs. Ryan.

I say *at first*, as she left me to my anger, my frustration, my thoughts, and the fear—not something I usually allowed. Then...

"We could storm the gates and break him out. It would be quite an experience," she suggested as luncheon was served, for which I had no taste whatsoever.

"I could call in a favor for that. Or we might simply have Mr. Munro take care of Abberline when he leaves Scotland Yard for the day, self-satisfied that he has Brodie in his clutches."

She seemed to have a healthy appetite for luncheon and her proposed scheme. She eyed me thoughtfully.

"Or have you decided to leave Brodie to his fate? I do suppose an arrangement could be provided by Sir Jamison, an annulment rather than a divorce, and be done with the man."

I looked at her sharply. Although by the brief and painful conversation with Brodie it did seem that he regretted my involvement.

"Or not," she added. "If you have set upon a plan? If you have not..."

I suddenly rose from the table, threw down my napkin, and went in search of Munro.

"Sir Avery made it clear that he wouldna be involved in the murder case," he said when I explained what I intended to do.

It did not include storming the gates of Scotland Yard, or having Munro assist Mr. Abberline in simply disappearing. Although that was tempting...

Sixteen

"AS I HAVE SAID, I cannot intervene in a personal matter such as the murder case that Brodie has pursued," Sir Avery Stanton of the Special Services reminded me from his desk in the Tower.

"What about a case that involves a man who has provided exemplary services, even at the risk of his own life?" I demanded as I circled his office once more, unable to sit still and unwilling to accept official statements.

As I had arrived at the formidable fortress earlier with Munro, I had experienced a feeling of dread that Brodie might very well find himself within those walls where it was said those who committed crime against the Crown were still taken. It seemed a good set of gallows never went overlooked.

I had pushed on, most determined. And now more than ever. I had never let an initial response get in my way, as I inspected the framed certificates on Sir Avery's wall and the letter below a Royal Warrant, signed by no less than Victoria herself.

"In service to the Realm," I read and the motto in Latin,

"*Semper Occultus—Always Secret,*" I translated from an agonizing year of studies.

"Service to the Realm," I repeated. "That would mean to the people of Britain, would it not?" I asked as I turned around.

Sir Avery watched me, much like a bug under a microscope. "It would," he finally replied.

"In secret," I added, according to the motto. He continued to watch me with a narrowed gaze. "Therefore, you are bound to provide service to the Realm—the *people* in this case Brodie, as long as it is done in secret."

"That is somewhat presumptuous, Lady Forsythe."

Brodie had warned me about bantering words with Sir Avery. He was intelligent, clever, and could be quite ruthless—all in the name of the Crown, after a brilliant military career, and his family was well-placed with connections, all the more that he had been chosen to head the new Special Services office.

Presumptuous perhaps, still I had a draw card, as those familiar with the game would say. My great-aunt was most willing, had even suggested that she might call in a favor to help in the matter.

"If an assistance was to be provided in secret, then it would not be presumptuous at all, but in keeping with the purpose of the office," I suggested.

As I said—intelligent, clever, and that other part, ruthless. And like the consummate diplomat that he could be, he sat there watching me, as if the bug—myself—might crawl out from under the glass and leave his office, never to bother him again.

"Assistance might be provided," he finally replied. "In exchange." And there it was. "*Quid pro quo,* Lady Forsythe. You seem to have some knowledge of the Latin language."

"Something for something."

"Precisely."

"What might that be?" I asked, keeping in mind that intelligence, cleverness, and ruthlessness.

Sir Avery stood then, hands thrust into the pockets of his trousers as he slowly rounded his desk.

"You are a person of some accomplishment. You have traveled widely and have a knowledge of at least two languages."

"Three," I corrected him. "With a passing knowledge of Arabic." When it came to asking directions and the cost of an item, and just enough to know if I was being taken advantage of. As now?

He smiled, and I thought that might not be a good thing.

"I stand corrected," he continued. "You have also proven yourself to be most resourceful when confronted with a certain situation, as well as proficient with fire-arms and a sword?" he added with obvious skepticism.

"The rapier," I provided, my suspicion deepening.

"Yes. And the ability to think independently. Most unusual for a woman."

I ignored that comment and continued to wait.

"I have a proposal for you," he continued. "One that, in consideration of your talents and skills, could be of use to me and the Agency. In exchange for assistance of the Agency in your investigation into the murder of Ellie Sutton, you will agree to participate in a case of critical importance to the Crown."

"The counterfeit case..." I started to remind him.

"We have made progress in that with the information you have already provided. That will be resolved. I am speaking of a new case, at a time of my choosing, and one particular to your abilities and your skills. *Quid pro quo*, Lady Forsythe."

A case of his choosing might mean anything and anywhere with the interests of the Crown in foreign places.

"I might continue on my own," I replied.

"You might, however that could take substantial time. And by what you have described to me of Mr. Brodie's present condition and circumstance, you might consider that he would not live long enough for you to see the matter done, whereas with my approval and Agency resources..."

He left the rest of it unspoken. There was no need.

I had described Brodie's situation, passing over the more gruesome details—it was far too painful emotionally to describe all of it. Even with that brief description he had come to the same conclusion that I had—that Brodie might not survive being imprisoned under Abberline's authority.

"I accept," I finally said.

"Do we need a contract, Lady Forsythe?"

"Only if there is the chance that you might refuse your part of the bargain," I replied. "For my part, you have my word."

"I will take it. And I will inform Mr. Sinclair that he is to make himself and Agency resources available to you."

"There is one additional matter."

"Only one?"

I ignored the comment. "It seems that Brodie has sustained several injuries in Mr. Abberline's care," I continued. "He needs medical attention and better accommodation than a steel cot in a room no bigger than a closet since there has been no proof of any crime." I kept a hold on my temper.

He was quiet for several moments. "I will see that Brodie's injuries are provided for. As to the accommodation..."

He made a gesture as if this part was out of his control.

"He is presently under the authority of the Chief Inspector, and it would be frowned upon for me to interfere."

He was playing politics. I wasn't.

"The Chief Inspector and the Agency are both under the authority of the Home Secretary," I pointed out.

I was relying on that intelligence and shrewdness to understand the unspoken, that I would not hesitate to contact the Home Secretary or anyone else who could assist in this situation.

"Surely there are more comfortable accommodations, particularly in consideration of his injuries."

Sir Avery nodded. "I will see that it is taken care of, and that Mr. Sinclair is available to assist your inquiries in this case. He can be available—"

"I prefer immediately," I said then.

Sir Avery smiled. "As you say, immediately. Where will you inquire next?"

"There was a man who may have seen something the night Stephen Matthews was killed. I want to find him and question him. And then I would like to speak with Sir Edward Matthews. He may be able to provide information about the night his son was killed as well."

"Argosy Trading Company. You believe the two murders are connected?"

"Ellie Sutton saw the murderer that night. It was the reason she left London. It is reasonable to assume that the murderer is still here in London and may be responsible for her death as well."

"Be careful with Matthews," he cautioned. "He's shrewd and he's been known to go around the rules from time to time."

"What sort of rules?"

"The sort that have made him a very wealthy man, and enriched the fortunes of the Crown. I suppose that is little

comfort with no one to pass it on to. Take it as a warning."
Then he added, "I would not want you to run afoul of the man
before you fulfill your part of our bargain."

"That was a long meetin'," Munro commented as I informed
him that we now had the assistance of the Agency in the matter
of Ellie Sutton's murder.

He gave me a look that I was familiar with from Brodie.

"The man musta had a great deal to say in that regard."

"Yes, and it's very possible that I may have just made a
bargain with the Devil," I replied and told him that we were to
meet with Alex, and now had the resources of the Agency.

"The Devil for certain," he commented and shook his
head. "If Brodie were here..."

That was precisely the point. Brodie was not here, and it
was already done.

We met with Alex for very near two hours. I explained what
we knew about Ellie Sutton's murder, and what Brodie had
shared about Stephen Matthews' murder when he was still
with the MET.

"And there has been a man seen at your town house?"

I gave him the description that Brodie had provided, and
then the clues that we had found.

"A man with a taste for brandy and the imprint of that
boot," Alex nodded.

"And a man—perhaps the same man—who wears fine
clothes and a bowler hat," Lucy Penworth added the notes to
the board in Alex's office after she joined us.

"What of the boy?" she asked.

"According to Brodie, he is safe, but he did not share where
he had taken him," I had her add to the notes.

"What about the inspector who continued to work that old case after Mr. Brodie left the MET?" Alex asked.

"He's dead," Munro replied. "He was killed the night Brodie was arrested by Abberline's people."

"That leaves the man Iverson to question from that night ten years earlier. The one whom you learned about from Mr. Burke. And Sir Edward. According to what you learned, he was there that night as well." Alex concluded.

"I can have someone I know check the Registry Office regarding Mr. Iverson. We work with them all the time. They have information on everyone—births deaths, burials," Lucy added.

It did seem that she had settled in quite well to her new position with the Agency.

I stood back from the board to make certain I hadn't failed to mention something.

Then, as if Brodie was standing there, I added three words that had assisted in solving past inquiry cases—motive, means, and opportunity.

It was rapidly approaching the evening hour, and I was learning a valuable lesson—the Special Services Agency never slept.

At least not when there was a situation, or a case, as it were, that apparently had been given top priority.

The hours were long and went longer into the night, even as other offices across London closed for the day.

I hadn't eaten since the night before, when I had joined Brodie in St. Giles, and I was going on raw nerves alone.

Munro brought food in from the tavern very near the Tower. I still had no appetite as I thought of that stark cell at the New Scotland Yard and that metal plate on the floor with a congealed mass that apparently was supposed to pass for food.

When confronted by a determined Scot...I ate.

It was very near eight o'clock in the evening when a young man knocked on the door of Alex's office and entered with a large paper envelope that had been delivered from the Registry Office, in spite of the fact they had closed hours before.

It seemed that Sir Avery's influence extended even after working hours.

The envelope contained a list, made on a writing machine with entries under the name Lucy had given them. It included the date of birth, date of marriage, number of children, and addresses where Thomas Iverson had lived, and included employment as a steward at the Clarendon Club. There was no date of death shown.

I had wanted to go to the club tonight, but both Alex and Munro persuaded me against it.

"He would not want ye to go there at night," Munro had informed me, somewhat kinder than I would have expected. He did have that same gruff manner when it came to these things. I discovered a softer side to him as I reluctantly agreed.

I had made my notes.

Lucy was to go to the newspaper archive in the morning and find out if there were further articles about Stephen Matthews' murder, while Alex was going to make inquiries with the MET. He'd use the connections of Sir Avery to try to learn when formal charges were to be filed against Brodie.

Everything that could be done for now, had been done. Still...I kept seeing Brodie in that cell. It was little consolation that Sir Avery had been by Alex's office earlier to let me know that he had sent a physician to New Scotland Yard to see to Brodie's wounds.

I was assured the man was a long-time associate, most

competent, and would not be turned away. Munro had accompanied the physician. Still, it was of little comfort.

I worried about Brodie, then I worried about Munro, considering some of the exploits I had heard about their youth on the streets of London. However, it seemed that Abberline had little interest in Munro now that he had the man he wanted...had wanted for ten years.

Munro had returned unscathed some hours later.

I had clasped my hands together to prevent them from shaking as he removed his jacket and a particularly nasty-looking knife that apparently the constables at Scotland Yard had either overlooked or were unable to find.

I reminded myself that they were dealing with a wily, much experienced person who exceeded them in experience when it came to the streets and *minor* criminal activities.

"How is he?" I demanded.

"He's had worse."

I couldn't imagine worse and still being alive.

"Ye want the whole of it?" he asked.

"Yes." I wanted to know all of it, so that I would never forget the sort of man Abberline was.

"He has a gash over one eye that required the physician to sew it up, and another on his head where one of them took the truncheon to him." He paused before going on.

"They took the boot to him when he was down. He has broken ribs, but wasn't coughing up blood."

That was a good thing?

"If there was blood, it would be that one of the ribs might have punctured a lung."

"And it seems when he was down, one of 'em stomped his right hand. The physician tried as best he could to set the bones right."

One of them? I saw Abberline's part in this.

"Did you speak with him?"

"Only a few words, as ye can well understand."

I wanted very much to ask if Brodie had spoken about my earlier visit.

"Did you tell him that we are continuing with the case to find Ellie Sutton's murderer?"

"There was no opportunity, as Abberline's people were present."

I nodded, then turned back to the desk in an attempt to compose myself. Tears wouldn't do Brodie any good.

I felt a hand on my shoulder. "He's had worse, miss."

I tried to wipe the tears away. I never cried!

Only since...Brodie.

"We'll find the man who did this, miss, and clear him."

I nodded as more tears slipped down my face.

It was well into the night when we finally left the Tower.

Alex made a driver available to us as Munro had sent Mr. Hastings back to Sussex Square after the trip to Scotland Yard with the physician Sir Avery had provided to see to Brodie's wounds.

We had a plan how we would proceed the next day and Alex assured me that he would keep us informed as to any formal charges made against Brodie in the matter of Ellie Sutton's death.

I ached down to my bones in a way I had never experienced before, not even after the death of my parents. Perhaps that was a blessing in young children, not fully understanding until later.

But even when I understood those things—my father's infidelities, the gambling, the ruin, and our mother's death too young—the pain of all of it was not like this.

I silently cursed Abberline for his treachery and determination to hurt someone for his own ambitions. And then cursed Brodie for the chances he took, for that damnable *Scottish stubbornness*, as my aunt had once described him.

"He is most clever, but can be somewhat obstinate...He is after all, a Scot...Most important, he can be trusted."

And somehow, in spite of that stubbornness, that overprotective way that was so often maddening, and his intrusion into my well-planned life...

Seventeen

I SLEPT LITTLE, and when I did, I dreamed about Brodie in that cell in Scotland Yard.

I rose, a headache threatening just there at the back of my head, and went into the adjoining bathroom across the way, the sky still quite dark beyond the windows. When I returned, a faint light had finally appeared and the headache had subsided during a hot bath.

I found Lily sitting expectantly at the end of my bed, Rupert at her feet. It did seem that she had a way with the hound. I received merely a roll of his eyes as I went to the wardrobe and found a skirt and blouse I might wear for the day. No doubt due to the fact that I had no sponge cake to offer.

"It was late at night when ye returned," she began. "Mr. Brodie was not with ye."

It seemed that she was still awake quite late.

I was aware that she was quite fond of Brodie, in that way of shared experiences, her curiosity of all things pertaining to our investigations, and the fact that she had no father figure in her life.

He had somehow stepped into that role. She needed that, even when it came as a reprimand about her manners—most particularly when it came to my great-aunt or myself—or his insistence that she pay attention to her lessons.

"*She is a bright one*," he said on more than one occasion. "*She reminds me of yerself. God help us all.*"

The compliment had brought color to her cheeks at the time, and I was reminded that, in spite of the fact that she was very nearly a young woman, there was a child inside who needed his presence in her life.

And now?

I saw the worry in the frown on her face.

"Wot will happen to Mr. Brodie?"

I smiled at the fact that she still referred to him as *Mr.* Brodie.

"We will simply see that he is proven innocent of the charges and released."

There was no point in glossing over the most serious facts of the situation. She had already heard enough to know about the encounter with Abberline's men.

"Will it be dangerous?"

Very likely, I thought. Abberline was most determined to see Brodie imprisoned for Ellie Sutton's murder, or possibly hanged.

She didn't wait for an answer. "I want to help."

"I know," I replied as I saw the stubborn set of her jaw.

"I'm not a child, and I can read and write now as well as ye can. And I'm not afraid of the police or anyone else! Didna I prove meself in yer last inquiry case?"

She most definitely had. We might have been too late in

resolving the case without her deciphering an important code, that had impressed even Alex Sinclair.

However, I would not endanger her in this. Not that my efforts would always be successful.

"I need you to do something far more important," I told her.

She looked at me suspiciously as I continued.

"My great-aunt—who is now your family as well—might take it upon herself to do something quite dangerous."

I didn't go into the fact that, with a little imagination, I could see her actually storming into Scotland Yard, perhaps with a weapon, and demanding Brodie's release.

A little drastic perhaps—still this was a woman who had a king, highwaymen, and apparently smugglers for ancestors. There was undoubtedly a book in all this.

To someone else it might seem ridiculous in the extreme, nevertheless...Having been raised by the woman, I would not have put anything past her, no matter how ill-advised, given her age. After all, at the age of eighty-six, she was going to Africa on safari.

"Dangerous," Lily repeated. "Like her driving the motor carriage?"

"More dangerous. I would not want to see her harmed or taken in by the police. However, I cannot be here if I am to help Brodie."

"Yer tryin' to get round me," she accused, her blue eyes so bright I thought there might be fire spitting from them at any moment.

"She's been like me own family, with you and Mr. Brodie. Ye know I wouldna let anythin' happen to her."

"I know," I admitted. "It is the reason I asking you to

remain here, and let Munro and me do what we must to clear Mr. Brodie."

She was thoughtful for several moments. I expected an argument. I would certainly have made one.

"Aye," she finally replied. "I'll stay here...but I expect to be included in yer next inquiry case."

A demand. It seems that I was surrounded by them. First from Sir Avery, which I would undoubtedly regret although the idea was intriguing, and now a slip of a girl who was far too intelligent and quite crafty.

"You are not to let her know about our arrangement," I insisted.

She agreed. "It will be our secret. Do ye think I need to carry a weapon while yer gone?"

Mrs. Ryan saw that we had plenty of hot coffee and scones as I met with Munro in his office to go over our plans once more.

By the time we left Sussex Square for the Clarendon Club at Regents Park, Lucy would have already gone to the newspaper archive to try to find any additional information about the murder of Stephen Matthews ten years earlier, and Alex was to contact Sir Laughton, my aunt's attorney, in the matter of having Brodie released.

I requested Mr. Hastings' services once more. It would go a long way to keeping my aunt at Sussex Square. Of course, there was no accounting for the possibility that she might take it upon herself to take the motor carriage into the city.

I thought of giving Lily the St. Christopher's medallion Brodie had given me, yet hated to part with it. And there was the possibility that it would take far more than St. Christopher to protect anyone my aunt encountered if she took it upon herself to visit Scotland Yard.

I had spoken with her regarding the fact that Alex would be working with Sir Laughton in the legal aspect of the situation. She had replied, slightly distracted as if her thoughts were elsewhere.

"He is the best man for the job...I do think it may be time to take the motor carriage out for a drive."

"Remember our bargain," I reminded Lily as Munro and I departed.

"I want to see Brodie," I told Munro as our coach pulled away from Sussex Square.

"It might be best to wait until Mr. Sinclair has spoken with yer aunt's attorney," he finally replied.

"Sir Avery arranged for me to see him before."

"It's not a matter of permission from Sir Avery," Munro replied.

"Then, what is it...?" But I knew. It wasn't that I couldn't see him...he didn't want to see *me*. That was obvious, and it cut like a knife.

"Ye need to understand," Munro tried to explain. "With the charges that Abberline intends to file against him and the injuries..."

Excuses. And while I did appreciate Munro's effort to ease the pain of the truth of it, it didn't change the fact that Brodie didn't want to see me.

I had asked him to trust me, and then had deliberately gone against his wishes.

Damned bloody stubborn Scot! As if I would simply ignore everything and leave him to take his chances with Abberline!

That was what I wanted to say but didn't as we approached closer to Regent's Park and the Clarendon Club.

"Since you have had business with the club in the past, you should speak with Mr. Ramsey to see if Mr. Iverson is about," I replied.

We were shown into the main entrance of the club when we arrived. Isaac Ramsey was a portly man with a sharp eye.

"Mr. Munro, to what do I owe the pleasure of your calling on me, with your last visit to deliver our order of Old Lodge whisky so recent? Has her ladyship increased the price of her whisky? If not, then I would prefer to put in an order before that happens."

As discussed, Munro introduced me and then explained we were there to ask a few questions in a matter of the incident some time ago and the murder of Stephen Matthews at the club.

"Mr. Iverson, you say. Yes, he's here today," Mr. Ramsey replied. "We're preparing for a birthday celebration for one of the members. A terrible tragedy about young Matthews. Unfortunate, even ten years ago."

Munro emphasized the importance that we speak with Mr. Iverson.

"I'll send for him. You can meet in the main hall where we're setting up for tonight."

Thomas Iverson was a short, thin man, with just the beginning of grey hair among the brown, and an expressionless demeanor that one might expect of a man who perhaps saw a great deal at the club and had learned to protect the privacy of those within those walls. And perhaps look the other way when he saw something?

The fact that he had been employed for a number of years spoke to his discretion in such matters. I did hope that he would be willing to share what had happened that night Stephen Matthews was killed.

Munro asked if he remembered the incident. Mr. Iverson glanced over at Mr. Ramsey.

"We don't discuss matters concerning our members," he replied what had obviously been well established, if those employed at the club wished to keep their jobs. Discretion at all costs.

Isaac Ramsey nodded, obviously satisfied that the reputation of the club would not be jeopardized, and left to attend matters for the evening celebration.

"A young man was murdered here at the club," Munro reminded him.

"That was a long time ago. I don't remember anything from that night."

Munro looked over at me. It did seem that he was not willing to cooperate.

"A young woman was with Mr. Matthews when he was murdered," I explained what I had been able to learn. "Afterward she managed to escape and then disappeared. According to the police report she saw the murderer that night."

He shook his head. "Will that be all, miss?"

"She was murdered three nights ago." In spite of Brodie's refusal to see me, I was not about to simply walk away from this. "Now a little boy is an orphan, and an innocent man has been accused of her murder. We're trying to find who did kill her and need your assistance."

"Murdered, you say. Poor thing. I've got a family of my own, two boys and a girl," Iverson replied.

He looked about and seeing that Mr. Ramsey was not about, "I remember that night. Total chaos, it was, when young Mr. Matthews was found and the poor girl screamin' for all to hear.

"They were in one of the upstairs apartments. I had served supper no more than an hour earlier when it happened. The other gentlemen made to get away as the police were called for."

"We were told that she saw the murderer," I explained. "She was then able to escape and left London, afraid for her life."

He shook his head. "You have to understand what it was like, what with the other employees, the members, their...guests. It was bedlam, it was. I had just returned upstairs to remove the plates from supper," he hesitated again. "There was someone on the floor, seemed odd to me at the time."

"How is that?" Munro asked.

"I didn't recognize him as one of the members; you get to know the regulars after a time. And the guests were usual-ly...ladies," he looked over at me when he said that.

"The young miss, though...she was different than most, almost shy, quiet in a way, pretty little thing. It seemed that Mister Stephen was most serious about her, not what one usually sees here.

"One of the housemaids said that she overheard a conversa-tion with his father, that he intended to marry the girl. Every-thing changed that night, and the girl disappeared. We heard the rumors that she saw who killed the young man and she was afraid for her life."

"What about the man you saw that night?" I asked. "Do you remember anything about what he looked like?"

"He was dressed quite handily, wore a fine suit of clothes. Made me think he might be a new member." He continued to remember.

A suit of clothes. It could have indeed simply been a member of the club that he saw attempting to leave a scandalous situation.

"Strange though," he said then.

"What is it?" I asked.

"When the gentlemen arrive for the evening, the staff take their hats and coats, to be returned later when they leave. That has been the custom for as long as I've been here—almost twenty years. It's like the members are arriving at a private residence, all proper. The man I saw was a short, stout fellow and still wore his hat up on the second floor, a round piece with a thin rim."

A bowler hat?

"More than one gentleman has such a hat," Munro commented as we left the club.

"But one that drew Mr. Iverson's attention? And on the second floor of the club near that private room where Ellie Sutton was with Stephen Matthews that night?"

And there was the other part of it...he had described the man he saw as *a short, stout man with a bowler hat*. The exact same description of the man Brodie had seen across from the town house in Mayfair.

Two different men with the same description, both seen after a murder ten years apart? A coincidence?

Eighteen

WE RETURNED to the Agency offices at the Tower of London. Alex Sinclair met us at the high street entrance with some urgency.

Something had obviously happened. I was almost afraid to ask what it was, my thoughts racing. And then there was just one thought—Brodie!

"What is it?" I demanded.

"Sir Avery has instructed me to immediately bring you to his office once you returned," he replied, that lock of dark hair over his forehead, and intense expression behind his glasses.

I could only think the worst.

What if Brodie's condition has worsened? Had those formal charges been read against him? What then would happen?

We followed Alex through the maze of passages and hallways of the Tower, past a yeoman warder's desk with only a glimpse through a narrow slit of window in the stone walls to a central courtyard beyond, and could only imagine what those who had been imprisoned inside through the centuries had experienced.

Was Brodie to have a similar fate?

In spite of changes in the Tower, it was still manned by yeoman warders, who lived in apartments within the walled fortress. Even though the fact that executions no longer took place at the Tower, there were still gallows, a reminder of the Tower's past.

Of course there were stories about the Tower. Three queens had been executed on the Tower green—Anne Boleyn, Catherine Howard, and Lady Jane Grey. Although there were those who argued that Lady Jane Grey had never been queen. It was one of those arguments over who was the rightful successor to the throne. As usual there was disagreement and...Off with their heads!

I had visions of the queen from Mr. Carroll's novel and shuddered at the thought. Then there were the stories of two young princes that were imprisoned there and never seen again, simply because of the happenstance of birth.

Sir Avery's office and the other offices of the Agency were in an area of the Tower that were once royal apartments near the river, with an entrance that had been used in past centuries by members of the royal household arriving by barge.

There was still a landing on the banks of the Thames, and Brodie and I had used the entrance in the past.

We eventually reached Sir Avery's office, and Alex knocked to announce our arrival. At Sir Avery's response, Alex escorted us into the office.

"Here you are, dear," a familiar voice greeted us. "We have been having a pleasant conversation. And now you and Mr. Munro have returned. Please do join us."

My great-aunt looked over from where she sat across from Sir Avery. Sir Jamison Laughton, her attorney, sat beside her.

At her other side sat the hound. Rupert immediately got up and greeted me with an insistent nudge of my hand, no doubt looking for food.

My aunt was dressed in a gown of royal-blue satin, trimmed with white satin at the edge of the sleeves and about the neck, a creation of Madame's for the Queen's golden jubilee a few years earlier.

It was an elegant design, somewhat over the top, I thought, for calling on the director of Special Services. And then there was the walking stick made of mahogany and topped with a circle of gold and precious stones that she held before her.

She had been forced to use it when she had previously injured her ankle and had been known to wield it about like a truncheon. She held it before her now with a bejeweled hand that included a ring set with another blue sapphire that was inherited from some long-lost ancestor.

She presented an impressive sight, and knowing my great-aunt, not without a purpose. My friend Templeton had nothing on her when it came to grand entrances.

And performances as well, I thought.

I had not spoken of Brodie's situation when I returned from Scotland Yard; there had been no time. Nor had I discussed the murder case we were following.

The less said, the better, as I did not want to concern her. However, I was reminded that it was never wise to underestimate her or what she was capable of.

"We have been discussing the situation," she said with a smile for Sir Avery. "I have expressed my deep concern over the manner in which Mr. Brodie has been treated in this," she continued. "It would appear, for anyone with a grain of intelligence, that given the somewhat difficult history between certain parties, liberties have been taken."

There was another smile.

"To be brief I have expressed to Sir Avery that all manner of justice must be observed, as any clear-thinking person would insist. To that end, and in light of certain actions on the part of certain individuals, I do fear for Mr. Brodie's safety and that he might be subjected to someone taking the law into their own hands."

I did wonder quite sarcastically who that might be.

"Sir Laughton has been good enough to accompany me," she continued. She glanced over at her attorney. There was that smile and I was again reminded of Alice's Adventures and that Cheshire cat.

"He has delivered an important correspondence regarding the matter," she explained.

"Just so," Sir Laughton commented with a look at Sir Avery.

Sir Avery nodded and indicated a piece of thick stationary on his desk. I briefly caught the royal seal.

"I have received a note from his Royal Highness, the Prince of Wales no less, that I am to take every precaution to guarantee the safety of Mr. Brodie until the situation can be resolved. And Sir Laughton is to confirm to His Royal Highness that it has been duly received and noted." Avery's mouth thinned.

"And what precisely does that mean?" I asked. "What is to be done?"

"I have already notified Scotland Yard that my office is assuming full responsibility for Mr. Brodie, and he is to be transferred here without delay."

I exchanged a look with Munro. At least Brodie would be

safe from any further injury on the part of Abberline, and his current injuries could be looked after.

"Lady Montgomery, Sir Laughton, I presume this concludes our business."

"Quite so," my aunt replied. "And I will expect confirmation once he has arrived. By telephone will do." She stood then, smiled, and swept past us with Sir Laughton.

"How did you manage that?" I asked as we returned to Alex Sinclair's office, Rupert ever hopeful for food.

My aunt patted my hand. "When one lives long enough, one learns very quickly how to deal with fools and imbeciles—not Sir Avery of course. He is intelligent and very shrewd in his own way. And quite handsome as well, don't you think?"

"About Brodie..." I reminded her. She held up a hand.

"I am aware of most of it, and the situation with Abberline will not be tolerated. Brodie is...very important to our family, and I will not believe that he is guilty of this murder.

"The Chief Inspector has proven himself to be disgusting, underhanded, and without the brains God gave a turnip. And too dull-witted to understand that he should not threaten me, or mine."

This with a voice that had sharpened like steel. I had seen it before, but I must say that I was impressed. I thought of the turnip. They had no brains, which was a perfect description.

"I have done nothing more than '*call out the cavalry*,' as Templeton would say after her trip to the western United States," she added. "Of course, in this instance, that consists of Sir Laughton and that directive from His Royal Highness." She turned to her attorney.

"We must be going. The hound did insist on accompanying us —such odd behavior." She paused, "I do hope Mr. Hastings has returned. I was tempted to drive the motor carriage. However Jamison talked me out of it," she continued. "It's quite open to the elements, and he explained that all sorts of disgusting things might be churned up from the street. I didn't want to spoil my gown, and my riding costume is not the presentation I wanted to make."

Of course, I thought.

Munro assured her that Mr. Hastings remained with the coach and team. I didn't mention that I was relieved that she had left the motor carriage at Sussex Square.

After they had gone, we went to Alex's office. The hound had gone in search of food. Considering the age of the Tower and all sorts of crawling creatures that might still be found, there was no telling what he might return with.

Lucy had returned as well from her search for any additional information in the newspaper archive.

"I found something very interesting," she said, opening a leather case. She retrieved a note pad.

"There was an article about the funeral for the young man, Stephen Christopher Matthews. The odd part is that there was no period of mourning like one might expect for someone from a family of the Matthews' position and all." She scanned through her notes.

"The article made reference to his death—but nothing about murder, on 2 April, 1881, at the age of twenty-one. Then, something odd in that same article. Remembrances were to be made to Mrs. Adelaide Matthews of Kent. There was no mention of Sir Edward Matthews.

"I thought that was quite odd as well and went back to the Registry Office and searched the family names." She turned over the page.

"There was an entry for Edward Matthews that included

date of birth, his parents and a sister. I found her date of marriage, and the names of three children.

"I then searched for Adelaide Matthews, his wife, and found her family name of Lewiston under the registration for their marriage on the fourteenth of June, 1859, and a record for when they lived in Kent. But there were no entries for the births of any children."

"There could have been a simple mistake," I suggested. "Perhaps it wasn't recorded at the time."

"I suppose that's possible," Lucy admitted. "But I went back over every entry for the family, right up to the most recent recorded for the past year. There is no record for Stephen Matthews."

Another coincidence?

It was late in the afternoon when we received word that Brodie had been released from Scotland Yard and was being brought to the Tower, under guard, on orders from Sir Avery after he received that note from His Royal Highness.

Sir Avery assured me that his injuries—courtesy of Chief Inspector Abberline—had been provided for, but all I could think of was the sight of him, bloodied and beaten in that cell at Scotland Yard.

It was very near seven o'clock in the evening when one of Sir Avery's people announced that a police van had arrived at the High Street entrance. I started down the hallway that led to that serpentine of passages. Munro stopped me with a hand at my arm.

"I'll go."

"I want to see him!" I protested.

He shook his head. "I know that well enough, but I also know the man. With what he's been through, what Abberline has done to him, its best ye wait for a while."

It was on the tip of my tongue to tell him to take a flying leap, or worse. I was worried and angry at what had been done to Brodie.

There was that little voice inside that warned me that Munro was undoubtedly right. The truth was that Brodie had sacrificed himself to make certain that I was safe, when we went to speak with Mr. Iverson.

He had then been viciously attacked and beaten by someone who wanted revenge against him for that murder case ten years ago. And his words when I went to Scotland Yard were still there.

He didn't want my help, and had told me to stay away, something in his voice that I had never heard before. It could have been the pain from his injuries that made him say it. But there had been something in that dark gaze, something cold and bleak...

"Yes, of course."

The problem was that I didn't understand. I only knew that something had changed.

I refused to give up on the case. A young woman had been brutally murdered and a boy orphaned. With or without Brodie I was going to find who had killed Ellie Sutton.

I could have returned to Sussex Square, but I didn't.

Lucy and I had made our notes on the board in Alex's office, listing everything we knew about the recent murder, and the one ten years earlier.

There was something there, something more that connected the two cases, and I was going to find it.

I spent long hours into the night in Alex's office, even after he and Lucy had left for the day.

The hound had returned with a contented expression and curled up under the desk. I probably didn't need to know what that meant or where the remains of a bloody carcass might be found.

Before leaving for the day, Alex had one of Sir Avery's people bring a cot to his office along with a pillow and blanket. It seemed that it was not unusual for those who worked for the Agency to stay over when a situation warranted it.

There was coffee and food, if stale biscuits could be considered food, left from a small kitchen down the hall.

Alex informed me that Brodie had been taken to what was called the infirmary when he arrived. There, his wounds would be checked and attended if necessary. He described it more as an office that contained only two beds.

It explained the ease and quick response of the *'physician'* Sir Avery had called upon. However, I didn't consider it a positive sign that the Agency had its own *infirmary*, as it was called.

I thought about going there, even after Munro's warning, if only to assure myself that Brodie was in fact there, then decided against it.

Sir Avery had worked late. He stopped by Alex's office before leaving.

"You are planning on staying the night?" he inquired with a look at the cot.

"Alex was good enough to make arrangements for me."

I had visions of needing something in writing, a royal decree or possibly a document signed by two witnesses. A little sarcasm there, but I supposed it was to be expected with everything that had happened.

Rupert had roused from under the desk and positioned himself between me and Sir Avery.

"Should I be concerned about the animal?"

"Not unless you make a threatening gesture," I replied. "He does have a dislike for that."

Sir Avery glanced at the wall board.

"Most interesting," he commented. "You've accumulated quite a lot of information."

"With assistance from Alex and Lucy."

"You seem to have a gift for investigating crimes." He looked at me thoughtfully. "I look forward to your work with the Agency, Lady Forsythe. Good evening."

I looked around for the invisible net that might have been laid to entrap me—merely a reaction, of course.

Still...I had made that promise in exchange for Brodie's care. I was not one to break my word, yet I couldn't help wondering what I might be getting myself into. And then there was the question—what would Brodie have to say in the matter?

"Any difficulty?" Munro inquired after Sir Avery had gone.

I was more than aware of Brodie's own thoughts toward Sir Avery—someone that he had once described as a spider continuously spinning a web. Not exactly a recommendation. It was more a caution of the man.

"Not at all." I hoped that I was right and didn't go into my own reservations about the bargain I had made with Sir Avery.

"You're leaving then?" I asked.

He was returning to Sussex Square. "To see that all is in order," he explained.

I suspected it might have something to do with my aunt's fascination with her motor carriage.

He glanced at the cot against the wall.

"He'll be all right, miss," he reassured me. "He's doin' well enough. The broken ribs are the worst of it. Give him time."

"Is there anything that I can bring with me when I return in the morning?"

My first thought was that there wasn't anything. Yet studying that board with Lucy's latest notes about what she had learned had most definitely raised new questions, and there was someone I wanted very much to speak with who might be able to answer some of those questions.

"There is something you can bring back with you..."

Nineteen

I ROSE EARLY after a fitful night, the hound nudging my hand.

No one was yet in the offices of the Agency except for those Alex had referred to as the *'night guard.'*

There were occasional sounds that echoed down the passage from above, as the yeoman warders stationed during the day had arrived from their respective apartments or flats to begin the day.

The hound made a somewhat urgent sound, and I unwrapped myself from the blanket that had twisted about me. I swung my legs over the edge of the cot to the stone floor.

There was no window in Alex's office, and therefore little light except from the hallway. No doubt to prevent anyone escaping, I thought drily.

I found the electric light on the desk and turned it on. The marvels of electricity still amazed me, especially here—modern inventions in a thousand-year-old fortress. I did wonder what my ancestor would have thought of it all.

Considering stories I had heard from my aunt about that

particular ancestor, he would have probably smashed the light bulb with his sword. After all, one could never be too careful when it came to one's enemies.

Rupert made another sound, and I decided we needed to go in search of hot coffee. I picked up the pot with only the dregs of coffee grinds, and turned toward the hall that led to the green.

He sounded quite urgent as we passed the infirmary and stone steps beyond that led into the upper level of the tower compound.

We encountered a warder, and I explained the urgency. He directed us to an outside area, and the hound bounded on ahead. When he returned, I retraced our steps back down into the area that contained the Agency offices.

I stopped outside the infirmary, my hand on the lever to the door, when it suddenly opened.

A lean man, approximately my height, with thinning hair and mutton-chop side-whiskers—I was always curious how that description came about, as he did not resemble a sheep in the slightest.

Obviously equally surprised at finding someone there at that time of the morning, he looked at me with a curious expression, grey eyes staring at me over the top of half-lens glasses.

"You must be Lady Forsythe," he said by way of greeting.

I did not recall previous introductions. It was obvious, however, by the stethoscope about his neck that he was a physician.

"It was late in the evening and we weren't properly intro-duced," he said at my obvious curiosity. "I'm Dr. Watson. I've been attending Mister Brodie. Dr. Daniel Watson," he added at my surprised reaction. "No relation to the gentleman in Sherlock Holmes stories, except for the coincidence of the name, and our profession of course. You're here regarding the patient." He angled the door open a few inches more.

"It was a long night after he finally settled. As you see, he is finally sleeping. He does have a formidable spirit."

Formidable. Now there was a word I had not thought of before.

"He'll be all right?" I inquired as I looked past him to where Brodie was lying quite still on one of those hospital beds.

"As I said, he is quite formidable. A broken rib can be most painful, and he appears to have at least two, possibly three. I managed to bandage him up to prevent too much movement on the van ride here last night.

"And then there are superficial wounds," he continued. "A deep cut over his left eye and a head wound. I stitched the cut. The head wound is the worst of it, still he doesn't seem to have any residual effect from that."

"You attended to his wounds at Scotland Yard."

He nodded. "He was in some difficulty then, from some sort of altercation on the street, I was told. Although it did seem a bit more severe than what I usually see."

An altercation on the street? It was not surprising that Abberline would have called it that, protecting himself against any suspicion that it might have been otherwise.

"I must say that Sir Avery was most insistent that he be given whatever care was needed. It was good that I was called in when I was. He had lost a good amount of blood."

Brodie had still not moved.

"When might I speak with him?" I asked.

"I gave him another dose of laudanum a short while ago. It's only now taken effect. It will be several more hours. Rest is best now, to let his body do its work.

"The human body is a remarkable thing," he went on to explain. "It has amazing restorative powers given a chance, once the bleeding has been stopped and wounds have been closed."

It was most encouraging.

"You've had experience with such things?"

"A bit of experience in Burma. You see most everything in war. It was there I met Sir Avery. We returned together, along with several others, and he persuaded me to join him in a new assignment he was taking on," he continued. "Hence the Agency," he said with an engaging smile. He gestured to the pot in my hand.

"It appears that you might be in search of coffee? Come along then," he said, closing the door behind him.

"With the hours I often keep, I have discovered where to find fresh, hot coffee. Is that fellow your escort?" he asked of the hound as he joined us.

Dr. Daniel Watson was most congenial and with a surprising sense of humor, a stark contrast to Sir Avery.

"One has to have a sense of humor when dealing with wounds, amputations, and very often death," he explained over hot coffee that did wonders for restoring my energy.

"I suspect the other choice might be to simply go insane. It can all be quite gruesome." He had looked at me, quite curious.

"It is most unusual to find a woman working for the Agency, aside from Miss Penworth, of course. She does have a special affinity for information-gathering. And then there are the ladies who come in to clean; several are wives of the warders. One doesn't usually encounter someone who actively pursues solving crimes."

It seemed that my agreement with Sir Avery had brought some attention.

"Mr. Brodie and I have a private inquiry firm," I explained. "He has worked with the Agency in the past, when a case has required it."

"Of course," he said with a gentle smile. "I didn't mean to speak out of turn."

Brodie still had not wakened when we left the 'commissary,' as it was called. Another name borrowed from the military.

Dr. Watson explained that many things at the Agency had been set up in military fashion.

"You can take a man out of the war, but not the war out of the man?" I commented.

"That is quite good, Miss Forsythe," he complimented.

Alex and Lucy had both arrived at the Tower offices when I returned to Alex's office.

He had decided to plot a time line of the events in the case of Ellie Sutton's murder. He then added a similar timeline for that ten-year-old murder of Stephen Matthews, while Lucy set about transcribing my notes into what she referred to as "a case file that was required by Sir Avery." It included my earlier notes and the more recent ones from the visit Munro and I had with Mr. Iverson.

Munro had returned as well, with the item I had asked him to bring.

It was very nearly eleven o'clock in the morning when I placed a telephone call to the Matthews residence in Kent, to inquire if Mrs. Matthews was available. I was informed that she had left some time earlier.

"She's gone to the florist's shop, then Highgate, the same as every week," her housekeeper added. "She won't return for several hours. Do you care to leave a message?"

Highgate.

I declined by simply saying that I would call again another time.

According to the information Lucy found at the registrar's office, Stephen Matthews was buried at the western cemetery there, I thought as the telephone call ended.

And Mrs. Matthews went there '*every week,*' according to her housekeeper.

I wanted very much to speak with Stephen Matthews' mother, yet hesitated to go to Highgate, and intrude on what I could only assume was something very emotional for her.

However, a young woman was dead, a small boy orphaned, and Brodie's life very much hung in the balance.

I was determined to learn not only who was behind this, but the reason. And time was critical, with the murderer still unknown and still out there.

Highgate Cemetery was in the north of London.

Munro nodded when I informed him that I wanted to go there, and the reason.

"Aye, but ye'll not go alone."

It was midafternoon when Mr. Hastings guided the team through the arched stone entrance of Highgate. We drove down an avenue with trees and shrubs past Egyptian sepulchers, mausoleums, and Gothic tombs, then arrived at a small stone building where a black hearse had just departed.

It disappeared along an adjacent pathway, with several coaches following behind. A small man who looked much like a troll that had stepped out from under a rock turned and nodded a greeting.

Munro explained that we were looking for a site where another individual was buried.

"Stephen Matthews." I gave him the name.

"Matthews?" he replied, then his expression changed. "Ah,

the grey lady. Comes here every week. Always dressed the same in a grey gown. Lewiston is the family name."

He then gave directions for us to continue along the path, then turn at the carriage path that had a tall oak tree with a weeping angel at the base. The Lewiston family plot and crypt were only a short distance on, a carved wood sign with the family name beside the main path.

With those directions, Mr. Hastings proceeded to guide the team to the area the little man had indicated.

"I don't much like these places," Munro commented.

I naturally had my own opinion of them—a boat, a torch, and a Viking sendoff seemed far more appealing.

Still, there was something peaceful about Highgate, with its winding carriageway and overhanging trees, much like a medieval forest.

Mr. Hastings drew the team to a stop behind another coach, and we stepped down.

"Do ye want me to go with ye?" Munro asked.

I could have sworn he was relieved when I told him I was quite all right on my own. I would never have imagined that he would be uneasy in such surroundings.

The hound had no such hesitation, but bounded off. I suppose it was a dog's paradise with abundant trees and bushes, and scents far different from the streets.

I had worn my split skirt and jacket with boots, my hair pulled back. I was not in the habit of wearing a black gown even if I owned one, which I did not.

My sister had declared me a heathen. "What will you wear when Aunt Antonia passes on?" she had once asked, quite serious.

I had promptly pointed out that our great-aunt would very

likely outlive us both, hence no need to be concerned what we would wear.

However, in the remote possibility that we *might* outlive her, I had informed Linnie that I would wear gypsy clothes, bells about my wrists and ankles, and dance barefoot in the moonlight, as my friend Templeton had once described she wanted to be sent off. And I would set the torch myself to the funerary barge carrying my great-aunt's body.

"There are times," Linnie had declared in response, "when I am positively certain that we are not related at all."

So there we were, my aunt and I for a Viking send-off, my sister for an impossibly boring interment in a crypt where the insects and rats would have their way, or possibly someone in the greater London Planning Department would decide decades later that her crypt had to be moved to make way for a rail station.

It did conjure up all sorts of images.

I navigated the pathway quite easily that led to a clearing with an enormous crypt in the center, surrounded by other monuments. The crypt was of the granite Gothic design with a wrought iron gate and quite old—a Lewiston ancestor by the inscription over the entrance.

The setting was peaceful, surrounded by trees, those family names, and the sad, drawn features of the woman who sat there.

She came every week since then, her housekeeper said, and brought flowers for the son she had lost. A son who had fallen in love with a young woman and fathered a child, and then was tragically murdered. And who, strangely enough, was buried in his mother's family crypt.

I passed other Lewiston monuments that went back through at least three generations, and then slowly approached a woman dressed in grey who sat beside a simply carved head-stone that read:

Stephen Christopher Lewiston
Beloved son
1860 to 1881

Not Matthews!

I couldn't help but feel that I had somehow stumbled upon another piece of the puzzle that was Ellie Sutton's death.

But what did it mean?

Twenty

I WAITED at the edge of the clearing. I might be anxious to learn what I could, however, contrary to my sister's declaration, I was not a heathen. Nor was I insensitive to other people's grief.

My own experience with such things were my parents. Our mother first of *'wasting disease,'* as the physician said at the time. To which our great-aunt called him a fool and highly incompetent. Still, that did nothing to ease the sense of loss of someone who had spent the last two years of her life confined to bed.

The other experience was with our father. The only thing I could say about that was that my sister and I were undoubtedly better off for it.

Cruel, I know, and Linnie has often reminded me of it. Nevertheless, I have no sympathy for someone who wasted the family fortunes, undoubtedly contributed to the death of our mother, and would have put my sister and me on the street if not for our great-aunt. Nor someone who then chose the coward's way out of the debacle he had created by taking his own life.

With that said, I did believe that a person's mourning was a private thing, and I didn't want to intrude on Mrs. Matthews.

I waited, until the sun angled lower through the canopy of trees, with the distinctive sound of a hound in the distance.

"It is very peaceful here," I commented.

Adelaide Matthews look up startled. She stared at me in confusion, her face pale and drawn.

"Do I know you?" she asked in a tear-filled voice.

How to begin a difficult conversation, I thought. I introduced myself and saw her confusion deepen.

"Lady Forsythe?"

"I telephoned your residence and was told that you were here. Forgive the intrusion, I know this must be very difficult."

"A young woman such as yourself? What would you know about how difficult this is, how painful, how empty my life is now...?"

Grief.

I supposed that it was different for everyone. I could have replied that I knew quite well what it was to lose someone I loved and the aftermath of loss that followed, but I did not.

I felt her pain, and the anguish I saw in the expression on her face. But this was not about me. It wasn't even about her. It was about a young woman's murder and a boy who was now orphaned. It was about Brodie.

"I'm making inquiries about the murder of Ellie Sutton."

That tear-filled gaze met mine. I could only imagine the chaos of emotions behind it. She rose suddenly, and I noticed the cane she used to steady herself.

"I must be going."

She slowly started across the clearing toward the foot path. I laid a hand on her arm.

The grey lady, the man at the cottage had described her. Most certainly an accurate description of the woman who was hardly more than a handful of years older than myself, and stared back at me now.

I explained that I was making inquiries on behalf of Angus Brodie, who was with the MET and had investigated her son's death ten years earlier, and now the murder of the young woman who was there the night her son was killed.

"I cannot help you." She pulled away and would have continued down the path.

I pulled the toy locomotive from my bag. "You gave this to Ellie Sutton's son."

She stopped and stared at the toy in my hand, a different emotion on her face now. She reached out and took the toy locomotive in trembling hands.

"Rory," she whispered, a faint broken sound. "Is he...?"

A name I hadn't known until that moment. I felt a deep pang of guilt for the distress I caused.

"He's safe," I assured her. "Mr. Brodie was there that night, afterward," I explained. "He made certain Ellie's son is safe."

She nodded as she stared down at the locomotive. Her gloved hands shook as she stroked the toy.

"I left this for to her to give to him...a birthday gift, even though I had no idea when his birthday might be."

I heard a sound from the brush nearby. She heard it as well, and the look on her face was startling, as if she thought someone else was there. Someone she was afraid of.

It was the hound. He appeared with a stick in his mouth.

"It's all right," I assured her. "He came with me."

She relaxed slightly. "Stephen was fond of dogs, but he

wasn't allowed to have one…" she said with a glance back at that headstone. "I really must be going. Thank you for bringing this. It means a great deal to me. I had hoped…" she started to say, then added, "I cannot stay."

"Mr. Brodie was seen there the night Ellie Sutton was killed," I told her then. "He is now facing charges for her murder."

There was something else in her eyes, something almost fearful.

"What do you want …?" she demanded in a voice that trembled.

"The name on the headstone should be Matthews…but it is not."

I thought she might simply turn and continue down the path, leaving me with my questions.

There was a part of me that wouldn't have blamed her. There was that other part of me that was determined to find answers.

"Rory is safe?" she asked.

Of all the things I expected, she surprised me. I assured her that he was as we returned to the coaches.

She asked for her driver to wait for her at the entrance to the cemetery. She was uneasy and most anxious. I exchanged a look with Munro. He assisted her into our coach.

"I'll be waitin' at the caretaker's cottage; the hound stays with ye," he said, then set off afoot.

Mr. Hastings stepped down from his seat atop the coach with the excuse that he needed to quiet the team. Rupert lay at our feet and promptly went to sleep.

Mrs. Matthews stared out the window of the coach, her gaze drawn back to the path and that grave in the clearing beyond.

"Stephen did so like animals. Does Rory like them?"

I replied that I had not the chance to meet him, and didn't know the answer to that.

She nodded and it was several moments before she continued. "That night Stephen left for the club, and my husband shortly thereafter. They'd had words, not for the first time. I knew that there was a young woman Stephen was quite taken with. He had met her at the club—not the usual place where a young man might meet an *acceptable* woman."

Something changed in her voice with that one word, a sad, bitter sound.

"He had spoken of marriage. I didn't know then that she was going to have a child. I learned about Rory later from...information my husband received."

I wanted to reach out at the broken sound of her voice and take her hands in mine to offer some comfort, but didn't. Nor did I think she would have accepted it.

"That last night...It was very late when my husband returned alone," she continued. "He didn't say anything about what had happened."

There were no tears now, only the sad expression on her face as she continued to stare out the window opening.

"It wasn't unusual for Stephen to stay the night at the club. I didn't learn what had happened until the next day, when Inspector Brodie came to our residence. He was...very kind. I learned afterward that Ellie apparently saw who killed Stephen and was forced to leave for her own safety. I wanted to find her..."

"But you didn't."

"I couldn't. Then just over a year ago, she reached out. She had returned to London after all these years...with her son."

"Why couldn't you look for her?" I asked.

It certainly seemed that the Matthews' wealth would have protected Ellie and her son, perhaps even made it possible to find the man who had killed Stephen Matthews.

"I couldn't because...my husband was not Stephen's father." She looked at me then. "He raised Stephen as his own, but there was always a...distance.

"I was not always old, and crippled. I was young once, like yourself, and in love," she continued.

It was not difficult to know what had happened, much like her son's situation.

"I didn't tell anyone I was with child. My father thought that another arrangement was far more acceptable than a match with the man I loved. Edward had built Argosy Shipping into a very successful company. It was considered a brilliant match."

And a very lucrative one, to be certain, I thought. One of those arranged situations for reasons that very often had nothing to do with a young woman's feelings.

"I tried everything to persuade my father against it...There was a tragic accident."

I was certain I knew the rest of it—the father of her child died.

"I was terrified of my father, of what would happen to my child. So, I accepted Edward's marriage proposal. Stephen was born seven-and-a-half months later— *early*, Edward told everyone, and presented himself as the proud father. But he knew.

"He wanted a son of his own, and I was determined to protect Stephen."

She'd had difficulty when she had Stephen, and it was almost four years before she again found herself pregnant.

Sir Edward should have been pleased. Instead, he was furious, unable to understand how she became pregnant after four years and accusing her of having taken a lover, as she had before they were married.

It was then the beatings began, leaving her badly bruised and with broken bones, and ended in the loss of the son he had so badly wanted.

The abuse was, I had learned through my sister's experience, all too common, but there was little that was done about it.

The reasons were different, but always with the same ending, rage taken out on those who most often couldn't defend themselves.

And then there was the financial reality of it all. A woman's wealth, be it inheritance or money she had earned, all passed to her husband, with rare exception. In my sister's case, her inheritance came through our great-aunt just as mine did.

"I was unable to have another child after that," she continued in that same sad voice. "For a time, Edward seemed to accept Stephen. He was given the finest education, indulged as fathers indulge their children, and I thought..."

And yet, horrible things were said that last night before Stephen was killed, the truth of his *'early'* birth flung in his face, as if it was his fault.

Sir Edward refused to accept a marriage to a young woman who very likely spread herself for every young man she came into contact with, repeating her disgrace of an illegitimate birth.

He told Stephen, in no uncertain terms, that he would either do exactly as he wanted, or he would be out on the street where he belonged. Difficult, painful words that could never be taken back.

"Stephen shared with me that she was going to have a child. I pleaded with Edward not to turn his back on

Stephen or our grandchild, knowing he would force me to do so as well," she said, looking out at that clearing once more.

"The weeks after Stephen was killed were very...I don't remember much of that time. Edward arranged for a physician to provide medication so that I could sleep. It seems that all I did was sleep.

"I do remember speaking with Edward about the young woman and the child she was going to have—Stephen's child. I insisted we couldn't turn our backs on her. He said that he would take care of everything. But she had disappeared.

"By then Mr. Brodie had left, and the inspector who took over the case was certain that Stephen was killed by a man who had entered the club that night with the entertainers, and robbery was very likely the reason he was killed."

She continued to press her husband about the need to find Ellie Sutton. But he insisted that she had disappeared.

"It was better that way, he told me, and that most likely Stephen was not the father of her child. I still wanted to find her. I had to know. Edward refused to speak of it. He became angry whenever I asked what progress he had made."

Had he become abusive over it? I wondered.

"He became...distant after that. He was rarely home. His excuse was the expansion of the business. He never spoke of Stephen after that, almost as if...he had never existed. When it came to arrangements to be made..." She hesitated, and I saw some other emotion on her face.

"He told me to make whatever arrangements I wanted."

She looked at me then, a new emotion on her face. Strength and determination that had given her the strength to survive the tragedy of her husband's neglect and abuse, and that tragic loss.

"I insisted that Stephen was to be buried here, under my family name," she continued.

And she had continued to come here every week since.

"I don't know how any of this might help Mr. Brodie now. As I said, he was very kind and understanding. I had hoped he might find the one who was responsible for Stephen's death, since no one else was able to find them.

"I tried to contact him after I learned that he had left the MET and he had his own private inquiry firm, with the hope of finding Ellie. But that was...difficult. I'm certain you understand with what I've already told you."

I could only imagine that Sir Edward would have objected strongly to any further inquiries that would only have caused him further embarrassment.

She looked down at the toy locomotive and her voice softened. "When Ellie Sutton returned, I had hoped that perhaps one day... She had sent round a note, to let me know that she had returned.

"I had heard the rumors, of course, that there was a child," she continued. "I sent this to the hotel where she worked and had enclosed a note telling her that it was for her son."

After a time she seemed to gather herself. "I would like very much to see my grandson. You will tell Mr. Brodie."

I looked out the window opening and realized that Rory was all that Adelaide Matthews had now. I assured her that I would tell Brodie, and thanked her for the information she had shared with me. It couldn't have been easy.

It had grown quite late, the sun low through the branches of the trees as I asked Mr. Hastings to take us back to the cottage.

Munro was waiting for us. He had spent the time I was

with Adelaide Matthews in conversation with the caretaker of this part of Highgate.

They had gotten along like old chums. It seemed the man was a Scot—Mackenzie by name. Imagine that.

"You were a long time with the Matthews woman," Munro commented after we delivered her back to her coach and driver.

"Were you able to learn anything from her that might be useful in helping Mr. Brodie?"

The truth was that I didn't know.

What I had learned was that Adelaide Matthews had suffered greatly in her marriage. She had then lost her son, and any opportunity to know her grandson. Until Ellie Sutton had returned.

I had Mr. Hastings take us to Mayfair. I was in need of additional clothing, and it was safe to assume that if we had been followed or someone was lurking about the town house, I was quite safe with both Munro and Rupert.

It was well into the evening when we arrived back at the Tower.

I went first to the infirmary where I discovered that Brodie was not there. Dr. Watson informed me that Brodie had spent the past several hours with Alex and Sir Avery, against the physician's advice.

"I was afraid that attempting to confine him to bed might cause further harm. He was most adamant about being up and about."

Adamant. I could only imagine. There was another word for it, or rather three, to be precise—bloody stubborn Scot!

I found him with Alex Sinclair and Lucy Penworth in Alex's office. As much as I was very glad to see him, I was inclined to agree with Dr. Watson.

The bruises on his face had taken on a blue-green color.

The bandage over his left eye concealed the cut from the beating that he had taken at Scotland Yard. As he stood before the board that Lucy and I had filled with information, he held himself in such a way that suggested any attempt to straighten himself would cause great pain.

It appeared that he had washed. The dried blood on his face and in his hair was gone, and he had acquired a clean pair of trousers and shirt. He didn't look at me, didn't so much as even acknowledge that I was there. My stomach knotted. He was angry, I could feel it. However, we were not alone and it would have been awkward to go to him. I saw Alex Sinclair's hand in his improved condition. All-in-all, a remarkable improvement from the last time I saw him in the infirmary.

Lucy and Alex both greeted me in that familiar way.

"I say," Alex then commented. "You've been gone for some time. Were you able to learn anything new?"

He knew me well enough by now to know that I had not spent the day shopping or taking luncheon with friends.

"I met with Mrs. Matthews," I replied, with a look at Brodie. "I wanted to know what she remembered from her son's murder ten years ago. I thought there might be something important that could be helpful now. It was very difficult. I feel sorry for her, with the loss of her son and grandson."

"Was there anything that might be useful?" Lucy asked.

"I'm not certain. I thought it could be useful to add the notes to the board." I looked again at Brodie. That dark gaze briefly met mine, then angled away.

"Her son is buried in her family plot at Highgate. Not under the Matthews family name, but under her name. It seems that there was a great deal of difficulty in the marriage. She shared that Stephen was not Edward Matthews' son."

"That couldn't have been easy for her," Lucy commented.

"It wasn't," I admitted with another look over at Brodie.

He had taken it all in, yet made no comment. Unusual, I thought, however he was obviously dealing with a great deal of pain. If he had been up for hours, against Dr. Watson's advice, he was undoubtedly exhausted as well.

I crossed the office to the board. I wanted to add my notes as I had not had a chance earlier to make note of what I'd learned that afternoon.

Brodie handed me the chalk he had been using. Our fingers briefly touched.

I could have been mistaken, but it seemed that he pulled his hand back quite suddenly as he went to a nearby chair and took great care as he eased down onto it.

It was just the pain and exhaustion, I thought, as Alex and Lucy told me what they had been able to learn.

Lucy had spent most of the day going through police archives hoping to learn more about the official investigation into Ellie Sutton's death.

"It's almost as if ..."

"As if what?" I asked.

"As if it isn't important," she said with a note of disgust. "It certainly hasn't been given any priority. And there have only been two mentions of it and then..." She looked over at Brodie.

"It has been followed up that the case is now closed."

"Of course. Chief Inspector Abberline is certain he has already found the murderer," I replied with another look at Brodie.

While Lucy searched the police reports, Alex had spent the day also searching their files, specifically their records of known criminals, for someone that fit the description of the man with the bowler hat.

"They keep fingerprints now, and descriptions of known

criminals, along with photographs. That doesn't include how a man is dressed and not all their files included photographs. That is a rather new aspect for them."

He had then searched through files the Agency had compiled over the past several years, but had found nothing.

"The man does seem to have skills that most persons wouldn't have. On a suggestion from Mr. Brodie, Sir Avery has provided me with permission for access to military records. The office of military records was closed by the time I returned today," Alex informed.

"I will be following that up tomorrow with Lucy's assistance."

I was beginning to think that those who claimed to have seen the man might be mistaken.

Except for Brodie. He had a keen eye for detail from his training with the MET and his earlier life on the street learning how to survive. He had often come upon a clue in an inquiry that no one had yet discovered.

"Aye," Munro commented. He had been quietly listening to what each had to say about what we had learned that day.

"Matthews has a reputation for bein' a hard man for those who work for him."

A hard man, but not unusual, I thought as I wondered what he might have seen the night Stephen Matthews was murdered.

"He might be able to tell us something from that night." I had no more finished the thought than Brodie objected.

"Ye'll not go to speak with the man!" He winced at the effort that took, seized with a fit of coughing that doubled him over.

When I would have gone to him, he waved me away.

The coughing subsided, and I was relieved that there was

no sign of blood, in spite of Dr. Watson's assurances that he didn't seem to have any internal bleeding from the beating he'd taken or the broken ribs.

"Are ye quite through givin' orders to everyone then?" Munro asked in a manner that only a very good friend would dare to risk.

"*Pian anns an asal,*" Brodie muttered in Scots Gaelic that conveyed a great deal just the way he said it.

Munro merely shrugged. Obviously not the first time he had heard it, and undoubtedly not the last.

"Aye, and ye are a horse's ass as well," he replied as he slipped an arm about Brodie's shoulders, the only place that hadn't suffered injury. "Now, do I have to throw ye over my shoulder to get ye to return to the infirmary before ye do yerself more harm?" Munro asked in a tone that suggested he would do just that, no matter the pain it caused.

Brodie leaned against him as they left the office, looking very much like two men who'd had a bit much to drink. Their progress was slow and measured with more than one curse between them.

I had updated Lucy and Alex on everything that I'd learned and made notes on the chalkboard. I then hurried to catch up with Munro and Brodie.

I hadn't seen Brodie alone since he was brought to the Tower two days earlier, barely conscious and mostly incoherent, and wanted very much to see him.

I was grateful for Dr. Watson's care, however I wanted to see for myself that he was recovering. And I wanted to discuss the case with him.

I had missed our conversations and while I was confident of my abilities, the truth was that I missed him terribly—the exchange of ideas, our conversations...

"Ye let her go alone?!" I heard Brodie say only a few yards ahead in the hallway. "Ye know what I told her!"

"She wasna alone," Munro replied. "And there was no danger."

What Brodie said next stopped me in the dimly lit hallway.

"Yer like a brother, but dinna go against me in this! I dinna want her part of this. Ye know the sort of man Matthews is. I have my reasons."

"I know well enough," Munro replied as their voices faded in the hallway as they continued toward the infirmary. But not so far away that I didn't hear what he said next.

"Ye should have told her from the beginnin'. She's a strong, braw woman. And this business with Matthews, yerself held here with charges against ye...? Ye need to trust her. There are those here who can assist. Ye have no choice."

"No!" Brodie replied. The rest of it faded as they reached the infirmary and the door closed behind them.

It did seem that our confrontation at Scotland Yard, when he was first arrested, wasn't merely a reaction to the pain or even the fact that he'd been arrested.

There was something more...some reason that he was adamant that I wasn't to involve myself. It was a little late for that, I thought, and not without frustration and no small amount of anger.

What was it? What hadn't he told me?

With everything that had happened, Brodie now under arrest and held here, virtually a prisoner at the Tower, he was still adamant that I wasn't to continue?

Bloody hell, I thought. I was not of a mind to be lectured, which I was certain would happen if I entered the infirmary now, asking his thoughts on what I had learned.

It was not the visit I thought we might have, once I was assured that he was going to live.

Bruises would eventually fade and ribs would heal, Dr. Watson had assured me. In the meantime...

Let him sit there with whatever it was he should have told me, imprisoned for all intents and purposes, I thought, with no small amount of my own anger. Perhaps it was a good place for him.

A young woman had been murdered, and a young boy was now an orphan. I had managed to get this far in the case and learned valuable information without his assistance. I would bloody well finish it, and clear him of charges!

I silently cursed all stubborn, pig-headed Scots!

Twenty-One

IT WAS MIDEVENING when I returned to Sussex Square with Munro and the hound.

Rupert immediately dashed off to the gardens and the forest beyond, doing what hounds do.

The ride from the Tower had been mostly silent.

Now, Munro reminded me that there were others at the Agency who would proceed with the case on Brodie's behalf. After all, Alex had the notes that had been made on the board in his office. The Agency, with his assistance, would take the next steps.

I didn't argue or attempt to persuade him otherwise. After all, Munro had been supportive of my involvement and had even argued the matter.

The silence on our return from the Tower had given me time to think, and I wasn't about to sit on my hands when I could help clear Brodie of murder. Either with or without his approval.

I thanked my aunt once more for her assistance in getting him removed from Abberline's supervision, a situation I was certain would have become only more dangerous for Brodie, considering the man's obsession with revenge. I didn't mention the difference of opinion between us regarding my involvement in the case.

We shared a dram of her very fine whisky, which I was much in need of with everything that had happened. It did help to soothe my earlier anger.

"What do you know about Argosy Shipping?" I asked over a second dram.

While she left her business affairs to Munro and her attorney, a woman who was reported to be wealthier than the Queen and had several enterprises including the distillery in Scotland, did have some business sense of things. Not to mention, she knew people.

"Hmmm, this is a particularly excellent production, don't you think?" she suggested as she took another sip of whisky.

I was not one to argue the matter.

"Argosy," she said with a thoughtful expression and another sip. "Quite successful an enterprise with Sir Edward's determination, of course."

"You know him?" I asked. It was not impossible that she might have encountered him and his wife at one of the social functions she attended.

"Met him once at Ascot. He attended with his son—dreadful business about that. It must be over ten years ago now that young Matthews was killed in that situation at the Clarendon Club. And no other children—a son, for an heir to the business," she added thoughtfully.

"What do you know of Mrs. Matthews?" I asked.

"I met the woman several years before at a benefit for orphan children that I sponsor. Lovely woman, very caring of the orphans, I thought. Then after her son's death she seemed to disappear, overwhelmed with grief I heard.

"Dreadful tragedy. There were other rumors, as there always are." She looked at me then. "About Sir Edward. There were rumors of affairs, and he was more determined than ever to make Argosy the premier shipping company."

"What do you know about the man?" I then asked.

Affairs were one thing, and not unexpected with the physical abuse that Adelaide Matthews had spoken of. But I needed to know more. It was important for what I had planned.

"Quite ruthless in his business dealings it seems. There are rumors that he intimidates those whose cargos his ships carry. He approached Mr. Munro some time back regarding shipments of our whisky. He wanted his company to have exclusive right to the cargos."

I had not heard this before, but then those were matters between my aunt and Munro.

"Sir Laughton knew of some past...situations for other cargos that seemed to disappear when they reached foreign ports. Often at great loss to the owners. And there were rumors that the cargos somehow found their way to markets abroad, with considerable profit to Matthews, of course.

"Sir Laughton advised against making any business arrangement with Matthews. He thought it much better to keep Old Lodge whisky exclusive where we could control the price. I daresay the man was correct. It has been a most lucrative arrangement."

Ruthless. Stolen cargos—that was the only way to describe it. Someone who had abused his wife, and turned his back on the only son he was likely to ever have over an affair and the child that came of it, and then refused to either acknowledge or help the child's mother.

What was such a man capable of? Had he willingly allowed Ellie Sutton to disappear with her claim that she saw the murderer that night?

What did he know about that night? And now Ellie Sutton was dead.

Were the two murders somehow connected?

Brodie was not responsible. That much I was certain of.

I finished the whisky in my glass and stood to go to my room.

My aunt took my hand in hers.

"You will take care, of course."

Once more, I was certain she had a certain way of knowing what I had decided to do. Or perhaps it was simply that she knew me so well.

Much like herself?

"Of course," I replied.

"And do take the hound with you when you leave in the morning," she added. "I will be off to have luncheon with my ladies."

I had asked that supper be brought up my room. It was waiting for me when I finally arrived—I had a great deal of work to do before tomorrow.

It was very near midnight when I finally stepped back from the chalkboard. I had added the additional notes from my meeting with Mrs. Matthews, and information my aunt had provided.

Rumors? Perhaps.

Sir Laughton, my aunt's lawyer, was known to be very thorough when it came to protecting the interest of his clients, and one client in particular. My aunt had known him for over forty years and he had never failed to protect her interests, along with Munro who managed her affairs from day-to-day.

I took a long bath in the adjoining chamber, then slipped beneath the covers on the bed.

It was not uncommon to have trouble sleeping, my thoughts churning with clues in a case. Except when I was with Brodie...

My plan was set. And oddly enough, I had no trouble sleeping.

I rose early the next morning and quickly dressed. It was barely half-past eight o'clock when I went downstairs and encountered Lily with Rupert. She had dressed as well.

"Yer leavin' now? Is it about Mr. Brodie?"

There were times the girl was too bright and far too intelligent.

"There are matters I need to attend to at the office." I thought it best not to go into the reason.

"I can help," she replied with far too much enthusiasm.

"I know—however, what about your lessons?"

The last thing I needed was to be concerned for her safety with what I intended to do. She made an immediate face.

"I can catch up when we return," she suggested.

A flimsy excuse at best, and she knew it. And it was doubtful that her tutor would simply be waiting idly for her to return. That was not how it worked.

"Not this time," I replied. "I will be meeting with business people. Quite boring, I assure you, very probably for several hours." Not precisely true; nevertheless, it worked.

I saw the change of expression, not quite a frown, but she was definitely resigned to remaining with her *'boring'* lessons.

"Perhaps you can persuade my aunt to take you to the zoo after her ladies' luncheon. There are many fascinating creatures there," I suggested. It was something that had been mentioned in the past.

"Her ladies' luncheon?" she said with a groan. "That will take hours and there's nothing to do. It's boring.

"They have been known to conduct a séance at their luncheons," I added.

"Séance?"

It appeared she had never heard of such a thing. Imagine that, with all her worldly experience.

"Contacting spirits from the other side, much like Templeton, often with surprising results."

"Do they appear? Like ghosts?"

"It's more of a hand on one's shoulder, a whisper in the ear, or a sudden unexpected sound that reaches through from the other side."

Her eyes were as large as tea saucers. "That could be exciting," she exclaimed.

Exciting, as opposed to a boring business meeting.

"Will ye be taking the hound?" she asked. "I dinna think he'd take to strange sounds. It might upset the ladies."

I agreed.

"Do ye think I should take the dirk I found in the sword room? Just in case one of them gets a bit rowdy."

I did hope she wasn't referring to the ladies.

I advised against it and explained that, in my experience, none had ever shown any sign of hostility. Of course that didn't include Wills—Sir William Shakespeare, who my friend Templeton claimed could get quite an attitude when he was upset about something.

Lily decided that she would take her chances with the ladies and any spirits they happened to conjure up.

Munro had left earlier on a matter for my aunt. When he

had still not returned, I asked Mr. Hastings to bring round the coach.

By the time he had readied the team, then arrived at the front entrance, Munro had still not returned. I left a note for him, then called for the hound and we set off for the Strand.

I had not been to the office in several days, however I could more easily place a telephone call from there. There were far too many ears about who might have overheard, had I placed the call from Sussex Square.

In addition, the Strand was not far from the place I hoped to visit, as well as the person I wanted to speak with.

The office was as I had left it days earlier. It didn't appear that anything had been disturbed.

Rupert lay near the door—guard dog on duty?

Amusing as that seemed to most people who encountered the hound, he had proven himself to be a trusted companion on more than one occasion, with an uncanny knowledge of the streets.

I had become acquainted with hunting dogs, including one named Rupert at an early age. While my father had reprimanded me more than once regarding making pets of the various hounds he kept at our country home, I had still proceeded to befriend them.

Rupert, the original, had been my adventure companion, so there was no surprise that I had established a friendship with the current Rupert, even though he was somewhat lacking in refinement. And more than a companion, he had proven to have amazing tracking skills, as well as a somewhat surly attitude when provoked.

Brodie had thought him to be quite useless, a scrounger who begged for food, until he had interceded in a dangerous situation twice on my behalf. They had a grudging acceptance of one another since.

They did seem to share some of the same habits—an affinity for the streets, knowledge of the best places to find food, and a penchant for wandering about at night in search of low-life characters. Not that I was comparing one to the other. Brodie would have grumbled at that.

The call I wanted to make and the person I wanted to visit as the next step in the investigation that I was determined would clear Brodie, was Sir Edward Matthews.

Argosy Shipping was well established throughout Britain. Sir Edward Matthews had built it up through the years, with ports and warehouses not only in London, but in Liverpool, Bristol, a warehouse and departure point in Southampton, Dublin, as well as a working partnership with the port at Le Havre in France for cargoes shipped abroad.

It was a shipping behemoth that had continued to spread over the past twenty years into the Far East. It was said that Sir Edward was determined to make it as successful as the East India Company had once been, with a growing fleet of sailing and steamship vessels.

The East India Company had been responsible for expanding British interests across the globe. They'd established what was for all intents and purposes branches of the government into foreign countries, that eventually became British territories that very often included armies to protect interests there.

After over one hundred years of dominance in the shipping trade and amid accusations of corruption, not to mention growing unrest and resentment within those territories, the government stepped in and had dissolved the company in 1874.

It seemed that Sir Edward Matthews with Argosy was determined to take the place as the foremost shipping company around the world, even with no heir apparent.

I was informed by a clerk at the shipping office at the port of London that Sir Edward was to depart for Liverpool before midday.

He was presently at the dockside offices overseeing the launch of a new steamship he had added to his fleet of cargo ships. It was suggested that if the matter was important, I would be able to reach him there.

It was half-past ten o'clock and I still had no word from Munro. I did hesitate about going on my own—I could almost hear Brodie's objections, considering the man with the bowler hat who had been seen on more than one occasion and at the town house. A man with a bowler hat that Mr. Iverson had mentioned seeing the night Stephen Matthews was killed at the Clarendon Club. And Ellie Sutton's murder ten years later, after being terrified by a man in a bowler hat?

How it was all connected was yet to be seen. With Brodie confined to the Tower and recovering from injuries courtesy of Mr. Abberline, it was up to Munro and me to determine exactly how it was connected.

Sir Edward had also been at the Clarendon Club the night Stephen Matthews was killed. What had he seen? Was there something he might know that could connect everything?

I might be grasping at straws, as the saying went. However, I was not willing to leave any stone unturned in helping clear Brodie of the charge of murder.

I placed a call to Sussex Square and was informed that Munro had not yet returned. I then waited an additional half hour. When he had still not appeared, I closed and locked the office

Rupert accompanied me to the sidewalk at the bottom of the stairs. Mr. Hastings had waited patiently with the team. I gave him the location of Argosy Shipping.

"The docks, miss?" he questioned.

I caught the hesitation at his voice. He had been in service with my aunt for many years, a man of impeccable reputation as well as skill in navigating the congested streets of London. Not to mention the somewhat *'unusual destinations'* my aunt had him take her. It appeared the London Docks were not part of her usual itinerary.

I assured him that it was correct. He opened the door of the coach and Rupert and I climbed aboard.

To say that Argosy was a behemoth of a company seemed to be an understatement as we arrived at their main office's dockside, very near where the East India Company once had their busiest enterprise.

The nearby docks and warehouses had long ago been stripped of the signage that was once visible to all along the river frontage. Yet it was still referred to as the East India Company in spite of the fact that the EIC had not occupied the site for almost twenty years.

Mr. Hastings delivered us to the offices of Argosy Shipping at the frontage street near the docks, and enquired if he should wait.

The clerk I had spoken with earlier had assured me that he would deliver my message to Sir Edward. There was no guarantee that he would still be there, of course, much less be willing to meet with me.

I asked Mr. Hastings to wait and left Rupert with him, since he could be a little intimidating, particularly when it came to men.

Inside the main office, I gave my name to the desk clerk. He remembered my earlier telephone call. I was asked to wait as another clerk was sent with a message to another part of the building.

It was a warehouse, lined up with others along the waterfront, the ground floor used as a business office and the main part of the two-story building extending back toward the docks.

It was some time before the clerk returned, and I was prepared that my request to meet with him might now be refused. I was surprised when the clerk announced that Sir Edward was pleased to meet with me and asked that I follow him to his private office.

The front office was much like any business office one might encounter with a front counter, clerks' desks, telephones, and a telegraph operator, no doubt for contacting foreign offices.

There was also an impressive global map that covered one entire wall, with several locations marked. No doubt those various ports where Matthews had shipping interests. Another wall contained a list of the names of ships, much like those I had seen on my travels, that contained arrival and departure dates.

Beyond the office was a rabbit's warren of passages and hallways, with wood walls and floors that one would expect of a warehouse. It included a massive set of overhead doors with signage that announced the main entrance of the warehouse by the dock just beyond.

I followed the clerk past to another set of doors that opened onto a lavishly furnished room that was in stark contrast to the part of the building I had just passed through.

There was a large desk, another global map on the wall behind it, with those same locations marked, and thick carpet underfoot. There was a telephone on the desk, next to a bank of a half-dozen speaking tubes that snaked across the desk and into the adjacent wall. Each had what appeared to be an electric call bell beneath the mouthpiece.

It was an octopus of innovation that no doubt connected Sir Edward to different locations of the vast Argosy business empire and allowed him to be informed of the daily arrival of those sailing and steamship vessels and their valuable cargoes.

After meeting with Adelaide Matthews, I had prepared myself to meet the man responsible for her accounts of abuse, an angry man who was prone to lose control over one matter or another, and had taken that anger out on her in the past.

The man who greeted me from behind the desk could not have been farther from that 'other' man, she had described.

Had it been nothing more than delusion after the death of a beloved son years before? Granted there was every possibility of difficulties between them, most particularly after what she had described as a violent argument that last night.

I was not unfamiliar with those who masked their true feelings and emotions. I was reminded of my sister's husband, who had deceived those closest to him and then very nearly got her killed.

Then there was our father, who had betrayed our mother and would have sent our family to ruin had it not been for our great-aunt, who became both mother and father to two orphaned girls when she was well into her sixties—a *grand adventure* she had called it, in that inimitable, somewhat eccentric way of hers.

Whom was I seeing now, I wondered as Sir Edward greeted me with a congenial smile and ease of familiarity.

"Lady Forsythe, this is a pleasure."

We exchanged the usual pleasantries as he indicated the

richly upholstered Queen Anne chair across from him at the desk.

"Mr. Bolding, whom you spoke with earlier, didn't indicate the reason for your request. To what do I owe the pleasure? As representative of her ladyship, perhaps? She may have mentioned that I would like very much to not only have her as an investor in Argosy—which could be most profitable for her—but also to handle cargoes of shipments from her various enterprises."

I replied that Mr. Munro saw to my great-aunt's business enterprises. This was regarding another matter which I hoped he might be able to assist with.

"Of course," he replied. "However I can be of assistance."

No doubt, I thought, still with the hope of acquiring my great-aunt's business.

I watched his face as I briefly explained that I assisted in inquiries, frequently beyond the interest of the MET, and that I was presently assisting in gathering information about the recent murder of a young woman in Charing Cross.

"I understand that a man has been arrested in the matter," he replied.

"Yes, however, he is not the murderer. It seems that the woman was being followed by someone who was described by those she worked with. I understand that you knew the victim from some time ago."

He drummed his fingers on the desktop, the only outward change in his demeanor.

"I meet many people in my business dealings, still...a woman? I don't recall the name."

"She was an acquaintance of your son," I replied. That brought a discernible reaction, the faintest tick on one cheek.

"I have no son, Lady Forsythe. My wife's son died some

time ago, a most difficult time, as I am certain you can understand..."

"According to information I was able to obtain, he was killed in an attack at the Clarendon Club ten years ago. The young woman who was with him at the time was Ellie Sutton. She was a witness to his murder and then left London a short time later."

A smile, but far different from the smile that had first greeted me. Most interesting.

"A colorful story for one of your novels, Miss Forsythe."

I caught the omission of my title. An oversight perhaps? Not that it bothered me. Or was it deliberate, perhaps a way of putting me in my place. And what was that, I wondered?

"It seems there may have been another witness that night, at least someone who was seen leaving the club immediately after Stephen Matthews' murder—someone who matched the description of the man who was seen only days ago following Ellie Sutton."

The smile deepened. "This is all very interesting, Miss Forsythe. However, that was ten years ago. Perhaps the persons who worked with Ellie Sutton are mistaken."

His hand flattened on the desk very near that bank of speaking tubes with those call buttons.

"A man with a stocky build who was said to wear a rather expensive suit of clothes and a bowler hat. Not exactly what one sees every day. Do you recall seeing someone that night ten years ago matching that same description? It could be useful in finding the murderer."

He rose from behind his desk. "I have no memory of anyone of that description, Miss Forsythe, and I must now ask you to leave. I have several appointments and am now late for one of them."

I caught the movement of his hand toward that bank of speaking tubes, but instead of lifting one to communicate with someone, he merely pressed the call button beneath the farthest one.

I rose, as it seemed that our meeting was definitely at an end.

"A man with that same description has also been seen following me," I told him.

"Yes, quite," he replied.

I caught a movement at the corner of my eye, and an impression of someone—a man of stocky build.

"Our meeting is at an end, Miss Forsythe."

His demeanor had changed completely along with his expression. For a moment I was certain I was looking into the cold, calculated gaze of the man who had abused and terrified his wife. A sudden movement behind me and an instinctive warning.

A few seconds more and I might have been able to defend myself. There weren't a few seconds more, as the blow exploded painfully at the back of my head. I saw stars, and tumbled down the rabbit hole into a black void...

Twenty-Two

BRODIE

"WHEN?" he demanded.

"I missed her by only a few minutes, according to the note she left at the office," Munro replied.

"Matthews!" Brodie spat out as he moved a little too quickly from the chair at the desk in Alex Sinclair's office and winced at the pain it brought.

"She met with the wife yesterday," Munro went on to explain. "Afterward, she was certain Sir Edward knew something from the night Stephen Matthews was killed that was part of the recent murder. I found it in her notes at Sussex Square."

Her damned notes! Brodie thought.

There were no accusations that Munro should have stayed with her, there was no time for that. She had not returned to the coach after that meeting with Matthews. If she was correct that the two murders were connected, she might be in grave danger.

What had she learned from Sir Edward? Something? Anything?

The fact that she had not returned from that meeting was proof enough that he was somehow involved. And the man had a ruthless reputation—he let nothing stand in his way.

There had long been suspicions of Matthews' business dealings. Munro knew only too well from handling Lady Montgomery's affairs. Those he couldn't persuade to do business with Argosy were then *'persuaded'* by other means.

In more than one instance, a merchant was either severely beaten or disappeared completely over a shipping transaction.

Lady Montgomery's business dealing had been the exception, with Munro steadfastly advising her not to do business with the man. And now Mikaela was in the middle of a dangerous situation and had disappeared.

Mr. Hastings had waited for over an hour for her to return from the appointment, then made inquiries inside the shipping office. He was informed that Sir Edward had left the building some time before, and there was no sign of her.

It was then he made the call from the shipping office to Sussex Square. He had arrived at the Tower just before Munro, along with that mangy, foul-smelling animal Mikaela was so fond of.

That was the other part of it, that Brodie couldn't ignore— the hound. He was usually docile during the day after spending the night on the street, content to find a place to sleep it off. But now the beast was restless, agitated, pacing back and forth in Alex Sinclair's office as if the damned animal sensed something was verra wrong.

"What's to be done?" Alex asked.

Brodie seized the coat Munro had brought for him the day

before and winced sharply as he pulled it on, then left the office for the larger one down the hall.

He didn't bother to request to see the man behind the door and didn't knock. The door slammed back against the inside wall.

"Get me out of here, now!" he demanded of Sir Avery.

Munro and Alex Sinclair had followed.

"What is it?" Sir Avery demanded. "What's happened?"

Alex quickly explained as Brodie again demanded. "Get me out of here, legal or otherwise. I'll not say it again."

"You're here at the courtesy of the Prince of Wales, and still under arrest," Sir Avery reminded him. "There are others who can handle this."

"I dinna care if it's the Queen herself." Brodie flung back at him. "And every second you waste arguin' may be too late for Mikaela. I'm leavin', whether ye permit it or not."

Curses filled the air as he left Sir Avery's office, and then made his way out of the Tower even as a dozen thoughts churned.

He had warned her, told her in no uncertain terms that he didn't want her involved in this.

She had been hurt, he saw it in her eyes. But there was that stubborn set to her chin even as she said nothing. She hadn't argued with him, had simply nodded and then left Scotland Yard.

There were reasons he didn't want her involved. Ellie Sutton's death was personal. But there were things he hadn't counted on—the man seen outside her town house in Mayfair, the information she had learned that the same man had been seen outside the hotel where Ellie worked, Brodie's arrest. And now Mikaela had disappeared.

Damned, stubborn...woman! Why couldn't she have listened to him?"

Munro handed the revolver to him as they arrived at the offices of Argosy Shipping.

The hound jumped down from the coach and raced ahead, nose to the pavement.

The answer was the same as Hastings had received—Matthews was gone, supposedly to an appointment. Brodie pushed his way past the clerk. Munro followed as Alex informed the clerk that they were with the Special Services Agency.

This part of the warehouse was a like a maze. It would have been near impossible to find their way without the hound. Nose to the floor, the animal appeared to know exactly where he was going, abruptly stopping before a set of large warehouse doors. He let out a sharp bark, then began to claw at the opening.

It was locked.

Munro fired two rounds into one of the doors, splintering the wood, and shattering the lock.

"Stand away," Munro told him. "Yer in no condition." He then seized the handle of one door and rolled it up at the opening. The hound was through the opening first.

He raced through the warehouse that opened dockside at the opposite end, darting among barrels and crates, howling as he picked up the scent, the sound echoing in through the building.

"She was here," Munro announced as the hound then raced out the opposite end of the warehouse and onto the dock.

They found him at the base of the gangplank where dockworkers unloaded cargo into the hold of an Argosy ship. He circled, stopped, then began crazily barking pointed up that wide gangplank. Brodie exchanged a look with Munro.

"How do ye want to do this?" Munro asked.

"I want to get her out of there." It was as simple as that.

"We'll need a diversion," Munro replied. "Like when we were lads on the street."

"Aye," Brodie replied.

"Ye'll be no good to me with broken ribs," Munro pointed out.

"Ye'll not go alone," Brodie informed him.

"I thought ye would say that. And there is the hound."

"I can help," Alex told them. "What sort of diversion is needed?"

Brodie exchanged a look with his friend.

"Come along, lad," Munro told Alex. "I'll show ye how it's done."

There was just a thin spiral of smoke from a pallet of cotton bales that had just been lowered onto the dock. As the wind came up off the water, smoke burst into flames amid shouts that suddenly went up among the workers off-loading the cargo. Smoke churned into a grey cloud and Brodie ran up the gangway, the hound right behind him.

Mikaela

There was something to be said for being dropped into a dank hole, the smell brackish, with water up over my ankles. That *something* would have rivaled the crudest seaman if there had been anyone else about. There wasn't.

I assumed that as I came up through the wave of throbbing pain in the back of my head, my mouth stuffed with a rag, my hands bound behind me.

I forced myself to think, ignoring the pain as I fought to stand, slipped into that brackish brine without the use of my hands to brace myself, then managed to push myself back into the corner of the angled wall at my back and an adjacent wall.

Brackish water, the smell of brine, oil, and the slow roll under my feet, and I realized where I had been taken. I was in the hold of a ship!

Everything else slowly slipped into place.

...That conversation with Adelaide Matthews the previous day; the abuse over the years; her husband's rage over Stephen Matthews' affair with Ellie Sutton and the child she was going to have.

...That last night at the club, a stocky man with a bowler hat seen leaving the club shortly after Stephen Matthews was found murdered, a man Ellie Sutton had seen that night.

...A man with that same description terrorizing her all these years later, and seen near the townhouse in Mayfair.

...My meeting with Sir Edward, the smile that had instantly changed to anger with my questions; the sudden movement of a stocky man behind me.

...Two people were now dead. Two murders ten years apart, linked by the events of that night.

And now?

I could only guess what my fate was to be. I had interfered, no doubt threatened Sir Edward with my questions. As for the man I had glimpsed just before I was struck? Would he return? Or would I simply be left in the hold of the ship, left to die as the ship left London for some foreign port hundreds of miles away?

Not precisely another adventure I would have liked to take.

My hands were bound and my throat was dry from the gag across my mouth. I couldn't see anything other than a thin sliver of light overhead which had to be the hatch. I couldn't even prevent myself tumbling into the water as the ship rose then slowly fell with the tide.

I heard shouts, the sound of someone running across the deck overhead, and what sounded like the bark of a dog, a familiar baying sound.

It came again, and I recognized that deep half bark, part howl of a hunting hound.

I tried to scream and choked on the gag. All I heard in my dark prison that was like a tomb, was that distinctive barking sound. That had to mean that someone was with him.

Desperate to catch the attention of whoever was up there with Rupert, I braced myself against that sloped wall of the hold and stomped my feet against the adjacent wall.

I lost my footing, slipped into the water once more, then pushed myself back up that sloped wall of the hold and once more stomped my boot against that wood wall.

I was exhausted, could hardly breathe for the gag in my mouth, and heard the sound of those on the deck overhead fading as they moved past.

I'm here! I wanted to shout. *Come back!*

Then the sound of bootsteps returned, louder this time, and more of them, along with the sound of the hound baying wildly.

That sliver of light at the edge of the hatch suddenly widened, then opened, light from the sky overhead glaring down into the hatch, painful on my eyes, as a ladder was lowered and someone slowly made their way down into the hold.

I held back. If it was Matthews or the man who had come up on me in his office...

The man on the ladder dropped into the water in the hold and cursed—first in English then in that broad Scots Gaelic.

"Mikaela! Where are ye, lass?"

The sound was muffled, a whimper, and I realized that it was myself. Strong hands closed around my upper arms and I collapsed against Brodie's shoulder.

A lantern appeared, held by Munro as he climbed down into the hold, while a dozen faces including Alex Sinclair and Rupert the hound, peered down after.

Brodie tugged the gag from my mouth as he held me against him. I stared at his bruised cheek and the cut over his left eye.

There was no time to say anything as Munro reached us.

"We had some assistance," he announced. "Sir Avery sent some of his people."

"Sir Edward?" I asked, my throat dry, my voice more like the croak of a frog.

Munro nodded. "According to one of Sir Avery's men, he was found not far away...along with a man with the bowler hat by the name of Howell, who has been in his employ over the last fifteen years or so. He *took care of things* for Sir Edward when he wanted something done, often outside the law."

Jacob Howell, who had once served in Her Majesty's service. From witness reports, it seemed that had included the murder of Stephen Matthews ten years earlier. And Ellie Sutton?

Twenty-Three

THERE WAS MORE, of course. There usually was when it came to murder and other crimes that somehow were part of it.

It was all connected, as Brodie and I had first thought. Still, finally emerging from the hold of the Matthews cargo ship, I leaned heavily against Brodie as we left the ship.

I had no idea where Mr. Hastings was directed to take us, until I saw white clapboard residences that lined the street in Mayfair.

Nothing was said as we arrived. Between the throbbing from the blow to the head I'd received, then being dragged down into the hold of the ship, I was in a sorry condition.

"Mrs. Ryan will be here shortly," was all Brodie said, as I leaned against him when my knees threatened to go out from under me, and I discovered that somewhere between the warehouse and the hold of the ship, I had acquired other bruises.

It seemed that Jacob Howell had no compunction about striking a woman. I'd obviously taken a slap to the face that resulted in a split lip.

Split lips healed, but not the memory. I could only lament that I hadn't enough time to retrieve the revolver in my bag when he came up behind me. I would have gladly ended his brutal habits. As for Sir Edward?

When I asked Brodie, he merely shook his head. Alex Sinclair was more forthcoming. It seems that Jacob Howell was not willing to take blame alone. Confronted by Brodie and Sir Avery's people, he had readily admitted to the killing not only of Stephen Matthews ten years earlier, but to the murder of Ellie Sutton as well, that was to have included young Rory.

No witnesses left behind, no one left to expose the even more chilling aspect of their deaths—that he had been hired by Sir Edward Matthews to "take care of things," for very lucrative compensation. To all intents and purposes, he was a hired assassin, whose job it was to eliminate anyone who stood in the way of Sir Edward Matthews' ambition. I was simply one more obstacle to *take care of.*

That was as much as I was able to take in, as we arrived at the town house in Mayfair.

Though he was hardly in any better condition than I was, Brodie escorted me upstairs.

I was a sorry mess. My reflection in the cheval mirror in my bedroom looked like someone I didn't know. Yet *'she'* was in there somewhere as he assisted me into the adjacent bathing room, then removed my soaked and muddied clothes.

I then found myself in that steam-filled showering compartment, as I braced myself against one wall, dizziness from the blow to the head threatening to send me to the floor.

Between the bruises, the lump on the back of my head the size of an egg, and split lip, I don't think I would have minded, except I would have missed Brodie's gentle care as he bathed me from my head to my toes, then just as gently dried me.

From there it was a very short distance, albeit it took slow effort, to the bed, where he tucked me under the covers. I was only vaguely aware he was there, then aware of nothing else.

I wakened slowly, thoughts returning even more slowly as I stared about the room.

I was in the bedroom at Mayfair, I realized, as the events of the day slowly climbed out of the fog of sleep.

A single electric light glowed faintly through the doorway to the adjoining bathing room, as my gaze slowly cleared on the shadow beside the bed—Brodie.

He had brought me back to Mayfair, washed away the mud, grime, and dried blood from my time in the hold of the ship, then left.

Somewhere in the hours between, he had returned, and now sat beside the bed, head back, handsome features along with an assortment of cuts and bruises, partially hidden in shadows in the room. Except for that dark gaze that slowly opened and fastened on me.

"You're here."

"Aye," he replied as he leaned toward the bed and gently stroked my forehead.

Other thoughts surfaced. "The charges against you? Abberline?"

"It's over."

I felt his finger gently brush my bloodied lip.

"Are you all right?" I asked, or at least as near as I could say the words. A split lip was new to me.

"Go back to sleep, lass."

I slowly nodded, reached for his hand, and slept.

❧

Brodie was gone when I wakened in the morning.

The other side of the bed was still neatly tucked. It appeared that he had spent the night in that chair.

I was stiff and sore as I rose slowly and took stock of my bruises. I grimaced at my reflection in the dressing table mirror. There was no concealing my bruised and swollen lip, however a bit of color added to my cheeks improved my pale complexion.

I had very nearly dressed, when there was a knock at the bedroom door, and Mrs. Ryan appeared. I was prepared for shock and then a lecture. There were neither, as she entered the room as if it was any other day, with a tray that included coffee and a tray of scones—the bracing aroma of the coffee was wonderful! And Rupert.

"It was all I could do to get the scones out of the oven," she commented with only a glance—albeit a slightly startled glance, then continued across to the sitting room, where she set the tray out of the hound's zealous attempts to steal a scone.

"He's had three already," she announced as she returned with a forced smile.

"Mr. Brodie?" I asked, ignoring her obvious curiosity and concern.

"He was here when I arrived last night, then left early this morning. Said there were things he needed to take care of." She went about the room, retrieving my soiled clothes from the night before with a frown.

"Did he say when he would return?"

"No, he didn't." She paused at the door. "I do remember him telling the driver to take him...to the Tower of London?" she added in that way that indicated she would have liked to ask more about that, and waited.

The Agency, I thought. Of course, he would go there first.

There was a vague memory of something I had asked him, about the charges against him and Abberline.

"My great-aunt?" I asked, aware of how gossip traveled. If she had heard anything of the events of the previous day, she might have been concerned.

"Mr. Brodie spoke with her and assured her that you were both quite all right. All things considered," she added with a single arched brow.

I thanked her for the coffee and scones, then asked her to call for a cab.

I finished dressing and pulled my hair up into a roll, my fingers brushing that knot at the back of my head.

There was someone I needed to see—Adelaide Matthews.

By now, I was fairly certain she would have been informed about the arrest of her husband.

It was more than that. I wanted to make certain that she was all right. The revelation that her husband had commissioned the murder of her son was going to be devastating, only adding to the pain and grief she'd experienced through the years.

Would she mourn what was essentially the end of her marriage? Or would she cling to it as some might, the only thing she had ever known of that relationship?

And what of the revelation that it was her husband who had ordered the death of her son all those years before, because of the scandal of fathering an illegitimate child with Ellie Sutton? Repeating the circumstance of his own birth from an affair that Adelaide had?

I thought of something Sir Walter Scott had written years before, *"What a tangled web we weave, when first we practice to deceive."*

Sir Edward had deceived so many people, and in the end caught in his own deceptions.

There would be the usual rumors and gossip, of course, not to mention the news of Sir Edward's arrest along with Jacob Howell, sensationalized in the dailies, as they reported the murder of both Ellie Sutton and the earlier murder of Stephen Matthews.

Were there others who had stood in the way of Sir Edward's ambitions? It was chilling to think that there might be others. Some of it would naturally come out as things had a way of doing. All of it over more than thirty years that Argosy Shipping had been expanding shipping across the globe, only time would tell. And perhaps some of it would never come to light.

Rupert and I enjoyed Mrs. Ryan's scones while we waited for the cab to arrive.

I ignored the driver's startled expression at my appearance, as I gave the destination of the Tower and we climbed aboard.

I arrived at the Tower and was greeted at the entrance by Lucy Penworth.

"Are you all right then, miss?" she asked with a curious glance in my direction as I followed her through the maze of hallways and passages.

"Alex was quite concerned about you, but Mr. Brodie assured him that you were all right."

"Is Brodie about then?"

"He was here early. I'm told that he met for some time with Sir Avery. Then he left. He told Alex there was something he needed to do outside the city."

Alex popped up out of his chair as we arrived at his little office. Quite spontaneous and then embarrassed for it, he threw his arms around my shoulders and hugged me. He stepped back and apologized profusely.

"It's just that you gave everyone a scare yesterday, abducted as you were, and put in that dreadful hold of the ship."

I would have smiled, however..."It will heal," I assured him about my badly bruised lip.

"Of course, and it does give you the appearance that no one would want to argue with you. I have some cosmetics, if you want to do a bit of a touch-up," Lucy added.

I had noticed that the freckles across her cheeks were less prominent of late.

"I quite like the look." Alex attempted to make light of my appearance.

"Is Sir Avery available?" I inquired.

"He did say that he would like to speak with you if you were to come into the offices today."

Alex escorted me to Sir Avery Stanton's office.

"I am so very glad that you are all right, Miss Forsythe," he added.

"Mikaela." I reminded him of my name, not the first time.

He blushed. "Of course."

I could see what Lucy Penworth found so endearing about him, with that lock of dark hair that spilled over his forehead and that slightly shy look behind the glasses.

Of course, there was that other side of him that had surprised both Brodie and me, and I wondered if she had discovered that yet. That fierce, brave side that had revealed itself not long ago.

Sir Avery rose from behind his desk and greeted me with a circumspect expression. He was pleased that I had survived the day before.

So good of him, I thought, in consideration of Brodie's

cautious demeanor toward the man—someone for whom Queen and country were more important than any one man. Or woman. I kept in mind the bargain I had made to have Brodie released from Scotland Yard, badly injured and in need of medical care.

I reminded myself that it was something to keep in mind, whenever Sir Avery chose to call in that bargain I had made with him.

"I have heard from no less than Lady Montgomery and the Prince of Wales on your behalf as well as Mr. Brodie's. You do have friends and connections in high places."

I smiled, as much as possible. I appreciated that he shared that with me. It might be advantageous at some time in the future.

"I want to thank you once more for intervening on his behalf."

That smile again, that for a moment reminded me of that Cheshire Cat.

"Mr. Brodie has provided valuable service in the past. I look forward to our continued relationship, as well as with you."

That particular aspect I had not yet shared with Brodie.

"The matter he needed to attend to is in Leeds," Sir Avery then provided. "Something most important to him. As for yourself, I am most pleased that you escaped mostly unharmed." He paused before continuing. "We have a lead in the counterfeiting case. It seems that we will be able to conclude that shortly." He looked at me.

"Will you be taking up your writing next? A new novel perhaps? Or will you be returning to the Strand with Brodie? Most unconventional for a lady of your position," he added.

"As I said—I am very pleased that you survived the ordeal. And as for Brodie..."

Unless I was mistaken, he waited to make certain he had my full attention.

"The charges against him have been stayed and will be removed, of course. He is far too valuable to the Agency to lose."

Brodie had warned me before about Sir Avery, what was said when they had met in the past, and what was clearly left unspoken.

"Of course, you told him about our arrangement when I will have the need to call on your particular talents."

That headache had returned and throbbed at the back of my head.

I thanked him for his concerns then left with a new under-standing of Brodie's reservations about the man.

Twenty-Four

TIME AWAY FROM THE CITY...

It was Munro who provided the answer to my question regarding where Brodie had gone when I arrived at Sussex Square to assure my great-aunt, and Lily of course, that I was quite all right.

My aunt had merely inspected me, then commented, "I have some cosmetics that will cover that, left by Templeton after a performance. After all I cannot go about the city in the motor carriage appearing like an old woman. One never knows whom one might encounter, perhaps a handsome man.

"It does cover quite nicely," she had continued. "Wrinkles in my case, and makes one feel quite lovely. By the way, I have not seen Mr. Brodie of late."

A hint for information, if ever there was one, which I avoided answering.

I could only imagine the benefit of the cosmetics, still I would most definitely sample some. The nasty bruise above my lip was the worst of it, not that I was usually concerned about such things. And it did bring startled looks from the servants. I could only imagine the comments others might offer.

"Crivvens!" Lily had exclaimed when she saw me. "I hope ye gave as good as ye got."

I hadn't thought of it that way. However, very near unconscious at the time, the best I was able to do was to kick out at the man I now knew as Jacob Howell, in a particularly vulnerable location when I had come to enough in the hold of the ship. That was when he had struck me across the face.

After all was said and done, what was in store for him now was far better than any blow I could have struck, even though it would have been most satisfying at the time.

Munro had just returned from business across the city. I found him at his office near the kitchens.

"Leeds. Brimley's son lives there with his family," he informed me when I asked if he knew where Brodie had gone.

A safe place, where Brodie had taken Rory, after his mother was killed.

I had not met the boy, of course, but I felt that instinctive tightness around my heart for what he had gone through, the loss of his mother, the horror he must have experienced the night she was murdered, not knowing what would happen to him. And there was the very real possibility that he might have been killed as well.

As I knew only too well, there were things that stayed with a person, no matter the passing of years, things that were never forgotten, but simply dealt with as best one could.

Munro waited, as if there was something more, then, "He should be back tomorrow."

I stayed the rest of the day, then night at Sussex Square, but couldn't help but think of Brodie, and how difficult it undoubtedly was to go to Leeds and explain to Rory Sutton that the man who had killed his mother had been found, and he no longer had to be afraid.

I listened to Lily's description of her latest studies, though not without the occasional roll of her eyes.

"Just get through your lessons," I encouraged her, what had worked for me very near her age. "Then you can choose whatever you would like to pursue next, perhaps travel..."

"I would like to work with you and Mr. Brodie," she announced.

Oh dear. I had exchanged a look with my great-aunt at that one.

"The apple does not fall far from the tree," Aunt Antonia merrily announced.

The next morning, I called to leave a message for Adelaide Matthews. After giving the servant my name, she picked up the call herself.

Her voice trembled at first. Yes, she had been called upon by a man from Sir Avery's office who had explained the events of the day before. Her voice grew stronger as she said that she would like very much to see me.

Afterward, I asked Mr. Hastings to bring round the coach to take me to the Matthews' home in Kent.

Adelaide Matthews was dressed in a deep, rich burgundy gown. There were circles under her eyes, but the soft smile was warm and...brave, I thought.

She was concerned for me after having learned some of the details of the confrontation with her husband and Jacob Howell.

"I met the man once," she revealed, with no small amount

of shock. "I had no way of knowing...but now..." Her voice broke softly.

"Edward was responsible for Stephen's..." She looked at me. "What about my grandson? When may I see him?"

I explained that Brodie had gone to Leeds, and that I hoped to see him later that day when he returned. He would undoubtedly want to make arrangements for her to see Rory.

"He is all I have left, you know," she said.

Upon leaving, I asked Mr. Hastings to take me to the office on the Strand.

Mr. Cavendish had returned to his usual place in the alcove at the foot of the stairs to the office. The hound leapt down from the coach as we arrived. His greeting for his old friend was to check for any food that might be about.

"And yerself?" Mr. Cavendish inquired with a narrowed look at me.

I assured him that I was quite all right. I had after all, applied some of my aunt's cosmetics before leaving Sussex Square.

"He's up at the office, sure enough," he told me then. "Returned a while earlier...he has someone with him, a young lad."

He had obviously brought Rory back to London with him. I heard their voices as I reached the landing at the top of the stairs then opened the door.

Two pairs of dark eyes fastened on me—one with that scar above his left brow only just beginning to heal, the other from a pale, solemn young face. Of the three of us, Brodie was the first to recover.

There was something in his voice as he introduced us.

"Rory, lad, this is Mikaela Forsythe." He looked at me then, the expression identical in both dark gazes.

His arm was around the boy's shoulders that were far too thin.

"It's all right," he gently told the boy. "She's a friend."

Rory nodded, then slowly approached. His face was thin as well, which made his eyes seem enormous, and his overlong dark hair was in need of a trim. But there was bravery in his expression, almost defiance in spite of what he'd been through, as he held out a hand.

"I am pleased to meet you, Miss Forsythe."

"And I am very pleased to meet you," I finally managed as I looked over his head at Brodie.

"Aye, lad," Brodie told him. "Ye've already met Mr. Cavendish below, and no doubt the hound has returned as well. Ye might ask the man to accompany ye to the public house, as I imagine yer near starved."

Rory nodded. "Does the hound bite?" he asked.

"No," I replied. "But he is most fond of biscuits and scones. Ask for some from Miss Effie at the Public House."

He nodded, then looked to Brodie once more.

"It's all right, lad. Yer safe enough now."

There was a long silence after he left. Brodie went to the window at the door and glanced below, much like a...worried parent.

He turned then. "There are things we need to talk about."

We sat across from each other at the desk, the way we had dozens of times. Only I sensed that this was different.

He had changed since that first inquiry case. There were faint flecks of grey among the thick dark hair that curled over the collar of his shirt. There seemed to be a permanent frown line at one corner of his mouth, and of course that cut above his left eye.

But there was something more...

"I wanted to tell ye, from the first of it but..." He shook his head, that dark gaze finally meeting mine.

"Everything happened quickly and he was in danger...Then ye were off on yer own..."

When I would have said something, he shook his head as he came out of the chair and paced across the office as I had seen dozens of times when something bothered him.

"The truth is..." he started to explain, then stopped.

When he seemed to be having some difficulty, I finished the thought. "Is he yours?"

He frowned. "I dinna know."

The words seemed caught there. He shook his head again.

"I told ye that I found Ellie Sutton work at a public house all those years ago. From there she found work at the club where she met young Matthews. Things had been difficult for them. His father didna approve of her and she had returned...for a while."

And she had returned to the one person who had helped her.

"We were together for a while, not long. Then Matthews sent word for her. It was obvious she had been hoping the whole time, though I tried to get her to understand how difficult it would be, the differences between them, the disapproval.

"Ye need to know that it wasna like what there is between us," he added.

As he explained, I suppose I had suspected as much the moment I saw Rory—that dark gaze and the dark hair.

"When she returned over a year ago," he continued. "I thought he might be mine at the time when I saw him," he continued. "But she insisted that Matthews was the father. She hoped after all the time that had passed it might be possible for the lad to know his family. It was the reason she came back."

It was a great deal to take in. Still, I was not naïve that he would have had relationships before. I had not considered that he might have a child. He continued to watch me with that intense gaze.

"I've spoken with Adelaide Matthews," I added. "She believes that he is her grandson. She would like very much to see him."

"Aye, in time," he replied. "He's come through a great deal."

Something he understood very well, having lost his mother very near the same age.

"There is no way to know for certain if he is mine," he said then. "But I intend to be part of his life."

I understood, and would have expected no less.

"We will figure it out together."

"It's more than ye bargained for, and I dinna expect ye to be part of it," he replied. "And there are other considerations. The lad needs to feel safe as he goes through this."

What was he trying to say? When I would have asked, he stopped me.

"This case...the other night, what could have happened. I have given it a great deal of thought. Ye went to someone who was dangerous, and ye could have been killed."

It was an old discussion, we'd had before. I thought we had at least reached an agreement about my involvement in our inquiry cases.

"I didn't know that at the time," I pointed out. What was he trying to say? What was happening?

His voice changed, halting, anger slipping in.

"I told ye to stay out of it! To stay away. I didna want yer help. And ye went to Matthews, knowing what ye did about the sort of man he was toward his own wife."

"It wasn't as if you could have gone there," I pointed out. "I thought he might know something about what happened that night at the Clarendon Club that could be useful to our case. And it wasn't as if I was alone, I had the revolver and Rupert was with me. I had also left a message for Munro."

"The hound? And what use was the revolver when Howell had ye bound and thrown into the hull of that ship?"

"The hound has proven himself on more than one occasion," I added. "And as I recall, Rupert led you and Munro to the hold of that ship."

"Ye didna do as I asked and it could have cost yer life! And now, yer to work for Sir Avery and the Agency in God knows what situations, when ye know my feelin's toward the man."

So that was what had him stirred up. I had hoped to speak with him first about it. Obviously, Sir Avery had already shared that with him.

"It was an agreement I made to have Dr. Watson see to your wounds after Abberline had you beaten," I reminded him. "According to the doctor, it very well saved your life!"

I was now on my feet, unable to comprehend how we had gotten from our conversation about Rory, to this.

"I was willing to agree to his terms to see it done. And I might add that you would have done the same!"

I went to the door. I was tired, angry, and hurt. He was equally angry, but it was what he had said—that he didn't expect me to be part of this new arrangement.

"Mikaela...!"

I heard the warning in his voice. I had heard it all before but not like this.

"You should have trusted me!" I told him, and slammed the door on my way out.

It seemed that Brodie and I had reached an impasse in our work together, and our relationship. It was not the first time, still this time was quite different.

Brodie didn't return to the town house. And I didn't return to the office on the Strand.

As one week slipped into another after the Matthews case was solved, I spent a great deal of time at Sussex Square assisting my aunt and Lily as they prepared for their departure for Africa.

They would be gone for almost four months, traveling first by steamship across the channel to Calais, then by packet to Lisbon, through the Strait of Gibraltar, and around northern Africa to Kenya.

It would be a full month before they arrived in Kenya, where they would stay at a compound frequented by other English travelers before departing on safari.

Lily had acquired a box camera. She was determined to take as many pictures as possible. I didn't bother to explain that there might be few places to acquire more film.

My aunt was still making decisions about which clothes to take with her, her favorite being the full hunting costume with pith helmet.

"We'll not be hunting for heaven's sake," she informed me. "Nevertheless, I do believe that pants and boots would be appropriate, don't you think, Mikaela dear? And then there are the suppers at Sir Laurence's compound, quite elegant affairs I'm told. I shall need the new gowns for that. I suppose the weather should be a consideration as well, as it will be quite warm, I am told."

I chose to stay out of this conversation. When I had been to

Africa, it had been by sailing ship across the Mediterranean to Cairo, down the Nile as far as we could travel, then into the desert of the Sahara—not an adventure I thought my great-aunt was up to, all things considered.

Through Munro, I was aware that after the initial scandal of charges against Sir Edward in the matter of the death of Ellie Sutton and Stephen Matthews ten years earlier, as well as Jacob Howell, that Brodie had taken Rory to see Adelaide Matthews, and she had asked to be allowed to see him often.

"It will take a while," Munro had told me, as if he was aware that there was something amiss between Brodie and me. "Ye know him better than any. Give it time."

I did give it time.

Adelaide Matthews had asked me to return, and I did. I liked her very much.

There was grief of course, much like an old injury that had been injured once more. But the wound would heal in time. And then there was Rory.

He was a frequent presence, and the grey pallor had disappeared from Adelaide's face, replaced by a smile of genuine happiness. It was time, I thought.

As for Rory, I arrived one afternoon to find him playing with the train set Adelaide had purchased for him. Lily had accompanied me when she heard where I was going that particular day, and it appeared that he was quite taken with his new 'friend.'

Adelaide had encouraged Lily to call again after she returned from safari. Rory had been fascinated about it. For her part, Lily had merely shrugged as we departed.

"He reminds me of someone," she commented. And that was all that was said.

Two weeks became three, and there was still no word from

Brodie. It did seem that our disagreement was most serious. I wasn't certain now that I knew him at all.

The week before Lily and my aunt were to depart, there was still no word from him.

I had thought a great deal about the *situation,* as I now thought of our estrangement. While I understood his concerns for Rory, I was not willing to accept that I had done anything wrong in going to Sir Avery regarding Brodie's incarceration, badly wounded, at Scotland Yard.

While I had dealt with that overbearing, stubborn Scottish demeanor in the past, I knew that I was right in what I had done. The problem was that he refused to see it.

Then, Lily and my aunt were to depart for Southampton the following day. I had made a decision and sat down and penned a note for Munro to take to Brodie. I intended to keep it brief, however there were things that needed to be said.

I have given our last conversation considerable thought. In spite of our work together, which resolved several difficult inquiries, it seems that we have reached an impasse.

I have decided to accompany Lily and my aunt to Africa. We will be gone for several months.

I wish you well in your work, and particularly with Rory. He seems a very fine young man.

I hesitated on how to close the message. Any endearment seemed somehow inappropriate under the circumstances.

I signed it simply, *"M".*

∾

Brodie was not at Southampton to see us off, and I had not expected it. My note had said all there was to say. There had been no response.

Munro had accompanied us to the port.

"Miss..." He started to say something in parting, then hesitated.

I had no idea what he would have said as I shook my head.

"It's quite all right, you know," I told him.

We boarded the steamship that was to take us to Calais, and then on to Kenya.

I did not look back.

Author Note

DEADLY BETRAYAL ended up being longer than previous episodes of Brodie and Mikaela's adventures in murder.

It marked a turning point in their relationship that the characters demanded. After all, they are two very different people and quite strong-minded in spite of similarities in their life experiences.

There were new inventions in 1891, that included the development of Lady Antonia's motor carriage—heaven help anyone who gets in her way. The first gasoline-powered motor carriage was patented by Carl Benz (the name may be familiar) with a three-wheeled vehicle in 1886. I have embellished the story to provide her ladyship with a four-wheeled motor carriage.

The telephone was in wide use by 1891, along with another invention, the speaking tube. It was a horned device linked by a tube (hence the name) from one part of a building to another, most usually business offices such as banks. In such situations, they also included an electric call button at the base of each speaking tube, to signal that a person was making contact with another.

By 1891, the East India Trading Company, which had the monopoly on shipping that had established Britain into foreign countries, had disappeared. The power of the EIC led to the expansion of the British Empire. It also led to rampant corruption, and perhaps that saying, "Absolute power corrupts absolutely." It was dissolved in 1874. The docks where the ships had arrived and departed were still referred to as the East India docks.

There were dozens of other shipping companies in Britain and abroad to fill the global void left by the EIC. Hence, Argosy Shipping, though purely fictional.

As explained, Brodie and Mikaela drove the change in their relationship at the end of Deadly Betrayal. Characters do have a way of taking over a story. I did attempt to convince them otherwise, but they insisted on having their way.

Do not despair—there is more in store for them with DEADLY SCANDAL. This will include that case that Mikaela is asked to take on by Sir Avery of the Agency. It provides a new aspect of their relationship, as they are forced to work together once more, albeit reluctantly, and Brodie is forced to make...wait for it...changes, if he is to win her back.

I do love it when a man must face his own shortcomings and make a decision on what matters most to him. However, we are talking about a stubborn Scot. And then there is the new aspect of their relationship—Rory. Who may or may not be Brodie's son.

Exciting things are coming. Next, DEADLY SCANDAL, for that most unlikely pair.

Also by Carla Simpson

Outlaws, Scoundrels & Lawmen

Desperado's Caress

Passion's Splendor

Silver Mistress

Memory and Desire

Desire's Flame

Silken Surrender

Angels, Devils, Rebels & Rogues

Ravished

Always My Love

Seductive Caress

Seduced

Deceived

About the Author

"I want to write a book... " she said.

"Then do it," he said.

And she did, and received two offers for that first book proposal.

A dozen historical romances later, and a prophecy from a gifted psychic and the Legacy Series was created, expanding to seven additional titles.

Along the way, two film options, and numerous book awards.

But wait, there's more a voice whispered, after a trip to Scotland and a visit to the standing stones in the far north, and as old as Stonehenge, sign posts the voice told her, and the Clan Fraser books that have followed that told the beginnings of the clan and the family she was part of...

And now... murder and mystery set against the backdrop of Victorian London in the new Angus Brodie and Mikaela Forsythe series, with an assortment of conspirators and murderers in the brave new world after the Industrial Revolution where terrorists threaten and the world spins closer to war.

When she is not exploring the Darkness of the fantasy world, or pursuing ancestors in ancient Scotland, she lives in the mountains near Yosemite National Park with bears and mountain lions, and plots murder and revenge.

And did I mention fierce, beautiful women and dangerous, handsome men?

They're there, waiting...

Join Carla's Newsletter